CHAPTER 1

The summer sun in Missouri was wicked and intense matched only by the unforgiving amount of humidity produced in the air that made waiting for the warrant to arrive almost unbearable. His bullet proof vest felt tight and stuck to his body through his sweat soaked T-shirt beneath. His sunglasses were constantly fogging from the water pouring off his head, down his cheeks and mingling with his breath as he exhaled. "Only one thing would make this trip worth the wait", Jack thought to himself, staring out the tiny rectangle window in the back door of the panel van, "Catching this guy and stopping him for good would be worth another 12 hours in the sweat box". He focused on putting an end to this investigation. He thought about all the pain and suffering caused by this psychopath and how close he was to ending his reign of terror. He tried to pull his mind away from the sauna he was sitting in and focus on the purpose and need for it all, but the unforgiving clock in his head was moving in slow motion.

"You doin alright sweety?" she asked with her southern drawl that Jack never could get used to. It made her sound like a simple local girl with no education or ties to the FBI. She sounded like a waitress on roller skates in an old 80s movie, floating up to your car window to take your order. But you would be wrong, he knew her ability and had worked multiple cases with her before. Cathy

Chambers was one of the best young agents they had on the East Coast and he was thankful to be teamed up with her on this case, but it still didn't shake the sound her voice made and the instant images of her in a tight pair of daisy dukes, cowboy boots and a tube top hopping off the back of an old beat up pickup with a beer in her hand. Not that he had ever seen that before, but for some reason, that's what he pictured when he heard her voice this time.

"Yep, just enjoying the weather you have down here. I am surprised anyone in these parts is overweight with this much heat." Jack replied.

She was something of a looker as well which made teaming up that much easier or difficult. It depended how you looked at it. Something about the southern girls with their blonde hair, bleached even lighter with the sun and the constant wet look to her skin from the heat, gave her a seductive and sensuous look to everything she did, all hours of the day. Special Agent, Jack Lawsen never mixed business and pleasure, but if he was going to break that cardinal rule, Special Agent, Cathy Chambers would be a good enough reason for him to do it.

"Honey, this is nothing, you should come down in August when the summer really begins. There are days when it's hard to think about wearing clothes." She replied back with a flirtatious tone and twinkle in her eye.

It was hard to imagine it hotter than this and it was only June! Jack didn't want to be here in August, with or without Cathy's clothes on. He wanted to be done with this case, and the south, and get back to the North West where the four seasons had meaning and distinctive differences in climate. If this crazy asshole hiding in the house hadn't started his shit in his part of the country, Jack would've never been assigned to this case and wasted

8 months chasing him all the way down to this hell hole, where they now had him cornered in a small suburban house.

He could sense everyone in the van was getting restless with the wait and trying their best to maintain a professional posture while the clock slowly ticked and the non-air-conditioned temperature inside the confined space grew by the minute. Looking around at the eight members of the Janesville Police Department SWAT team that he and Cathy had been given for the raid, Jack felt like an old man.

The men looked confident enough in their ability, but seriously doubted they had any real world experience doing the job. By the looks of them, the oldest man, a Sargent, was no more than 28. He assumed the majority of the training any of them had received was in a classroom or worse online. A few of them had a prior military look. This didn't surprise Jack. Law enforcement was a standard path most veterans took after the service, but that didn't change the situation they were in now and the very real threat that was waiting inside the house. This wasn't the sands of the Middle East or mountains of Afghanistan. The man they were after was a mentally unstable killing machine and there were lives at risk. He needed the men to be on their A-game here and didn't have time for heroes or acts of valor.

All the information he had on the man inside indicated he would defiantly be armed, but would most likely be alone. He didn't have any accomplice's that he knew of or had discovered during his investigation and the guy preferred to work with blades. That didn't mean there wasn't a firearm in the house or he didn't have one for backup and there were still two women missing from the trail of bodies he had followed leading him down here from Portland. He hoped he would find them alive when he finally got inside, but it wasn't in this guy's MO to leave witnesses. Fourteen women in total had been raped and murdered on his little killing spree heading south, adding more images to plague Jacks already dark filled nightmares.

Cathy adjusted her own sweat soaked vest across from him on the bench and he could tell the stifling heat was getting to her as well, even though she wouldn't admit it. A small glint of happiness rose in his eyes at the thought of her being a little uncomfortable. Misery loved company and he was glad to see he wasn't the only one suffering. Jack was pleased to know that his age wouldn't be the reason he was uncomfortable. He had 10 years on Cathy and twice that on the SWAT team, but he never let that slow him down. He wasn't a fitness freak and counted calories, but he wasn't a fat slob that gave up on life either. Jack could and would always hold his own with the young but this heat was becoming unbearable. This case couldn't be over soon enough.

His phone vibrated in his pocket, stopping his assessment of the team and thermometer in his mind that was pushing the mercury levels. He withdrew it and swiped a sweat soaked thumb across the screen to unlock the device. It took three attempts before it worked and when it did, his calendar popped up instead of the message.

"Fucking phone!" he muttered to himself as he wiped his hand on his pants and tried moving the app off the page to pull up the message.

Another app opened, one that consisted of driving directions and asked for him to input his location with a women's voice he could only imagine was from Europe. He shook the phone and furiously swiped at the screen again. He hated the phone. It was issued to him six months ago from the FBI and loaded with a ton of shit he had no idea how to use. The director insisted he sign for it and that it would streamline things and make his investigations easier. Jack didn't see how it was making anything easier, the damn thing had a glass screen on it that you had to be careful with not to break and when you could manage to get the right thing up on the screen, the glare off any and all light caught the glass making it unreadable, not to mention the print was so small you needed a magnifying glass to read it. This of course was only possible if you knew what you were doing. 9 times out of 10 he didn't. Technology was the way of the future, he wasn't blind to it, but some of it didn't make a lot of sense. He had solved hundreds of cases before the smart phone, and hundreds after that with only a flip phone. All this so called "advancement" didn't seem to make the bad guys any easier to catch or change the barbaric nature of them all. You still had to use your instincts and do the leg work.

Cathy could see the issue he was having and reached across the van taking the phone from him. Within three seconds, she handed it back with the message displaying the approval of the warrant filling the screen in print large enough for him to read.

She gave him a small wink and adjusted herself one last time in the seat getting ready for Jack to give the go ahead. She knew Jack, and his dislike for technology. She also knew that he was the most capable agent she had worked with and didn't hold this handicap against him. If anything it was what made him stand out above the rest. He didn't rely on the newest gadget or latest advancement in criminology investigation. Jack got out and beat the brush. He did the research, legwork and wasn't afraid to get his hands dirty to solve a case. His reputation was what most agents yearned for and her partnering up with him was an opportunity she would not let go to waste.

"We got it, call in the order to the other two teams to stand to. We go on the front door first, wait for our call to hit the back. Street team hold on the four corners and watch the exits." Jack said into his mike attached to the top of his vest. "This ends today. No matter what, this guy does not get away. Understood."

Nods came from each of the men in the van as Jack made eye contact with them. He ended on Cathy and she smirked at him with a nod in agreement.

The doors swung open and the bright mid-day sun flooded inside blinding them all temporarily from the darkness of the van. Four men on each side piled out the back doors and moved from the street, up the driveway to the front of the small country style rancher sitting at the end of a peaceful small suburban cul-de-sac. The men were moving low and ready and as professional as could be expected for a small town unit. He and Cathy lined up at the back of the 2 lines of four opposite the door that was flanked by benches with flower pots on them.

Jack looked down the line to the man in front. It was silent. No sound came from in the home and nothing from beyond. The streets were quiet for midday traffic. Jack looked back out at the Van he had just spent the better half of the day in. Besides it and the black clad men holding weapons around him, the place looked normal and peaceful. Nobody would have ever known what was behind this door. The evil in the world could go on right beside you and you would never know.

Jack pulled back from the street view to the lead man and gave him thumbs up. The lead man, a short wide guy, stepped directly in front of the door with an oversized sledge hammer. It looked like something from a carnival with a massive head at the end of a 4 foot handle wrapped with steel bands. He raised it high above his head and glanced over at Jack one last time. He gave a nod and the hammer came down hard fast and accurate on the door knob. It fell to the ground with a clang splintering the door and jam upon impact. The man threw his entire body at the door and it caved inward as he fell inside to the ground. The two teams zippered inside the opening fast and seamless, each one peeling left then right, shouting out commands to each other and anyone that was in the house to follow to the letter.

Jack and Cathy moved in after the team had cleared the first room. He could hear the back door cave in and shouts coming from the back of the house indicating the rear team had entered and was working its way toward them.

The house was quaint and simple. Family portraits hung from the walls in every room. The coziness of southern living could be felt from the lace coasters on the tables to the pitcher of lemonade sitting on the kitchen counter. Three pair of worn out cowboy boots were displayed on a shelf in the living room surrounded by photos of horses ridden by the same faces hanging on the walls. Knitted and crocheted blankets were draped over the backs of the couch and love seat and the small coffee table in-between had a bowl of mixed nuts with an ancient looking chessboard resting on it.

In no way did it seem to be a home harboring a psychopathic killer or a place where you would go to find one. It looked like any other family home, held onto for generations after the city had grown up around it. The pictures on the walls displayed at least three generations of family with the same faces separated by decades of memories.

Jack knew that the two missing women were not in any of the photos so that could mean more were being held if someone was home when the killer arrived. That is of course if the missing women were alive when the killer got here. Which was still up in the air. All he did know was that they were missing and had been spotted 200 miles from here almost a week ago. Beyond that, it was hope that kept them alive in Jacks mind.

From the back of the house emerged a member from the rear team and they met halfway down the hall at the door to the basement. Jack pointed at it and moved his hand in a circle above his head ending the motion pointing at the door. The team followed the instruction and lined up again with the short wide man in the lead. Time was short; the sounds from them entering and clearing the house from above would send the maniac below into action. They had precious seconds before screams would be heard. Jack was really hoping to find them upstairs and have this over with, but now, with the element of surprise gone, speed was his only chance at getting anyone down there out alive and he needed to move fast. He could see the worry in Cathy's face as they lined up again on the basement door. He knew she was thinking the same thing he was, they were too late.

Jack gave the nod and the man smashed through the door again with the hammer and this time, pulled back off to the left, allowing the team past instead of rushing inward down the stairs. The four man stack flooded down the staircase into the darkness with Jack in the lead and into a hail of bullets.

CHAPTER 2

This was always his favorite time of year. The snow was knocking at the door and forest had given up its lush green color to the skeletal remains of limbs and trunks. They reminded him of the cold bitter winter to come. Everything seemed to slow and move at half speed. Even in school, the teachers didn't seem to focus on cramming the useless knowledge into the minds of their youth during this time. They too realize that this was a time to bundle up and await the change in season. It was an inevitable thing that you couldn't change, only prepare and await the coming stillness and cold for months to come.

What the season did bring was Halloween and a break from school. For some reason this holiday was recognized and celebrated the world over. He didn't know if it was real or fake or if it held some sort of ritualistic meaning, but what he did know was he didn't have to go to school and was allowed to beg for candy from total strangers. This made him anticipate the night and the day more than other children his age, but for reasons and purposes beyond their understanding.

For Vincent it was a time where he could be like any other child. A time to put on a costume and blend in with all the other ghouls, goblins and ghosts roaming the streets without anyone knowing who he was. He could be like all the other kids, greedily moving from house to house begging for candy with outstretched buckets and bags all the while keeping count of his loot and planning what to eat first when he arrived home from the evening.

His plan was always the same. He would get home, run to his room, lock the door and poor out the candy into a large pile on his floor. He would separate every piece according to type. Chocolate would be separated into types. Snickers from 3 Musketeers, from Reece's Peanut Butter Cups, from Mars Bars from Mr. Good Bars, candy bars with nuts from bars without. Hard candy into sweet and sour. Single pieces separate from packages with multiple. Homemade treats separate from fruit. Gum separate from taffy. It was a process that required time and focus. After the separation was done, then the inventory would begin. The count of each type was tracked and recorded in his mind. He never forgot. He could remember his haul from 3 years ago to this day down to the flavor of lollipop.

The thing that separated Vincent from the other children was his chauffer and large black car that awaited him on the block at the end of the street. All the other children were accompanied by parents always watchful from the sidewalks or patiently sitting in their station wagons watching them and enjoying the nights feeling and event with their children. The kids would scurry from the house to the car to show their parents and then off to the next house. For Vincent it was a strange site. The hugging and smiles, the laughter and happy faces of both parents and children were something he didn't understand. It's not like the children were accomplishing some astonishing task. They were simply begging. Putting out their hands for free stuff and the parents were happy with them doing it. It made no sense to him but it was an accepted behavior one day a year so he partook. His driver, Charles, would wait silently and then drive him home without uttering a single syllable. It was his life and what he had grown used to.

In all honesty it wasn't Vincent that wanted to participate in the event. It was his mother that convinced his father to send him to public school where he was subject to such pagan holidays. He remembered the argument they had 2 years, 3 months and 11 days ago. She said he was strange and different from other kids. Said he needed interaction with kids his age. His father simply grunted and walked from the room.

Apparently mom won the dispute because the next day, Charles dropped him into a mass of idiotic, unorganized chaos that was called School. The children all ran about in multicolored clothes. Some bright, some checkered, some striped. Some wore uniforms with letters on them and others dressed in short skirts with makeup. Everyone seemed to be in a hurry to get somewhere or talk to someone. A loud obnoxious bell rang out every hour signaling the gates to be opened or closed and floods of children to poor out into the hallways, scrambling like bees in a hive from locker to locker then back into different rooms, all within 60 seconds leaving the before mentioned hallways empty and void for 50 minutes.

Vincent melted into the background as much as possible. He wasn't stupid and understood what the teachers required of him and he played their game to keep them from ever devoting his name to memory. He was never late or too early. He never sat at the front or back of a class. He never volunteered or joined a club and he kept his grades at a steady B average so that attention would not be drawn his way by being too smart or lacking in a subject and requiring extra help.

Friends were out of the question; very few if any of the children could possibly understand him and his way of thinking. This whole school process was nothing more than a requirement of life. A passage you had to take to move forward in society. No sense of enjoyment or pleasure was found in it. He felt the same way with food. You eat to survive. Without food you would shrivel up and waste away. Your strength would leave you and eventually you die. So he ate. Nothing was particularly enjoyable about it. Sometimes the taste of a different food would make his senses burst with excitement for a short time then it would pass and he would simply resort back to his staples of necessity to survive.

But Halloween was his one time to let down his reserves and blend with the other children. He could observe them up close without being stared at with accusing questioning eyes by the others. Nobody knew who he was behind the Chewbacca mask. He was just another kid trying to look like some big hairy beast that was in a movie just released called Star Wars. He himself had never seen the film and had no desire to, but since everyone around him was talking about it he figured he would blend better dressed like the creature.

After a very short time he discovered that many of the children felt that Chewbacca creature was a good costume as he passed one after another on the sidewalks. Other creatures he assumed from the Sci-Fi movie could be seen as well as the staple night creatures associated with the holiday.

So much could be learned from observing the unorganized movements of these people. Why did they feel the need to run back and forth giggling like idiots to one another or talk so feverishly about things that had no meaning? Like it was a serious thing or act that could change the world. They were oblivious to the real world, what mattered and what didn't. This tissue thin hold on reality that they had was so apparent to him but invisible to everyone else.

The year was 1980; he was 13 now and felt every bit of 30. He knew he was smarter and better than all the morons surrounding him and felt that his life needed a change. He needed to move on and fast. Unfortunately in this world, he was bound by certain rules and restrictions beyond his ability to change. The first of which was his age. For some unknown reason, 18 years was deemed appropriate enough to live on your own, go to war, vote and have the ability to go to jail.

He wondered who deemed this age to be 18? Why not 17 or 19? Is it because 18 is an even number? Or was it because most children had graduated from high school by this time and were destined to be removed from under the yoke of parental control? What about those that went on to college? Would their ability to become an adult be put on hold until a degree was secured? What if they wanted to be a Doctor? They go to school for 8 more years, by that time they could be 26 years old and still have never done anything but school in life. How is that any different from him on his own now? School is school isn't it? The pursuit of higher education whether it be basic math or brain surgery is still school. It's learning something more than you knew before and therefore, you are not in the mainstream of life but under the protective umbrella of education and learning. How could you be expected to be any different than him now?

He read books daily, every topic and subject he could get his hands on. His intellect was far greater than any of the children in his school by far and he knew without question that his teachers were below him as well. At times he had to fight his inner desire to correct his teachers as they spewed out nonsense and incorrect information to the soft minded children around him.

So it couldn't be school that determined the mysterious number 18. It had to be something more meaningful. These thoughts ran through his mind as he settled into the leather seats of the large car driven by Charles. His time with the costumed commoners was over as Charles had indicated by flashing the lights at him after returning from another house and receiving yet another donation of candy from strangers. It was time to return home.

The hour was approaching 9 o'clock and he knew his father was already in his large study separate from anyone else in the house. He could picture him sitting in the large brown leather chair near the fireplace sipping a drink out of his square, crystal cut glass with two ice cubes rattling around inside and staring into the flames. He would often sneak down stairs and peer in at him and watch him for hours just sit and drink and stare at the flickering heat. This was the extent of the interaction he had with his father. If he wasn't at work or away on a business trip, he was in this room, silently pondering over subjects in his mind that only he could understand.

Mother would be in the lower entertaining room drinking wine and listening to her records over and over. She would do this until well after he was asleep. Many nights the sounds and rhythmic noise floating up through the house would be the last thing he would hear before drifting off to sleep. He thought the music all sounded the same, but his mother assured him that the artists were different and each song had its own meaning. Some vast

14

and deep bringing you to tears while others were simple and happy, making even the cloudiest day seem bright.

To Vincent he could never tell the difference. It was all noise, plain and simple. It was a distraction from his mind and the reality around him. It blurred out his senses and prevented him from focusing on his personal desires and thoughts. If anything, music was more of a distraction than school was.

Why allow this to happen, he thought. Why put something in your body that hinders you and slows your judgement like his father did with alcohol? Why allow this sound to take over your mind and stop the pursuit of knowledge that he found in his books? It was a waste. He vowed to never be as weak as either of his parents.

After an hour, the car slowly rolled to a stop and waited at the large Iron Gate that separated his home from the rest of the world. Two men exited a shack on the right side of the gate and pulled it open after Charles gave them a wave. The gate reminded him of a prison. He had read about them in his encyclopedia set. There were many prisons around the country. He had never seen one in person, but after the description given in print he deduced that he himself was a prisoner in one. It was a simple definition; A walled perimeter with infrastructure to house people and guarded to prevent entering or exiting without permission. An interior structure built to contain, house and feed people under protection without allowing them to leave and holding to strict routine day in and out. To take out of the public eye. His home was a prison. He was its sole inmate and he was tired of being held captive.

The car rolled forward and the two men holding the gate tipped their heads down at him as the car passed

through. He imagined they were freezing. The
temperature had dropped in the last few hours at least 10
degrees and the wind had picked up. He wondered what
would make a man stand in a small shack for 12 hours just
to open and shut a gate for a child. Pathetic, he thought.
Maybe they were paid well, maybe his father made them
do it. He didn't know and didn't care enough to continue
thinking about it.

The driveway up to the house took 5 minutes to
traverse as it winded and twisted through trees. Every
100 feet or so there were lampposts on the sides that
looked like something out of a Sherlock Holmes novel,
illuminating the large paved road around them. The
forest beyond the drive was more like a park than a forest.
Huge trees shot from the ground into the sky and the
ground around them was vacant of anything but thick
green grass, carefully manicured by dozens of people
daily, employed by his father. It looked like a cemetery
for giants as the light illuminated only the base of the trees
through the inky blackness of night as far as it would
allow you to see.

He could see the last bend in the drive as the light
from the house illuminated the clouds above it on the hill.
Rounding the turn it came into view and stood mammoth
through the windshield. It grew in size the closer the car
got. 4 Stories of brick and masonry work towered above
the circular driveway in front. It didn't belong here.
Maybe on a Dukes estate in Europe from that long ago
time of horses and carriage's, but not in Upper New York
state. He had heard people refer to a house this size as a
Mansion or Estate. Even once he overheard his Father
on the phone in his office talk about the family holdings,
but in no way was it ever called a home or house.

A man in a black suit and tie came down the long rows of marble front steps to meet the car as it pulled to a stop opening the door for him. He was a tall, stick built man, older than his father but seemed healthier in some way.

Arthur was his name. He lived in the guest house across the property. You couldn't see it from here and it was a good 20 minute walk to get there. Mom said he was in charge of the estate and responsible for all its workings, day in and out. Vincent didn't really know what that meant but he figured that Arthur lived for free and mowed the lawn or something.

"How was your Trick or Treating Master Vincent?" he asked with a smile reaching for his bucket of candy.

Trick or Treating. What an obscured way to describe what he was doing. He wasn't tricking anyone about anything except maybe for his identity and as far as treats went, he could only assume it meant the candy he was peddling for like a street dwelling homeless vagrant from complete strangers. They should call it Undercover Begging, not Trick or treating for god's sake!

"Good, is Mom Up?" was his reply, pulling back the bucket from his outstretched hand. It was his after all, he had done all the work to get it, and he wasn't going to hand it over to Arthur.

"Yes sir, she is in the Lounge and your father is in his office. Would you like me to fetch them for you?"

"No thanks. I will just go to bed."

"Very good sir." He replied back and shut the door.

The car pulled away immediately and vanished into the enormous garage connected to the eastern wing of the Estate home. The light flooded out from within one of the 8 doors as it rose up, illuminating the cobblestones in front and Vincent could see the shiny colors and shapes of all the other vehicles parked inside. His father was fascinated with the automobile and had over 50 different types and styles tucked away behind the walls of his garage. Every kind from Jaguars and Rolls Royce to more modern cars like Corvettes and Ferraris. He knew each kind, make and model. He of course was never allowed to touch them and he had only been inside the garage one time to stare at them, but that was enough to devote them to memory and look them up in his vast book collection. To him it seemed a waste of money. None of them ever left the building. They simply sat there getting wiped down daily by people with nothing better to do with life than polish another man's car.

Arthur held open one of the massive rounded wooden doors for him to enter, like he wasn't capable to do it on his own. Inside, the cavernous space of the Fourier was not warm or snug as a home should be. Nothing about the space was inviting or welcoming, instead it was empty, cold and vacant of feeling or hominess. It was his prison. Across the vast entry room sat two large staircases hugging the side walls of the room leading up to the second floor in a slow gradual arc ending at the second floor landing and to his bedroom. Each step covered from top to bottom in a red velvet carpet that was never appealing to barefoot walking. The rounded handrails were dark oak with large golden orbs on top and bottom of the newel posts. On the upper landing in between the two staircases stood a sculpture of a woman with no arms. She was naked from the waste up and her stone nipples stood out at him as he walked by. Vincent hated the thing.

His mother told him it was a beautiful piece of art that his father had purchased for her in Europe and shipped here on one of his many business trips overseas. Apparently the thing was really old and was worth a lot of money. To him it looked like an armless naked woman that was in his way constantly staring at him as he passed by.

"Would you like me to have a snack made for you sir?" Arthur asked.

How sad, you live for free at my parents' home and you can't even make me a snack yourself, you would have someone else do it.

"No thanks, I'm tired, just going to turn in."

"Very good sir. Have a pleasant night sleep and Happy Halloween." He replied back with a half nod toward him.

Arthur turned to his left and walked away through a set of double doors leading into the kitchen and off to the East Wing. Vincent figured he was going to make himself something to eat and then go to his house for the night. No doubt he would sneak a bottle of wine and some food on his way. What a pathetic way to live. Sneak around, head down, doing another man's bidding. Always at his beck and call and stealing food in the night like a rat while living in another man's home.

As he ascended the stairs he could hear the faint sounds of music echoing down the long hallways above him. His mother would remain upstairs until well after he was asleep. She would give up her self-destructive wave through the day around midnight and wake around noon the next day to begin her intoxicated ritual of music, wine and solidarity again. It was her life. He had no desire to see her or his father and knew that it wouldn't be difficult to avoid either of them until he decided it was time.

CHAPTER 3

He was happy to finally be in his bedroom and done with this night of ridiculous childhood make believe and parental dreams of youth past that in no way appealed to him. Of the hundreds of different rooms in the prison, this was his and the only constant he had. Unlike the extravagant and meaningless decoration of the rest of the house, his walls were lined with his books. His Treasure! The one thing his father was good for was always allowing him to get whatever new piece of literature he desired from the book store in town. Autobiographies , Science Fiction, Murder mysteries, Educational books and every other kind of reading you could want was sitting on the shelves waiting for him. He even had a set of human anatomy books that you would routinely see on a Doctors shelf in his office, not a 13 year old boy's room. He had read them all cover to cover already and was striving to find more. Until then he would re-read his favorites.

As Vincent undressed and discarded his costume he admired the knowledge that surrounded him. He had read every word between the covers lining the walls already and most of those he had been through twice. His thirst for the unknown was a consuming force that pushed him deeper into the pages. Apparently children didn't begin to read until the age 6 and it was limited to small children's books like Cat in the Hat or See Spot

Run. By age 6 Vincent had read the Adventures of Huckleberry Fin and 20,000 leagues under the Sea by Jules Vern. For some reason his parents didn't pay any attention to this little phenomenon. Or maybe they expected it. Either way, it didn't really matter to him, he continued on his road of knowledge.

Unlike other nights, tonight he would vary in his ritual of getting ready for bed and reading himself to sleep. This night he had made other plans, plans that would change his life forever and get him out of this prison for good. Tonight's actions would be vaulting him into the world outside the walls so he could carve his own path and be allowed to change the world how he saw fit.

With costume on the floor at the foot of his bed exactly where he wanted it to be and pajamas on, he lay on the floor and separated his candy the way he had decided earlier in the night. Small piles were segregated in a circle on his floor by size, type and amounts. This was a necessary part of the plan. All had to remain in order without change in routine. It's what he suspected any child would do with the sugary haul from the night. Some of the candy that didn't fit into specific categories were opened and flushed down the toilet while the wrappers were placed about in pre-determined places on his floor.

He didn't want to eat them, but couldn't allow them to mingle, out of order with the rest and some residue of candy consumption must to be seen. After all, what childe wouldn't eat some or all of his candy on Halloween night when his parents weren't looking.

Planning and attention to detail was what he had learned from his books. Nothing could be out of place or stand out to draw attention. All had to look normal and without question. He moved across the room to his desk in the far corner against the window. It was a large wooden thing with an oval top that rolled up exposing a neatly organized working area, complete with pens, pencils and a pad of paper on his writing area. His school books were placed on the right side, biggest to smallest in a tidy, even pile. He had already done his homework for the weekend. It was the first thing he did upon returning home from school. This wasn't out of the ordinary, he always did it first. It was his way of being in control and not the incompetent teachers that gave him duties beyond their power or authority to complete. Getting his work done as soon as he was home was a way of ridding himself of this.

The darkness of night had overcome the horizon with clouds blocking out the dimming moon light through the window behind the desk. Only tiny dots of light winding across the black tapestry of the hillside lining the drive up to Estate could be seen. The wind howled on the glass outside searching for a way inside. The weather report in the paper was correct; there would be a storm tonight. He could sense the wetness outside and knew that before long rain would be tapping on the glass.

He pulled out the chair and crawled down under the desk. With a sock over his hand like a child's version of a puppet he reached up to the backside, under the top drawer and withdrew the large knife taped to the back of it. It was a very obscure and menacing looking thing. The tip was broken off leaving a blunt half inch wedge of rusted and pock marked steel at the end of the 6 inch blade. Initials were carved into the worn and cracked wooden handle, JG. He had no idea what they stood for, maybe John Gacey or Jimmy Green. Possibly Jodi Gresham, he didn't care. All he did know was it couldn't belong to his parents or anyone from the home. It could in no way be attached to anything his parents owned.

That's why he stole it from the toolbox of a construction crew 8 months ago that were doing work on his father's pool house. He was sure they had no idea it was missing and wouldn't care if they did discover it gone. Besides even if they did, enough time had passed that if it was noticed, they had given up the search. Planning was the key to everything.

Careful not to touch any part of the knife with his bare hand, he set it down on the floor next to the candy with his sock glove and opened his backpack. In a tiny compartment tucked away on the bottom of the bag he withdrew 2 pair of white latex gloves he had stolen from his last visit to the school nurse for the annual flu shot administration 3 months ago. He took two pair because he knew through his reading that a good detective could pull the prints if only one pair was worn by a suspect depending on ambient temperature of the room as well as his own body heat and prolonged use. It was a long shot, but it had been done in the past, he wasn't going to take that chance so two pair were secured.

Preparation was just as important as planning.

The large grandfather clock standing in the downstairs office bonged out 11 chimes, notifying the house an all residing in it of the current time. It was faint by the time the sound reverberated up to his room, but his hearing was perfect and he knew the time was growing near. His father was surely done by now staring mindlessly into the flickering orange light and had retired to his bed. Soon he would be sound asleep dreaming of his future wealth. Within the next hour his mother would stumble upstairs, collapse next to him and with the assistance of the alcohol would pass into a coma like sleep for the next 9 hours or more.

Since it was a Friday night and his father normally did not work on the weekends he assumed they both would consume more than the normal amount of alcohol and planned on sleeping in later than usual on the morning after. This all played perfectly into Vincent's plans.

Like any of the greats in history, from Jack the Ripper to Adolf Hitler, planning and preparation was paramount for proper execution. He had been planning and preparing for this the last year and a half. Every detail played through his head daily as he traced his steps home and back from school. He would scrutinize every plan he made and all the possible outcomes, both good and bad to the end. Some plans were discarded quickly; others took months to determine their inferiority then replaced by something better.

The window began to tick as the rain pelted it from the outside leaving small splashes of water on the smooth glass. Soon, the drizzle would turn to a down pour and the thunderous clap of the storm would boom above the house drowning any sound from inside. Tonight would be the night and it seemed like Mother Nature herself was agreeing with him and his decisions.

Across the room opposite his bathroom was the door to his closet, inside hung rows of clothing separated by season. Hundreds of colors, sizes and shapes filled the room that he was certain dwarfed most bedrooms kids his age lived in. Heavy jackets and long sleeve shirts on the right side closest to the door for the fall and winter hung motionless as he swung the door open. Across the back was a row of short sleeve polo shirts and button ups. Miscellaneous styles of slacks and summer pants hung alongside them according to compatibility and style. None of these clothes he liked. His mother picked out most of them and well over half still had the high quality and overpriced tags hanging from a sleeve or pant line. On the left wall was a series of shelves that resembled a honey comb more than a closet organizing system. Each cube was two foot square and filled with its own specific item. Nothing intermixed. T-shirts took up two cubes, underwear one, socks one, pajama sets two, shorts and hats and gloves in two.

Vincent knew he had too many clothes and surely there were other people much more in need of his garments than him, but it was out of the question to donate a thing. If he grew out of something it was thrown into the incinerator in the basement. His father loathed the idea of someone digging through the garbage and discovering something he had paid for and keeping it as their own. He would rather it be destroyed before giving it to the beggars of this world. Maybe it was this way of thinking or code that promoted the wealth his family had. He didn't know, but he didn't agree with it and it would end tonight.

Below the cubes of perfectly stacked clothing was a tri-level shelf with shoes on it, again, organized by style and function down to the laces. A tennis shoe would not be seen sitting next to a pair of dress shoes, nor would a pair of rubber boots be next to an evening loafer for around the house. Everything had its place and was arranged accordingly.

Vincent pulled on the shoe rack and scooted it out into the center of the closet. Behind it, against the wall was a loose board in the paneling. He retrieved the broken tipped knife from the floor and with his sock glove on again he pried the board loose. Careful to not create a mess with splinters, he eased it out of place and gently set it next to the shoe rack. From inside the darkness of the hole left by the board, he withdrew a green and gold colored gym bag. He set the bag down, replaced the board, made sure it was snug and let no debris fall to the floor, then moved the shoes back in place. He carefully moved back out of the closet through the open door carrying the bag and knife in hand while observing the area before him to ensure nothing seemed out of place or disturbed.

He stepped around the piles of candy, careful not to mix any together with a careless footstep and placed the bag and knife next to the gloves on the foot of the bed. He went to the bathroom and flipped the light on. The marble floor and glistening sinks sparkled back at him with cleanliness and wealth when illuminated by the lights. The bathroom was enormous for a boy his age and had no real purpose in a house that had fourteen others spread out among its massive floor plan. He figured everyone that knew him thought him to be a spoiled kid; he did not feel that way. He didn't partake in the lavish lifestyle his parents did, nor did he find any more comfort in clothing that cost ten times what the normal kid wore. He was forced into this life. He never asked for it and if anything, he was being held captive by these people, who were preventing him from moving on with his own wants and desires.

Opposite the sinks, lay a large bank of cupboards. He retrieved his chair from the desk and placed it under the cupboards. He stood on it and opened the top most door. Inside were standard bathroom necessities. Rolls of toilet paper, extra tissue boxes, cleaning agents and a box of rags used by the house cleaners filled the space. Vincent scooted the box aside and reached into the far back of the space. He withdrew an old white towel. To anyone else, it seemed to be no more than a spare cleaning rag that had fallen to the far back of the space and that was the idea. Placing the box back to its exact position as well as the other supplies and closing the door, Vincent moved back to the bedroom with the towel and chair. He placed the chair back at the desk exactly where it was before, right down to the dimples in the carpet and laid the towel open across the foot of his bed.

Lightning split the sky outside in a strobing flash instantly exposing everything hiding in the darkness behind the windows and he tensed waiting for the crash of thunder to follow. Seconds later the window shook with a boom as the sky let go a clap from heaven. The rain pelted the window now in furious blows carried by the wind. He smiled to himself because the world was meeting his needs for the evening. The plan was working perfectly. Tonight was the night.

With the old towel lying flat on the foot of his bed, Vincent emptied the contents of the bag from his closet on it and arranged them neatly. He then placed the knife on the towel as well as the gloves. He took off his pajamas, folded them neatly and placed them next to his turned down blanket and looked down at the tools that would unlock his future. He ran it over in his head again. Each step, every detail, one by one, to not miss anything or leave a question for anyone. It had to be flawless, perfect and without question. The gong from the clock reminded him of the hour and time for the execution part of the plan.

Planning, preparation and Execution. Each one invaluable without the other.

He was naked and moved to the door cracking it slightly listening for the sound of his mother's music. It was silent. Somewhere in the last hour she had either passed out and let the record end on its own or turned it off and retired to bed with his Father. Either way, by the time he arrived, she would be long gone to this world. He was sure that even the thunder could not wake either of them. Easing the door shut and holding the knob to limit the sound of it clicking back into place, he returned to the bed.

The items from the bed were not his; nothing on the foot of the bed was. It was secured for this night over time from different people and places, all according to the plan. One by one he would gain a piece and select a separate location to hide it. This way if it was discovered by accident it would not seem so strange, an item by itself was just that. Nothing to raise alarm, but altogether, a person may be able to come to a very possible conclusion and that would not benefit him.

The shoes sitting on the towel he pulled from the bag were a size twelve. Four sizes larger than him. He had stolen them from the locker room at school, along with the running pants and matching hoodie sweatshirt 11 months ago. The roll of toilet paper he secured from a restaurant he and his parents went to three months ago and the masking tape was from the schools front office where he swiped it when nobody was looking two months ago. Each item alone seemed like nothing, but together formed the perfect plan. The pants and hoodie were fit for someone two feet taller and 70 lbs. heavier than him, but that's what the tape was for. He pulled the pants up and wrapped the tape around his waist as a belt. The bottoms of the legs he taped tight to his ankles. The hoodie hung down past his waste and the sleeves were six inches too long. The tape fixed that problem as well. The toilet paper was used to stuff the toes of the shoes so that his feet would fit snug and they wouldn't fly off. He put on both pair of gloves and used the tape to secure them over the sleeves of the sweatshirt.

Vincent moved across the room to the mirror and examined his work. Turning slowly from left to right he looked for any gaps to the skin or areas where something may come untucked. He bent to the ground touching his toes then as high as he could in the air testing the dexterity of his new outfit. Everything seemed to be in order and hold. He pulled the hood over his head and cinched the two pull cords down tight, securing them in a simple bowknot under his chin. The tiny hole of flesh that remained circled his eyes, cheeks, chin and mouth. It was perfect. The reflection in the mirror revealed a small person in oversized green and gold trimmed clothes with gobs' of tape around each limb and waist. It was impossible to distinguish age or sex let alone hair color or any other distinguishing feature under the ridiculous, sagging and clumsy looking outfit.

He placed the knife in the hoodies front pouch. The remaining tape, toilet paper and towel were stuffed into the bag then zipped shut. He picked up his folded pajamas, walked to the bathroom door, careful not to disturb the candy or wrappers placed on the floor, picked up his slippers and place them with his pajamas on the sink. Moving back to the bed, he grabbed the bag and walked out the bedroom door. He turned back to give the room another check. Nothing was out of place that was not planned. The candy remained on the floor, sporadic wrappers placed nearby. His costume lay on the floor next to the bed and it was turned down for his night as it always was.

Perfect planning, leads to perfect execution.

He flipped off the light, left the door cracked and moved into the darkness of the upstairs halls and took his first step toward his new future. A future of his own making and desire.

CHAPTER 4

The upstairs hallway led out from his room down the corridor to the double staircase landing where the armless naked woman with stone nipples stood motionless watching the downstairs entry and front doors looking for Vincent. Beyond the landing, down the opposite hallway lined with doors on both sides, stood a set of sliding doors covered in mirrored glass. Pushing the illuminated arrow on the wall beside, they slowly slid open revealing an elevator large enough for 3 to 4 people. Inside, he pressed the button for the top floor.

As Vincent looked at his reflection in the mirrored walled box with brass handrail at waist level, he was surprised to see the calmness in his own eyes. He always knew this night would come, and that it would be meticulously planned and perfectly executed, but he had certain reservations about feelings and appearance during the time it was to be accomplished. It was the human factor in any operation that could ruin the best laid plans. The one thing you couldn't count on or foresee and plan for. But he looked fine, no sweat beading on his cheeks, his eyes were not bloodshot or squinted with worry. He looked as calm as he did every morning when he went to school. This was nothing more than a task that must be completed, like his homework or brushing his teeth, he simply returned to the job at hand and continued on. This was going to be easier than he thought.

The elevator moved slow and silent. It was a state of the art thing his father put in for his mother to use. She had fallen and hurt herself multiple times in the past trying to use the stairs at the other end of the house after an evening of records and wine. So the solution was to spend unknown amounts of money to install an elevator, not take away the bottle. Sad he thought, but that was another reason he needed to move on.

As the light flicked on number three, Vincent set the bag on the floor and scooted to the far corner of the small space. He double checked the tightness of his cinched down hood and bow knot under his chin. He couldn't have it come loose and possibly fall over his eyes, obscuring his vision at an inopportune time. It all seemed to be in order and as tight as possible.

The light went out on three and four illuminated. Vincent withdrew the broken tipped knife from his front pouch and held it in his right hand down at his side. The blade was incredibly dull and was of no use to slice with. A stabbing downward plunge was the only purpose of a tool like this. The wooden grip felt strange in his hand through the doubled up surgical gloves. He could make out the small cracks in the handle against his palm, as he rolled it around reconfirming the grip. He smiled to himself at the warmth it produced in his body. The simple tool in his hand seemed to warm him from its touch. It was clear to him that this was right and what he was destined to do.

The light went out on number four and the doors opened. Vincent didn't even feel the ride stop. It was state of the art, he thought to himself. His father must have spent a fortune on this thing.

The upper level of the home belonged to his parents exclusively. It consisted of 3 bathrooms, the master bedroom, an office, library, sundeck and pool/spa room and guest room. Altogether he figured it was larger than most people's entire home, but his parents deemed their lives in the need of such lavish living. This was something he did not understand and was tired of being forced to live.

Instead of a landing with stairs, the hallway from the elevator led to an enormous set of double doors. The colors of the upper floor were brighter than the rest of the house. The carpet was a light blue with matching walls and ceiling which arched above with clouds painted across it. It was as if you were outside looking into a clear summer day. The pictures on the walls were of old farm houses and children at play. Aside from it being his parents dwelling, this was actually a warming place in the home.

One of the large oval wooden doors was half open, as it always was. He figured his mother was never fully capable of closing it in her state when the evening was done. The soft glow of light barely illuminated the multicolored blue carpet of the room inside. From the direction the light came, Vincent knew it was from the master bathroom. She must have left it on after using it before passing out in bed.

He pushed the door inward enough to squeeze through without allowing it to creak as it did when pushed fully open. Standing inside the threshold, he stood motionless, staring into the blackest part of the room, allowing his eyes to adjust to the darkness.

According to everything he had read, your eyes were made up of cones and rods. Cones were responsible for taking in light and filtering it for your vision during the day and rods were used to see in the dark. It took a maximum of twenty minutes for your rods to adjust to the darkness and be at their top performance. Vincent stood perfectly still in the dim glow for the required amount of time, until his vision was crisp and the before blackness of the room now displayed shapes and depth enough to move without detection.

The bed emerged from the dark with two motionless shapes on top of it. The large desk in the corner with chair became clear as well as the couch and ottoman on the far wall. He could see his mother's shoes lying on the floor where she had kicked them off on her way to the bathroom. His father's evening robe was draped across the end of the bed with his slippers neatly placed below it on the floor.

Their room was enormous. He looked up at the ceiling and even with his vision adjusted to the night, he could not make out the curves or end of it above him. Directly to his right stood another statue, smaller than the many others in the home but still too large for its place in the room. This portrayed a woman with wings, reaching upward toward the sky with both arms. She was on her tip toes and seemed to be stretching as far as possible. Her completely white features seemed to glow in the darkness as the fingers in her hands were balancing a large crystal ball. He had never thought about it before, but maybe she was an angel. Maybe she was sent here to protect his parents from their inevitable fate that they had brought upon themselves. Or, maybe she was nothing more than an overpriced piece of stone that was purchased and hauled up here by his mother to irritate him yet again on the way they chose to live their life.

He could feel his temper flare and the knife in his hand begin to shake. It wasn't his nerves, he wasn't losing them or coming apart with anticipation, it was anger, anger at the fact that he had been held here for so long, anger that they were oblivious to him and what he could do. He was destined for more than this. They would hold him back no longer.

Vincent moved to his father's side of the bed, gliding through the room like a wraith, silent and unseen among the shadows. He pictured the human anatomy in his mind, focused on the upper torso and everything underneath. The heart, lungs and upper cavity all protected by the chest plate and rib cage, human bone molded and formed to be its very own armor for the body. He knew his father was six foot three inches tall and weighed at least 230 lbs. He wasn't a giant of a man, like the people you saw in the newspapers or magazines bulging with muscle, but he would easily crush a boy his size if he was given the chance to react.

The form on the bed before him was face down. He had stood here many nights before and knew that his father preferred this position. He knew flipping him over was out of the question because of the chance at waking him and had planned accordingly.

The human spine consisted of 36 vertebrae, from the lower back above the buttock extending up to the base of the skull where the two weakest of them all resided. In most cases it required less than 5 lbs. of pressure to dislodge one of these two, rendering immediate paralysis. With a little more pressure, the vertebrae would move completely out of position from the rest, severing the nerves to the brain and killing you instantly. This was what happened when you were hung. Vincent knew that it wouldn't take more than one or two good strikes to accomplish this and if done correctly, his mother wouldn't be disturbed, but a half of an inch high he would be hitting the skull and doing no more than waking his father with a bump on the head. An inch low and the knife would hit a larger vertebrae in the spine and stop cold, more than likely his hand would slip off the handle from the force of the knifes sudden stop on the hard bone and slide down across the blade, slicing his fingers and thwarting everything he had meticulously planned.

For the last 6 months he had practiced on the accuracy of his strike and grip strength. Over and over he would swing his ruler down onto the tiny "x" he made on the floor in the corner of his closet. Hundreds, possibly thousands of times he repeated the exercise and made contact with the exact point each time. He had placed so many strikes into the carpet that he had worn a small divot out of the fabric to the bare, hard floor below. He had cleverly set one corner of the shoe rack to be held responsible for the deterioration in the fabric. By the time this night came, he was capable of delivering a full power swing directly down upon the same spot 5 times in a row in less than 5 seconds. Perfect practice and planning made for perfect and proper execution.

The broken tip of the blade shadowed itself against the far wall in his peripheral vision like the devil's long fingernail pointing down at its rightful soul before he brought it down on the small spot below the hair, above the collar of his father's sleep shirt, piercing the skin and cracking into the tiny space between bones in the neck. His father's entire body jolted in an electric shock. Both arms shot straight out to his sides and his legs flexed straight as if he was completing a belly flop from a high dive onto the bed. It was the only movement he made. Only a small grunt sound like an animal adjusting itself in sleep escaped from him for a brief moment, and then air leaving his lungs. It had worked perfectly.

Vincent looked across the bed at the still form next to his now lifeless father. She didn't move. Even the spasmodic jump of his right arm touching her side didn't bring her out of her intoxicated slumber. He knew it wouldn't.

The hole oozed out blood when he removed the blade in a slow stream up and out, leaking down both sides of the back of his neck pooling on the mattress around him. He knew once the heart stopped pumping, so would the blood and the mess would be minimal. No more than a pint would be left on the mattress, leaving at least 4 inside the body.

His Mother always slept on her back with her jaw half agape, like she was waiting for someone to feed her in her sleep. She sometimes snored while in this position especially after overdoing it with the wine and records, adding to his disgust for them both. Unfortunately for her, she would not go as quick or painless as his Father did. With only her throat visible, the rest of her body was safe under layers of heavy hand made comforters and blankets, leaving it as his only choice and point of entry.

There are no immediate answers in the jugular. By severing it, the person will either exsanguinate themselves from loss of blood or choke to death from lack of oxygen. Either way it would not be quick and could last for up to a minute before the body shut down from lack of blood or air and during this time they would flail and try to stop what was happening in a frenzied, chaotic manner. He knew this and is why he saved her for last. He couldn't risk waking his father with her flopping about fighting for life.

He gave one final look down at her face before he struck. Not because he was having second thoughts and her memories might alter his decision, it was more because he wanted to make sure his aim was perfect and precise. He didn't want to risk a last second move from her and the knife glancing off her chin or landing in her mouth. She wasn't a large woman, but if faced with life or death, Vincent was sure that he would lose the initial fight with her and the prospects of his future would be destroyed. It was a risk he would take. He had waited this long, he could wait another second to ensure she wasn't about to move.

The first impact sank to the hilt of the knife. All six inches disappeared into the small divot at the top of a person's chest just below the throat called the Jugular Notch or Hollow of the throat. He was off slightly with his aim as he could tell by the lack of air exiting her mouth and adjusted immediately. The crimson spray pumped up and out of the hole he created when he withdrew the blade and his mother's eyes snapped open revealing shock and pain with a half muffled scream escaping her lips. The blade came down a second time, faster and harder, cutting off the scream to a gurgle as he could tell the larynx had been severed by the blow this time. Out and in repeatedly he struck. His face was speckled with red velvet mist and both arms were soaked with her blood. He could feel the hoodies material soak up the blood and stick to his arms underneath. She flopped on the bed for only a moment trying to fend off the attack and hold her throat closed at the same time to no avail, and then went still.

Vincent left the blade hanging out of the mangled mess that was her throat and checked her pulse. After a minute of silence and feeling for a beat he knew she was dead. He stepped into the pool of blood forming on the floor beneath the bed with both feet. He turned and walked to the door, leaving bloody tracks behind him soaking into the carpet. He grabbed ahold of it a foot above the handle with a glove stained hand and pulled it fully open. It squeaked on the hinges past the point he knew they would. He walked down the hall to the elevator and rode it to the lower level and crossed the entry way to the front door.

He wiped as much blood as possible on the handle leading outside and stepped down the stairs into the well-kept and manicured lawn. Standing in the downpour of rain, Vincent stripped out of his clothes and used the towel he removed from the bag to wipe all the remaining blood from his face and body where it had soaked through.

Naked, standing in the rain in the darkest hours of the night, he tucked the gloves, clothes, and shoes back into the bag he had stolen and moved back up the stairs barefoot, careful to not step in any of the bloody sneaker tracks or touch a thing. He remained on the marble floor as much as possible to avoid the carpet. He knew that imprints could be used as evidence and only the most resent would remain visible on the carpet.

Inside the entry way, he used the towel one last time and dried himself completely off then replaced it in the bag. It was only two large steps across the marble floor before he reached the huge rug that filled the foyer. Once on it, he wiped his clean wet feet dry and proceeded to the back staircase, leading down to the basement, always double checking behind him for traces of his bare foot prints.

Walking through the house naked was a strange feeling. He felt vulnerable, but powerful at the same time.

Everything around him was his now, he would control his own destiny and there was nothing anyone could do about it.

In the basement sat the massive black cast iron boiler responsible for providing heat to the entire estate. The front door was 2 foot wide and high, it pulsed with heat and the ever ticking sounds of the fire from within. Donning the oversized fireproof gloves used to operate the thing the huge door swung open with ease on well-built hinges and Vincent tossed the bag into the blaze. He scooped a few shovels of coal from the nearby pile on top to ensure its complete destruction. The heat from inside illuminated his body in an orange glow and licked at him with tongues of fiery heat. Using the leather gloves again, he shut the door and opened all the vents to fuel the blaze to its fullest ability and returned to the upper entry way using the stairs again, all the while looking at each step to ensure no smudges or tracks were visible.

The clock in the study bonged out 3 audible notes, indicating 0300 in the morning. Vincent had finished his last rounds of cleanliness of any water and smudges related to his return into the home. Careful to not disturb any of the bloody tracks or his room's preparation he retired to bed after a nice warming shower to remove any last traces he may have missed in his own bathroom. Again, this was a norm for Vincent, showering before bed was standard. He donned his pajamas and curled up under his blankets for the most pleasant night's sleep he had ever had. He knew within 2 hours, Arthur would find the door ajar and see the prints leading to the grass and follow them to his parents' room and seconds later would burst into his bedroom to check on his own safety. He would find me sleeping soundly in a false sugar coma, oblivious to the evening's events. Then his life could finally begin. Perfect planning, leads to perfect Execution.

CHAPTER 5

The coffee this time of night was consumed for purpose and function more than taste. The pot, with stainless steel bottom like you would see at an all-night diner sat stalwart and alone on the back table in the breakroom with black, hot tar settling motionless a quarter way up the side. She was tired, but had hours to go before she could leave for the night or morning, whichever it was when it happened and she desperately needed something to keep her going. Two packets of sugar and a good three second poor of cream cut the bitterness down to the tolerable level. She cringed at the first swallow of the slightly warm brew she had concocted and added additional packets without thought.

Too many days and nights had been spent in rooms like this, she thought to herself, looking around at the pale grey walls with chipping paint clinging to the edges where ceiling and floor met, the green padded backs of the chairs around the metal tables looked out of date and worn from years of use but the same in some way. It was as basic a room as you could think of, void of any emotion, good or bad. Simply put, it was a waiting room.

"Agent Chambers?" Came a voice from beyond the open door to the room, "You have a call, Agent."

She turned toward him, a young agent, maybe 24 or 28 years old at the most. She felt old and alone standing in the empty space, with only the worn out coffee pot working in the corner chugging and ticking from the heat beneath it providing her company. It was a new world, a younger generation of agents popping up like flowerers in the spring. One day they weren't there, the next, the hallways were full of them, each one scurrying about trying to impress the boss or solve a case to enhance their career. Jones, she thought, Special Agent Marcus Jones was his name. She had been here about 3 months now and still had a hard time remembering his name or any others for that matter. They all looked the same. This case was stumping her and it wasn't something she was used to.

"Thanks Jones" she said as he turned and disappeared before the words could settle on his ears.

Youth, she thought to herself. Never, when she was a young agent, would she leave the room without being dismissed by her superior. You were too nervous about doing the right thing or failing to meet the standards, but, it was a new time, a new way of doing things with a new generation of people. They were all entitled to more than they deserved and didn't feel the need to earn any of it. They could read about all the greats on line and stream documentary's any time they wanted more information. The world was changing, it was something she was having difficulty adjusting to.

She walked out of the break room into the mass of offices, glass doors and cubicles. This time of night, the area held only a handful of staff working late cases or finishing up on past due reports. Unlike her, most of them were trivial matters and starter cases to cut their teeth on and gain experience. Simple Fraud and missing person cases was the most they had. It resembled a learning center more than it did an FBI field office.

She was awaiting a call from the lab, giving her a much needed break on a case that had been eluding her for months now and trying her patience at the same time. The place was far from home and she missed her real office, apartment and more than the suitcase of clothing she brought with her.

Each cubical she passed looked the same with nothing more than a few pictures or desktop bobbles to distinguish one from another. Same blue carpeted 5 foot divider walls, only inches separating you from the next with no door for privacy. Same government purchased chairs and desks filled the identical boxes with any lack of decorative ability or individuality. It was what young agents had to endure and at least that was still standard. She was sure it wouldn't last and the new it wouldn't be long before each newbie would get their own offices with the way things were going.

Her office, loaned to her for the case, was a large glass walled enclosure at the end of the room that had an adjoining briefing area attached to it. It was reserved for Lead Agents assigned temporarily to spearhead a case. The view from her desk looked out over the open blue maze of young agents. She opened the door, and sat behind her desk. The light on her phone was aglow and blinking at her in a pale orange light, she snatched the receiver up, and hit the button.

"Special Agent Chambers." She said without emotion or question.

"Agent Chambers, Pat here. I'm sorry to say, all the prints you sent in from the Wilson case matched only the deceased occupants of the home."

"Shit, what about the blood drops leaving the apartment or the DNA on the sheets?" she answered back, upset at the lack of findings and another dead end.

"No ma'am, same as the prints. Everything in the home belonged there, one way or the other. No foreign prints or DNA found." He said in a half defensive mode.

Cathy could picture Pat Simmons sitting at his desk down in the lab right now. His squinted little eyes behind those thick coke bottle glasses, pocket protector bulging with multi colored pens and a nerdy white lab coat that was a size to small. Completely clueless about what really happened outside the confines of his lab and the risks that real agents took daily. He, as well as the rest of the nerds down stairs had no idea how good they had it being isolated from the real threat agents were put in. They could call themselves FBI only by way of the name on their paycheck. They were sheltered and taken care of by the government and didn't have a backbone among the lot of em. But, unfortunately for her, they were damn good at their job and would find something if something was to be found. But this case eluded them and her alike.

"Agent Chambers? Ma'am, are you still there?" She heard him half begging for acknowledgment or approval through the earpiece.

"Yeah Pat, I'm here. Listen I'm going to send a couple guys back over to the Wilson's place to go over everything again. If they find something I will get it to you ASAP for analysis. Until then, go over everything you have again, the blood, prints and fibers we found, cross reference them with the Atlanta killings. Something must connect the two, look for what isn't there."

"Not a problem, Special Agent Chambers, not a problem at all, we are here to hel............"

She hung up before he could finish his monolog about helping them solve crime and battle the forces of evil. She could picture them all sitting together on the weekends in one of their tiny apartments sipping Zima's, wearing FBI T-shirts and watching CSI episodes over and over, getting pumped up on what they called fighting crime.

It was late, and she knew sleep wasn't an option. This case was weighing on her. It wasn't the worst she had seen but it was the cleanest. Nothing was left, not one damn clue. Nobody saw a thing and nobody knew a thing. For over three months now she had been stuck here on a possible connection to an Atlanta triple homicide. So far the only connection between the two cases was the lack of evidence.

The ages were different, the locations as opposite as night and day, mode of death changed and the only common thing was how clean each crime scene was. Not one finger or foot print, no trace of forced entry found and the cause of death varied. In Atlanta a husband, wife and 4 year old son were butchered with a large Chef knife from the block in the homes' kitchen. They lived in a quaint little suburb surrounded by other middle class working families. He was a manager at the local Home Depot and the wife was a stay at home mother that made a little extra cash, selling homemade crafts on EBay.

The Denver case was two coeds living in an apartment they shared while working their way through college. One was drowned in the bathtub the other was smothered with a pillow on the bed. She had nothing solid on both cases and no leads.

Rising from her chair and pulling her jacket on, she walked out of the office and down the hall to the elevator. If she couldn't come up with an answer in her office then she would go find it somewhere else, and the only place she knew could help was the crime scene. Sitting around and waiting wasn't something Cathy did well.

The elevator ride down to the parking garage struck a tinge of hunger in her stomach. Maybe it was the habit of grabbing a bite to eat when she left work or the fact that she really hadn't eaten at thing since she came to work 22 hours ago. Coffee and chewing gum didn't seem to fill the void as much as it used to. A quick stop at the 24 hour café 3 blocks from the office would suffice before she headed over to the Wilson place. Hell, maybe it would help her clear her head a little she thought.

The doors opened and she stepped out into the chilly early morning Denver air. It was fresh and smelled of the distant mountains as the wind carried the cold pine with it across the plains through the town. It chilled her to the bone. It was moments like this she missed Missouri and the warmth of the weather. Year round you could get by without a heavy jacket or hat, but here, it was standard issue when you woke up each morning.

Her Jeep was parked at the far end of the garage. It was a well-lit structure with nicely painted lines and curbs void of the standard scuff marks and rubs you would find back home. Denver was a large city but maintained a younger, cleaner image than the east coast. It was seen in the store windows, unlocked doors and cleanliness of everything. The car was a rental from the airport and her Director insisted she get the 4 Wheel Drive even though it was only September. Apparently it could snow here in September. The thought of snow was crazy and ran across her mind as the 2015 Jeep fired up with the push of a button and the smell of the new car made her smile. For a moment she forgot about the case and the hunger in her stomach. For just a moment she thought about driving out of the garage and heading east. Just drive and drive back to the heat and warmth of the south. Tell the

FBI it was a dead end, nothing could be found and get back to her old stomping ground.

The phone in her pocket vibrated, jolting her out of the far off thought. She pulled it out and glanced at the number. The area code was one she didn't immediately recognize. Tapping the button on the dash, answering through the Jeeps audio system which had connected automatically, she said "Hello?"

"Yes, hello, I'm looking for Special Agent Chambers." A man's voice answered through the vehicles BOSE, speakers. A voice she didn't recognize.

"This is, who am I talking to?" She asked back, talking to the dashboard as she buckled her seatbelt.

"Ma'am this is Sheriff Frank Johns of Klamath Falls Oregon, I was given your number from a Director Allen in Atlanta. He said to get in touch with you on a case we have up here."

Anger immediately filled her with the last statement coming out of the speakers. What the hell was Director Allen doing, sending her another case when she wasn't even close to finishing this one and why in Oregon! WTF? Is what the youth of America would say.

"I'm sorry, Sheriff Johns, is it? Are you certain that Director Allen wanted you to contact me about this?" She snapped back quickly, staring at her speakers in the Jeep as if they were somehow responsible for the outlandish request.

"Umm, yes Ma'am, Director Allen gave me your name and number specifically. He said you were close and could swing by to take a look." Johns answered back.

"Well, Sheriff, I am nowhere near Oregon and I really don't know where Klamath Falls is, but I assure you, it would be extremely difficult for me to swing by as I am in Denver Colorado at this time, not to mention I am working a case here that is occupying more of my time than I want already. I know there is a Field Office in Portland, perhaps they could assist you. Would you like me to give you the number?"

"Agent Chambers, ma'am, I have already been in contact with Portland, they put me through to the switchboard in DC and then to Director Allen in Atlanta. That's how I was routed to you."

The three toned beeping sound emanated above his voice but behind it, through the speakers. From the display screen on the dashboard, Allen's name popped up with the words Incoming call, blinking above it. She felt her temperature rise as nerves shot down her arms to the tips of her fingers.

"Sheriff, I will call you back, I have another call." She said, cutting off the explanation he was giving her for the reasons of his request and searching her out.

If Allen was calling, it could only mean one thing. He did pass off another case to her and was calling to explain the reasons as he would know she would be pissed. She had worked under him for years and never had an issue with his leadership or style of management. He was a fair man across the board with all the agents, but recently, she felt the short straw was landing in her lap more than anyone else's.

Tapping the screen on the flashing name and number she spoke. "Oregon? Are you serious?"

His voice was calm and sounded more like a manager than the man she knew. "Cathy, there has been a murder in Klamath Falls with the same M.O. as the case you are on now. It happened yesterday around midnight. Could be the freshest scene we have. I need you to get up there and take a look."

"What MO? How could you possibly think these are connected? I still don't know if Denver has anything to do with Atlanta and now you're sending me to Oregon on another case? What about the Portland office, can't they go look at it?"

"They are on the way, but you are lead on this. You have been working it for months now and Portland doesn't have a lot of experienced agents in this field."

"I have been working a murder of college students in Colorado and a separate case across the country, not a family in Oregon! That's like a thousand miles away from here. There's no way they are connected!" She could hear the anger in her voice and it surprised her slightly. Maybe it was the cold, maybe it was the hour and lack of sleep, or maybe it was just being stumped on a case with no leads. Either way she felt bad immediately and was thinking of how to respond when his voice came out of the speakers again.

"I know what you're thinking Cathy. I know it's not your part of the country, but you're my best in the field and if these cases are connected we may be looking at a long distance serial here. Take a break from Denver and fly up to Oregon, give it a look with fresh eyes, go over the scene and tell me what you think. If it's nothing, leave it in the hands of the Portland crew and I will buy you dinner when you get back. OK?"

She knew she would go with or without the promise of dinner, it's who she was, but it was nice to hear him ask so nicely instead of giving her an order. She had been with the FBI long enough to be spared that kind of treatment and she knew he knew it.

"Fine" she said with a tired tinge in her voice, "I will leave tomorrow morning, but I am expecting a meal with real cloth napkins, not a burger and shake."

"You got it; your itinerary should be in your mailbox now. You leave in 4 hours. Thanks again Cathy."

The call ended before she could protest to the departure time leaving the Jeep silent. The soft even purr of the engine gently vibrating her seat was all that filled the evening around her. She looked out the window at the dark night and wondered how cold Oregon would be this time of year. She missed home and wanted this case to be over. Four hour notice to stop a case and start another one wasn't the curve ball that bothered her. The possibility that Allen believed they could have a killer that traveled 1000 miles between crimes was something she couldn't comprehend.

Serial killers didn't stray that far from home. Maybe a state line would get crossed from time to time on a spree but never 1000 miles. Even if they did spread across the normal distances between killings, the mode usually remained the same. Rape, molestation, mutilation, stabbing, shooting or strangling. Something was common. The cases were opposite in style, location and reasoning. If these were connected it would be the first she or the FBI has ever heard of.

A couple swipes on her phone and the number from Klamath Falls popped up from recent calls. She pressed connect and waited.

"Klamath Falls Sheriff depart, Sheriff Johns speaking, how may I help you?" came through the Jeeps speakers.

"Sherriff, this is Special Agent Chambers, I will be there tomorrow morning. Send me the address and have someone to brief me when I arrive. Sheriff I need you to seal off the area and do not allow anyone in until I arrive."

CHAPTER 6

The road unfolded through the windshield in shadowed layers of repetition and waves. Mile after mile of blacktop rolled past with little difference separating one spot from the next. This highway running across the county was vastly undeveloped and therefore unpopulated. It was because of this it was his preferred route to take. He enjoyed the drive, it gave him hours of silent reflection that he so desperately needed after his task was complete. A car would pass him heading off the other direction once an hour or less limiting his exposure or risk of recollection to the lowest possible denominator possible. To anyone else, he was simply a car traveling from one place to another, anonymous and routine in this vast country. He strived to present the appearance of normality and the mundane as so many other people traveling across the country looked.

From its appearance on the outside, the vehicle was as basic and bland as anything else you would see. With its cream/tan colored paint and 15 year old body style, nobody would give it a second glance for the envy of ownership or remorse for the owner, either way; It simply said to anyone seeing him pass by, look away, nothing to see here.

It was straight, clean and very functional. Nothing was broken or missing to alert the unwanted attention of the police, and because it was a station wagon, he could blend in about anyplace he went without being devoted to memory. He prided himself on the attention to detail he took with it to not attract attention. It was all carefully calculated in advance. From the pre-positioned door dings to the Jesus fish bumper sticker on the back indicating his religious preference. He could hide in plain site with no worries whatsoever.

Beneath the dull paint and sad body style was a different story altogether. The engine was a supercharged V8 interceptor designed for police vehicles that he purchased brand new and had installed by a mechanic down in Arizona. He remembered the guy giving him the puzzled look while he placed the order. Nobody in their right mind would want such a powerful engine in such a sad example of a vehicle. I guess not many people want that kind of performance out of a 94 Ford Taurus Station Wagon, but they were not Vincent. The suspension was modified to handle turns and jolts equivalent to a race car along with a possi- traction rear end for control and traction in all kinds of terrain and the ability to carry extra weight without the appearance from the outside being obvious. A small shop outside of Denver was recruited to complete this task of the modification process.

The fuel tank was removed and replaced with an aftermarket custom tank with a capacity of 200 gallons. With the cruise control set at a steady, safe and non-identifying speed of 65 MPH, he could get 30 miles per gallon. This gave him a driving range of 5000 miles plus or minus depending on traffic and if he needed it, the Air-conditioner. The mechanic in a small shop outside of Redding California told him he could be an over the road driver with it, after he finished installing the tank.

The rear of the vehicle was equipped with two full size spare tires, a roll away Jack and enough misc. belts, hoses, fuses and bulbs to fix whatever minor issues he could foresee while on the road if something happened. Overall, the vehicle served its purpose well and had been trouble free for years now. Vincent saw no reason for this trip to be any different.

The sign on the side of the highway stated the next service was 75 miles away. He glanced at the small bag sitting next to him on the passenger seat containing bottles of water and snacks. The fuel gauge was still over half full and he didn't feel any road fatigue that the people on the radio continued to preach about. He wouldn't need to stop in the next 75 miles or the next place after that. If he maintained his speed and the weather held out, he would make it home by tomorrow afternoon with no problem.

He adjusted himself in the custom seats he had installed, feeling the gel that filled them conform and mold to his new body position. If the temperature outside changed too drastically or he felt a twinge in his back because of the prolonged sitting, he could adjust the temperature of the seats with the push of a button. For his lumbar and legs, the seats were equipped with massage bearings that would roll and vibrate in seven different settings to alleviate any pains and keep his blood circulating after days of sitting behind the wheel.

He felt the need to urinate again. This upset him at the weakness of his body. He controlled his body, not the other way around. Sleep, was easy to master. He was able to go four days without sleep. Five to six if he really wanted to push it, but his attention would slip and he wouldn't be operating at 100 percent in the later stages of consciousness if he went that long. However the need to evacuate his bowels was something he was unable to control longer than a day at a time. Besides the pain, which he could subdue more than most people the medical issues that could arise from holding back your urine for extended periods was something he would not risk.

Vincent hit the cruise control button on the wheel and retrieved a small funnel from the center console. Reaching down between the seat and the console he pulled up a half inch diameter tube and attached the funnel to it. Unzipping his fly, he held the funnel against his crotch and relieved himself. To any passing motorist, not that there were any, it would seem like road wash, splashing up from the rear tires as the tube transported his urine along the bottom of the car and disposed of it directly in front of the rear tire, completely concealed from anyone farther than a foot from his car. It was something he had come up with after his first trip and realized that the human body, no matter how focused or disciplined, still needed to eliminate waste over time.

Finishing up, he zipped his fly closed, grabbed a bottle of water, poured it down the tube flushing away the urine smell and remnants of his waste, disconnected the funnel, replaced it in the console and blew through the tube to ensure it was completely evacuated, then stuffed it back down into its resting place under his seat. He moved the seat back and regained control of the car by disengaging the cruise. He was good for another 8 hours he thought to himself and eased back into the seat letting his thoughts take him back to the last couple days in Oregon.

CHAPTER 7

Klamath Falls turned out colder than Denver. She realized quickly that her jacket, suitable for Denver wouldn't suffice up here as a gust of wind hit her, cutting through the material when she stepped out of the car onto the side of the road in the grey evening haze. The bite of frosted air reminded her again of the time she had spent on this case and how she longed to be done with it and back to the warmth of the south.

The small home nestled just off the highway against the mountain surrounded by police tape was buzzing with people in uniform coming and going. It looked like some fairy tale giant had wrapped the place up in a yellow ribbon. Klamath Falls Police Dept. must have had a surplus of the police issued tape and were doing their best to use up every foot it. From the looks of the sporadic and chaotic movements of unorganized men and women scurrying around with no apparent direction or structure, she knew the small town had never seen a homicide like this and had no idea how to handle it, which was most likely the real reason she was called in to lend a hand from Allen.

Cathy pulled her collar up and tucked her head as low as she could to protect from the biting wind and keep in the little bit of rapidly escaping warmth she had remaining from the ride to the airport and pressed on toward the house. The sooner she got inside, and determined this was just a murder without any attachment to her case the better. She was certain it was a simple matter of shock and awe from a small town department dealing with the ever increasing barbaric nature this world was heading in. They were just not ready yet.

The home sat a hundred yards off the road directly across a large lake and looked as if it was constructed directly into the side of the mountain. She assumed it was called Klamath Lake being within such close proximity of the only town it only made sense. The evening wind picked up waves of cold moisture blowing across it seemingly focused directly at her as it pounded at her walking across the road. The remnants of burnt road flare ash littered the highway as far as she could see and the police had closed off the right hand lane using it for a staging area to park vehicles. The scene was almost two days old by now but you wouldn't know it by the amount of congestion around the home.

A young looking deputy approached her when she neared the police line and held out his hand.

"I'm sorry ma'am, this is a crime scene, and you can't come in here." He stuttered with as much authority as he could muster.

From his stance and demeanor, she could tell he had never been in a situation like this, nor had he ever needed to tell anyone to stop doing anything before in his life. His uniform looked clean, but a size to large and from the slack material hanging around the sides, he wasn't wearing a vest and weighed maybe a buck twenty at best. The gun belt wrapped around his tiny waste was from a long ago era with a worn brass double buckle and browning leather from years of use by other officers showing through the black around the edges. The revolver resting in the holster was hung low and huge on the man's frame and pulled down one side of the belt. She had a hard time believing the belt didn't slide down around his ankles. It looked out of place for today's law enforcement and completely alien on such a small man. Every department she could think of used semi-automatic pistol and none of them had the old leather belts any more. Synthetic and Velcro was the way of the future but it seemed Klamath falls didn't conform well. The clip on tie, around his scrawny neck was huge in comparison to his build which only made the star on his chest seem like a toy bought at a children's costume store all that much fake. All in all, it was hard to think of him as a cop let alone any kind of authority figure.

"Deputy, Waterberry is it? I am Special Agent Chambers, FBI. I need to get into the house and take a look around. " She said staring at the jumble of letters crammed onto his blue name tag, hanging from his right shirt pocket.

"Oh, I'm sorry ma'am, I mean agent, come right in." he said, pulling the tape up over her head.

Jesus, she thought. No ID check, no proof of who she was, no radio call for authorization and he used his shooting hand to raise the ribbon offering her his pistol side for the taking. This guy was an accident waiting to happen! Never mind the fact a strong breeze could knock him down, he was completely oblivious to his job. This had to be the real reason Allen sent her out here.

The home was different than the case she was on in Denver or Atlanta. This was a rural home, 10 miles from town. The closest neighbor was a half mile down the road in either direction. She knew it was a simple case of incompetence on the Oregon Departments side and they just wanted the Feds to get involved because they couldn't handle it. So far, nothing seemed to connect them.

Standing on the front steps of the home was a large man with 20 extra pounds hanging over the same style leather belt as Deputy Waterberry. He wore a large, puffy, down filled jacket that said Sheriff across the back in oversized white letters with an oversized star embroidered on the front. He was bald with a bright red head from the cold nipping at it and his ears and nose tips radiating the same shades or darker. An oversized white mustache extended down around the edges of his mouth and tied into a scruffy looking goatee that needed some trimming.

"Agent Chambers?" He asked, stepping down from the top step and offering his plump and oversized hand to her as if she was unable to climb the stairs herself.

"You must be Sheriff Johns." She replied, taking his hand and stepping up to the deck with him.

She was a good four inches taller than him and at least 80 pounds lighter, not to mention 20 years younger. He had a weathered grandpa's look to his face more than a Sheriff. His blue eyes were crisp and sure but she could see the worry and confusion behind them. She was certain that in all his years as a police officer, this was something he had no way of understanding and was thankful for her being here.

"Thank you for coming so quickly, we are kind of at a loss here. This thing is more than my department has ever handled or seen for that matter. I appreciate whatever help you can give us." He said while giving a half nod in the direction of Deputy Waterberry standing behind the tape pulling up his belt again and adjusting the star on his chest.

"Well, Sherriff, let's see what you got inside and then I will tell you what I can and can't help with."

"Your Director said this could be a serial case and maybe your guy has moved up here. Do you think that's true?" He asked excitedly as he moved out of the way on the porch.

Her temper flared at the question. What was Allen thinking telling this hick anything about her other case or planting the seed of a serial? She was sure this was nothing more than some local, getting fed up with the weather and giving in to his cabin fever by killing a random family or something. Nothing about the location or home led to any kind of connection up to this point and Allen hadn't even been out here to see the scene in person.

"Sheriff, I am sure we can figure something out on your case, but as far as what I am working on in Denver, I assure you, so far I see no reason that these cases have anything common." She answered back to him with as much control she could muster.

The front door was open and no splintered wood or cracked glass appeared on first glance indicating forced entry, as she followed him inside. The living room was large with huge bay windows lining the front with a view of the lake. If it wasn't for the highway right in front of the home, it would be a nice view she thought, if you could stand the cold that is. A large stone fireplace filled the far wall of the room with two couches evenly spaced on either side of it. No television was apparent in the room and it had an old, retired person vibe to it.

"Sheriff, who lived here?" She asked looking at the first room.

"Mr. and Mrs. Anderson." He said.

"Just them? No children, no grandchildren?"

"No, no, they had children and grandchildren, four kids and seven grandkids I believe, but it was only the two of them that lived here now. Kids moved out years ago and they have stayed here alone ever since. Hell, they been here for as long as I remember, they used to babysit me when I was a kid."

Again, she thought, completely different than her other cases. This was an old retired couple living in the country. Denver was two young college girls renting a place of their own downtown, working as waitresses on the weekends. Atlanta was a family in a suburb with a working husband and stay home wife. Aside from the distance separating the cases nothing else seemed to bring them any closer to each other than before.

"If you'll follow me Agent, I will show you what we found." He said with a low voice, as if he would be disturbing her or the dead people in the home if he spoke any louder.

A hallway exited the living room opposite the far couch and off to her right was an oval opening that served as an entrance to a kitchen. Nothing in either room shouted out home invasion or breaking and entering. It simply looked like an old retired couple's home. No upturned furniture or broken dishes were strewn about. No blood or signs of a struggle. It was an old retired couple's home. Plain and simple.

She followed Johns as he walked down the hall and turned right at the end out of sight. The walls of the hallway were lined with photos of people in all different seasons and ages. Some young, some old. Baby's, adult, military, weddings and what looked like reunions. Winter photos with the lake in the background and summer shots with flowers in bloom. Some were old still framed in black and white and other appeared to be taken with a digital camera and looked no more than a few months old. At the end of the hall she turned the direction Johns did and started climbing up a narrow set of stairs. Again, the walls on both sides of the stairs were littered with photos of people in all stages of life, giving the home a feeling of warmth and security.

She caught up with him at the end of an upper hall standing in front of a door at the far end. He was still and immovable. The red color of his face and head had faded and was now pale in the dimly lit hallway. She could see the fear in his face and the desire he had to not enter the room. He knew these people and this was hard for him. She could sense it and really didn't blame him much. Small town law enforcement generally kept the honest people honest and didn't have to deal with this kind of thing. It was more of a job of honor and friendship than authority and enforcement.

"Sheriff, if you don't mind, I would like to go in and take a look around alone, with fresh eyes."

She could see the relief in him as his posture deflated slightly taking in a breath and giving her a nod of thanks and understanding while stepping aside.

"Of course Ma'am, I will be downstairs if you need something."

She nodded back at him and watched him waddle down the hall, disappearing down the stairs at the end. He never turned back or looked at anything but the carpeted floor in front as he went. He was out of his element and too close to these people to be any good in the investigation.

Donning her gloves, she turned the knob and stepped inside. It was like stepping back in time, every piece of furniture in the room seemed to be a hundred years old, but in perfect condition. Lace doilies and coasters sat on nightstands protecting the wood finish wherever they were needed. The queen size bed against the wall sat on an old iron frame with rounded metal rungs around the foot and head. A wooden chest with padded top sat against the end of the bed. Everything was neat, clean and organized. Nothing seemed to be out of place or disarray. If it wasn't for the dead man in the bed and the woman on the floor in a pool of blood, the place was picture perfect.

CHAPTER 8

The powder used by the Departments Crime Scene
team lingered in the air with a chalky school room scent.
A quick glance at the door told her the team was
inexperienced and new to lifting prints. The residue was
everywhere. If her team was brought in there was no
doubt the scene would be compromised beyond recovery
of anything holding up in court. The carpet was clean and
free of anything giving it the appearance of an unkempt
home, but the multiple tracks in and out solidified her
assumption of an inept investigation team.

As carefully as possible, trying not to disturb what
was left of the scene that could be salvaged as evidence;
she approached the woman on the floor. The body was
face down in blood. She was wearing what her
grandmother used to call a sleepy. A long white night
gown with no sleeves that was floor length. It was an
older generation of dress fitting with the home. The
women had a full head of short cut white hair that was
tinted pink around the back.

The cause of death appeared to be multiple blows
to the back of the skull with a hammer that was lying on
the floor next to the body. Her nails were clean and free
of skin, so there was very little if any struggle or fighting
back. Urine smell rose from the body the closer she got.
As all people do, your bowels give up control of all

muscles when your heart stops and it lets go. Leaving your last moments on earth dirty and embarrassing. It was difficult to get used to and she could see why Johns had such a hard time seeing it happen to someone he knew so well and didn't blame him for making a hasty retreat.

Both bodies were only slightly bloated. Given the time of death reported to her being 32 hours ago, she assumed the cold temperature had assisted in delaying the natural order of decomposition. The pool of blood was still, cold and had changed to the dark black color that blood does when it sits for any length of time. Very little spatter was seen higher than the edge of the bed which told her the lady was pushed down and struck while on the ground, ending her life. She could count 3 distinct impacts on the back of her skull, each one producing its own tiny pool of dark crimson mixed with grey matted, sticky hair.

The man on the bed laid spread eagle with arms and legs out to his sides as if he was taking a Nestea plunge. No blood splattered the comforters or sheets around him. Only a single waffle style impact between his eyes from what appeared to be the same hammer used to murder his wife.   The lack of blood in the waffle marks indicated that he was killed first then his wife.   Both scenes before her looked quick, without a struggle and done with a simple purpose by a very strong person. Whoever came into this home, came here to kill these people.

Cathy moved to the bathroom and through the room looking for entry points or any other clue to how the perp entered. Windows were shut and locked from the inside. No doors were kicked in or locks scraped up from being pried open. Nothing was looted, or ransacked. No drawers hung open and nothing appeared to be missing. The only things out of place were the dead people in the room. She returned to the hammer and examined it up close. It was old, and well used. The wooden handle was worn smooth from years of use with a "TA" burned into the bottom.

She set it back down and exited the room. She had seen enough and only had one question to solidify her decision.

At the end of the hallway, the Sheriff and two different deputies stood in the living room, talking with open notebooks in their hands. She imagined the town of Klamath Falls was without any police services right now, since 3 deputies and the Sheriff were all here. The department couldn't have more than that on any one shift and the town would have to do without until this was over she supposed.

"Sheriff, what was Mr. Anderson's first name?" She asked, interrupting him in mid-sentence.

"Tom", he said," Tom and Aggie Anderson, great people. What do you think Agent? Can you help us out here? Any ideas on who did it?"

"The hammer upstairs, is that one of Tom's?" She asked.

"Yes ma'am" he replied, "He was a bit of a handyman after his retirement, kept him busy around the community. Did most of it for a homemade pie or just out of the goodness of his heart, didn't know him to take much else in payment."

"Thank you Sheriff, I need to make a few calls, but before that, I will need your people to vacate the house now and secure the outside until my people can sweep it."

"You Feds are gonna take the case?" He asked with an excited tone in his voice.

"Well, Sheriff, we are going to go over it ourselves to see if there is anymore the scene can tell us that you and your men may have missed, but yeah, we are going to be here for a while."

"Yes Ma'am, I will get my guys out and wrap the place up right away, and thank you!" Johns replied in a voice that was trembling with excitement.

She could see the relief in his eyes and hear it in his voice. He was in way over his head and had tapped out his limited experience a day ago. Swiping the phone's screen and double tapping the phone icon, she waited for the dial tone.

"Hello?" came a tired man's voice on the other end.

"Allen, its Cathy, did I wake you?"

"Almost" He said, "its eleven o'clock, I was almost out. What's up, any news from Oregon?"

"I got no sympathy for you" she said, "You sent me up here and it's only nine on this side of the country, so you better get used to it, but I think you may have been right about this thing. No sign of entry or struggle, no clues, nothing out of place to indicate a struggle or robbery and the murder weapon belonged to the victims, same as the other two. There is a possibility this is the same guy. "

The phone was quiet for a minute before he responded. "Shit!"

"I know" she said, "I've never had one like this. There was nothing to connect them. The manner of death changed from drowning to stabbing to bludgeoning and the victims themselves couldn't get more opposite. The only thing that remained constant was weapons used for the crimes belonged to the deceased and the time table between each one began to display a pattern. It has been

3 months from Atlanta to Denver and now two for the Oregon case. If this is the same guy, he's on some sort of cross-country killing spree and he is speeding things up."

"What do you need up there?" He asked, "I can have a team up tomorrow morning if you need them".

"Allen, I've been on this for months now with no leads and a lot of dead ends. I am one of your best, that's why you put me on this case, and I have nothing more to go on than I did on day one. These cases are clean with more questions than answers or leads. This could be our first real break; I don't need a bunch of young agents trying to step all over me to get ahead or further their career. I need a seasoned, experienced agent, someone who knows how to find what isn't there and track this guy down using old school methods. I need Jack."

The phone was silent for a moment. She stood in the freezing, wet wind blowing across the lake wondering if she had lost connection, then finally he spoke.

"He's retired Cathy, besides; I doubt we could find him. He fell off the grid 4 years ago after the Missouri thing, not to mention he's pushing 50 now."

"I don't care how old he is Allen, you're 51 and still think you can run the department like a man half your age. Jack tracked that crazy son of a bitch across the country and saved that women by doing it, not to mention the countless more he would've murdered if the bastard had escaped. He had a stack of files with all the cases he had solved over the years larger than most units have together. He is the best at this, retired or not, you and I know it. Find him, or tell me where to look and I will. I got the Sheriff up here, sealing the place until I can get inside and go over it in detail, with Jack. The bodies will be put on ice in the morgue until a full autopsy can be completed by our people, but the scene will stay as is." She half ordered into the phone.

"Washington" he said without any further argument. He knew it was a lost cause with her to argue and she was the best he had now that Jack had retired. They both knew it. If she felt she needed Jack, he wouldn't disagree.

"Last address we had was a post office box in a town called Metaline Falls, Washington. It's a rock throw from the Canadian Border and a hundred miles from anywhere. The nearest airport is in Spokane, over 100 miles south. You have two days to see if you can find him, if not, get back down there and use the team I send you to go through that home. They will start on the bodies while you find Jack. If you're right about this guy, you have less than a month to find him and stop him before he hits again."

"Thanks Allen, I will let you know." She hung up, and walked toward her car. "Where the hell his Metaline Falls", she asked herself as she fought to keep the wind off her face.

CHAPTER 9

Attention to detail with a methodical and patient focus in life gave him peace and purpose. It allowed him time to recover from the long trip across country and set his life back into the order he required it to be. He never could understand how people passed through life with no direction or commitments, letting any wind of change blow them to a new destination without the power or self-control enough to stay the course. Most of them were so weak minded they enjoyed the change and embraced it. This was chaos to Vincent.

With every stroke of the vacuum across the floorboards and seat backs, Vincent thought about his next ten moves and the last twenty he had made. It is what kept him alive and always moving ahead, ever reaching for perfection. Every inch of the vehicle would be cleaned; every crack, seam and vent would be meticulously wiped down and sanitized. This ritual could take up to eleven hours depending on the time he had spent in the car. Most people thought that paying twenty or thirty dollars and having a machine scrub down the outside of their car while a couple of undereducated drones of society swept out the inside with a brush constituted as cleaning. How wrong they were.

The carpeting inside was attached with minute Velcro tabs that he would detach and discard. New carpet flooring, custom made and fresh out of the plastic would be installed when he was finished. The seat covers were trashed as well and replaced with new ones from the cabinet against the back wall of the garage containing multiple boxes of them. Dash mat, steering wheel cover and all control knobs were pulled off as well and replaced.

In the world of technology and forensics, fingerprints were a thing of the past. DNA was the future and it could be obtained in many forms. A simple hair follicle was as distinct as blood type. Nail clippings or skin flakes held the same individual print and could be used as iron clad evidence if discovered. Even sweat and oil transferred to a surface can be pulled with the right equipment and traced back to a single person in this world of over 6 billion.

Vincent knew this and adjusted his life accordingly. Long sleeve shirts and pants were worn at all times. Knee high socks, stretched to the fullest up his leg under his pants with hiking style boots that provide ankle support and protection tied tight and secure was mandatory. His head was shaved as well as the rest of his body, leaving him completely void of hair. A ritualistic routine of bathing and personal hygiene was applied daily with body scrub and scent blocking shampoos. To avoid standing out, he often wore hats to blend in with his surroundings or at times, even a wig. He did not go out much, but when he did his true form was unrecognizable and his disguise was something no one would remember or take notice to. This was his standard and he executed it perfectly.

The car was rolled onto a set of ramps so he could get underneath and wash off every bit of road grime clinging to the undercarriage from different states he travelled through. When he finished with the tires, they looked brand new, free from even the tiniest pebble. Each individual tread seam was cleaned with a q-tip leaving all four spotless and free of debris. Overall, aside from the year and make of the vehicle, it looked brand new inside and out when complete.

Almost an entire day later, Vincent stood at the door to the storage unit and rechecked his surroundings. The car was clean, and prepped for his next outing. The garage was wiped down again and spotless as well. The large double bagged garbage sacks full of the materials he used to clean sat next to him and it would be disposed of in the dumpster 4 blocks away, but never the same one twice. He rolled the door shut, replaced the industrial strength padlock and walked out of the storage unit, leaving it until his next mission.

It was an old place off the normal thoroughfare of traffic and commercialized businesses. It had no cameras to monitor people coming or going and no computerized card system to allow access. The owners were older and had operated the place for years. They preferred cash and required no background check for services or any real identification for using the facility. A single guard patrolled the area once or twice a day for security purposes and he was sure the man was far from qualified in the security world. It was more of a necessity to keep their insurance premiums low. The place was perfect for him and his needs.

As he walked the side streets with the large bags in hand and small day pack on his back, Vincent watched cars as they passed and made sure to look the other way or take alternate routes whenever too much traffic started congesting on the streets. He never walked in front of ATM machines and avoided all traffic light controlled intersections as he knew cameras were stationed there, monitoring everything.

At times his walk home took him hours to complete, depending on the traffic or time of day. This never bothered him and he actually enjoyed the game he played with society. They had no idea who he was or what he had done. They were oblivious to his power and how easily he could make each of them disappear.

Tonight's walk went smooth and before long he disposed of the waste and was at the marina. Using his key to unlock the security gate, he walked out to the end of the dock to his boat. She was perfect. His one true home that nobody could take. His sanctuary of solitude and security.

The couple in Oregon was just what he needed. It had been too long since his last road trip and was looking forward to the memories he would have from this one. After a quick shower and meal, he would settle in with a good book and fall asleep to replay the events over and over again in his mind.

CHAPTER 10

The airport was smaller than most annexes of others she had been in across the country. The only reason it was called Spokane International had to be because of the couple flights a month over the border to Canada. It was clean and quiet. No sleeping passengers awaiting layovers from missed flights lying on the floor or lines of people pushing ahead to skip their seating position while boarding. Nobody seemed to be in a hurry or rush to get anywhere. It was as if the entire place was running at half the speed of other airports. She was shocked to see the smiles on the faces of gate agents this time of the morning. It was only 6 AM and half the shops were closed. The other half only served coffee but regardless of the ungodly hour and lack of conveniences, the people seemed to be happy and cheerful.

Cathy began to wonder if this was real or some kind of a staged movie set. Even the security screening personnel coming into the boarding area had on smiles and were holding actual conversations with the passengers as they de-shoed and emptied the contents of their pockets or unpacked laptops for the upcoming checks. Nobody was rude or in a flurry of hectic unorganized chaos as you so commonly see at these intersections. Hello, have a great flight and talk of the local football team was all you could hear from security as they processed the passengers. The atmosphere was light and fluid. Almost cheerful.

Before long she found herself standing on a sidewalk outside the airport with the keys to her rental car in hand. The de-boarding and transit through went smooth and without issue. The AVIS rental agency had her keys and paperwork ready and waiting for her. It was shocking to Cathy at the atmosphere the place had.

She looked back at the glass doors and realized the entire building wasn't more than 100 feet deep from the sidewalk outside to boarding the plane. She began to understand why Jack picked such a place to settle at. It was just like him. A fully functional and capable airport without all the crap the rest seemed to have. The outside as well as inside had a 10 year old look about it. Not run down or needing repairs, just back in time a decade. Everything was clean and well kept. Fresh paint or freshly washed, lined the sidewalks and curbs. The trees around the parking area were well trimmed and she couldn't see a piece of trash anywhere. The place was set back to a time where a person's attitude and personality went further and meant more than the kind of clothes they were wearing or smart phone they were using. It was every bit the kind of place that Jack would fit in.

Aside from the bitter cold and the location it had to the rest of the civilized world, seemed like a place perfect for retirement. She found the rental car office and stepped inside.

The woman at the counter was just as cheerful as the others she had encountered in the airport. She told Cathy about her family and kids. She brought up skiing and hunting and all the fun thing to do up here in the winter. The woman talked nonstop while she pulled up the reservation and filled in the forms for her.

Cathy could barely get a word in and before long she found herself behind the wheel of the SUV. She punched in the address she received from Allen upon landing on Jacks last known location and pulled out on the road.

She followed the directions being given to her and thought about the cases as she drove. She thought about the family in Atlanta and how they were murdered so brutally without care or remorse for the age of the victims. The guy, whoever he was didn't care about sex or greed. He didn't seem to be motivated by the carnage of the act. It almost seemed like a hit from a professional accept that there was no connection between them to come to that conclusion.

The family in Atlanta, two co-eds in Denver and an old retired couple in Oregon. Absolutely nothing to relate them except the distance and lack of evidence.

She took a turn indicated by her GPS and pressed on through winter covered landscape. She wondered what Jack would look like now and if he would remember her. Would he want to help her or just tell her to kick rocks? The last time she saw him he was in a hospital bed recovering from the multiple gunshots he received during his last case. He was conscious but pretty heavily doped up. It wasn't long after that and she returned to be debriefed on the case and Jack went back to Portland then soon after retired. She hadn't seen him since. Jack was the best agent she had worked with. He had a way of dominating any scene he was on and maintain control in all situations. He could think like criminal they were chasing and had the ability to anticipate his moves like nobody she had ever seen. Even in Missouri, when they breached the basement stairs of that home. Jack was the first one down into the darkness of that hell pit and the last one standing.

Cathy could still smell the musky mix of blood, burnt gun powder and sweat that filled the basement of that house. She remembered the sounds of Jack barking orders at someone out of site to her. She remembered the sound of gun shots and women screaming. She felt the weight of the man in front of her fall backwards against her as he was littered with bullets from the darkness below. It pushed her down and she tumbled off the side of the stairs to the hard concrete floor of the basement below.

She rolled her shoulders subconsciously behind the wheel of the rental at the memory and the broken bones she stained from the fall. She remembered the look in the man's eyes as she landed in front of him as vulnerable as a baby seal. She saw the hatred and lust for death on his face as he raised his weapon directly at her.

The phones' GPS beeped out a pre-recorded message stating she would need to make a right turn in 2 miles. She snapped back to the snow covered road through the windshield. All she could see was more of the same she had seen for the last 3 hours. Trees, lots of them all covered in snow. The road had changed from a 4 lane to a 2 lane hours ago and from a paved road to a half maintained gravel road 1 hour ago and now for the last 30 min she was on a less than maintained dirt road covered in snow. She couldn't believe she had kept the SUV on the road with her mind riding the waves of the past and not focusing on the present. The ruts from an earlier vehicle was the only thing she had to go by now to distinguish the road from the snow covered forest floor to the left and right. If there was a turn coming up on the right, she couldn't see it yet.

Maybe looking for Jack wasn't the best idea. Maybe she wasn't ready to relive the past and she should just turn back and find this guy on her own. The GPS beeped again informing her of the turn in 100 meters. She looked through the windshield and passenger window at the wall of trees and snow on the right and couldn't make out any opening large enough for the car to possibly pass through. She eased up on the accelerator and slowed to a crawl as the trees passed by. She squinted through the falling flakes looking for the road that the GPS was telling her was there. Another 50 meters of white wilderness went by and then a small opening in the snowbank on the side appeared.

She immediately stepped on the brake and the car slid sideways to a stop with the front tires resting dangerously close to the edge of the road. Reversing back and taking a second look at the opening in the forest she was thankful she selected the 4 wheel drive rental. The break in the snow was small, but large enough for a car to go through. It appeared to have been plowed before, but not today. The snow covering the road was almost 4 inches deep and no tracks from a previous vehicles could be seen.

Cathy double checked her phones GPS and discovered that the international No Service icon was flashing in the top right corner. Of course, she thought to herself. Why would Jack live anywhere where people could use technology? Turning around on the narrow track wasn't an option so forward was where she was going.

She pushed the 4X4 lock icon on the dashboard and turned into the opening. The drive was slow and narrow. She kept the forward momentum of the vehicle just fast enough to not slip or spin but still continue forward with control. The crunching fresh snow under her tires was all she could hear as she focused on the narrow path cut through the white powder. What seemed like forever passed before the tunnel effect of the snow covered limbs above her opened and she could see a small cabin nestled up against the mountainside on the edge of a small field. A thin trail of smoke drifted up from the chimney disappearing into the white sky above. It looked like one of those old fashioned hallmark cards her parents used to get when she was a kid. The cabin was small but had a very new and functional look about it. The closer she got the more things emerged from the surroundings.

First was the garage or shop set behind the cabin. It was larger than the house itself and looked almost out of place in the rustic setting of the cabin. It wasn't wood like the cabin but made of steel with a tall ceiling and straight rigid walls. Next was a windmill standing above the house up the mountain behind it. It stood tall and futuristic against the wild landscape below. It looked to belong out on the desert flats in Arizona, not up in the snow covered mountains of the northwest. Without the wind mill, the scene was what she expected to see knowing Jack. He always talked about the mountains and the seclusion they brought. The homestead was quiet and clean. The forest surrounded it and even with the cold snow covering everything it had a warm cozy appeal.

Cathy pulled up to the front of the home and stopped the car. She zipped her jacket up as high as possible and put on the gloves sitting on the passenger seat. She was hoping this was the correct place and someone wouldn't come running out of the house brandishing a shotgun because of her intrusion. Who knows how many visitors people out here received, but if it was Jacks place, she didn't have any idea what to say.

As soon as the driver's door was cracked the cold winter wind rushed inside chilling her to the bone. She ducked her head down protecting herself all she could and made for the front door of the cabin. She was on the first step of the porch leading to the door when it opened and a large black lab came bounding out straight at her. The initial response to something like this would be to jump back and run for the car, but Cathy new any sudden moves on the ice covered steps would result in a slip and fall. Then she would be on the ground with the dog over the top of her in the snow.

"Stop!" She yelled and held up her right hand in whatever defense it might provide. The dog was big, but had a happy playful look about it more than the Cujo dog your mind automatically resorted to in these situations. Immediately, the dog stopped, sat down and cocked its head to the side while looking down at her from the top step. The dog seemed surprised at her command and didn't know what to do. Cathy took a slow step back toward the car, keeping her eyes on the dog.

"Good dog" she said, "You stay right there."

The dog looked down from the porch watching her as she left the steps and rounded the front of the SUV. She made it to the driver's door without a growl or the dog moving off the porch. It just watched her with intent curiosity.

Cathy got the SUV's door open in just enough time to see a man walk out behind the dog from inside the cabin. It was Jack. He filled the doorway with his form and patted the dog on the head. She could see him smile at her and give her a small wink like he used to.

"Do I need to come out and get you?" He calmly said to her.

"I don't know, does that thing bite?" She asked back, from the other side of her car.

"Max?" He asked. The dog looked up at the mention of his name. "Max couldn't hurt anyone on purpose. He's a puppy wrapped up in a big dog suit. You got nothing to worry about girl. Now get in here. You're letting out all my heat."

Cathy shut the car door and headed up the steps. Max stood at the top, waiting for her with his tail wagging. She made it to the top and he welcomed her with lots of sniffs and pushes with his head. She gave him a pat and pushed past into the house out of the cold. Turning to shut the door behind her she saw Max busy marking the tires on her car before bouncing off into the snow out of site.

The inside of the cabin was warm and cozy. A large rock fireplace sat against the far right wall with the crackle and pop of wood burning inside. Huge floor to ceiling windows embraced it on either side with the cold winter landscape trapped outside as a backdrop. A worn brown leather couch and matching chair sat in front of the fireplace with a wooden coffee table sitting in between them. On top of the table was a book, opened to a certain page lying face down next to a chessboard that appeared to be in play. To the left of her was a small room with an ancient looking desk against the wall with windows behind it covered in papers and files. The walls of the room were covered in bookshelves filled with hundreds of different titles. A staircase was directly in front of her leading to an upstairs loft out of site. Jack stood at the kitchen counter on the far side of the stairs filling a cup from a coffee pot.

He looked about the same as she remembered him 4 years ago aside from the plaid shirt and Levis. The last time she saw him, he was in a suit an tie. He had the same large frame of a man that worked hard all his life. Broad shoulders, trim waste and a weather worn face. His hair had turned a shade lighter to a salt and pepper look, but he could pass for a man 10 years younger without issue.

"Coffee?" He asked without turning around.

"Sure" She answered pulling off her coat and gloves.

"Well" Jack said, "What can I do for you girl?"

"Right to it as always." She said.

"I don't get any visitors up here. Matter of fact, the last person that stopped by was my neighbor 5 miles away. He needed help getting his horses back after a storm put a tree across his fence line and scattered them to the horizon. That was 4 months ago. So I figure you showing up out of the blue has to mean you need something. So what is it?" Jack asked handing her the cup.

"It's good to see you Jack, you look good." She said ignoring his shortness and taking the cup with both hands. "I like your place. It's just how I imagined it when you talked about it."

"Thanks. It's a work in progress, always something needing to be done. Keeps me busy." He said. "What up girl?"

"I came up here to ask for your help Jack."

"That's pretty obvious." He said. "I didn't think you were here to visit. What do ya need girl?"

"A case Jack, a hard case. It has me stumped and I was thinking you might be able to shed some light on it."

"I have been out of the game for year's girl. Haven't thought that way for a long time and been up here off the grid enjoying the retired life has made me forget a lot of that shit. I am sure the FBI has plenty resources at their disposal to help you solve whatever it is you have gotten into that would prove a lot more helpful than an old fossil like me might be."

"Well, that's part of the problem. I have exhausted a lot of those resources you're talking about and they got me nowhere. We have been through all the paces on this thing and turned up nothing both forensically and identity wise. You are the last thing I can think of to help on this." She said.

"It's good to know I rate last on your list." He smirked.

"Not me" She answered back. "Allen was the reason it took so long to get ahold of you. I knew I needed help 3 months ago, and mentioned it then, but Allen wasn't on board with the idea. Now, things have changed."

"What does Allen have to do with any of this?" Jack asked.

"He's the director now and after months of me turning up with nothing to go on, he finally agreed to me asking for your help."

"Holy Shit, he made director? You gotta be kidding me!" Jack spat out.

"Yep, he's the man now. Calling all the shots and he wasn't big on me bringing you back into the fold let me tell you."

"You're not bringing me back into anything yet girl. Right now we are just two old friends talking about old times. You haven't told me anything and I haven't agreed to anything."

"It's bad Jack, real bad and I have nothing. No leads, no clues, not even a direction to start looking." She said moving to the couch and sitting down closer to the fire.

Jack walked over to the chair and sat down across from her. The fire felt good from this distance. He could hear the frustration in her voice and see the anger in her eyes. Cathy was a young, talented and resourceful agent when he was with the FBI. She worked hard in the world of men to climb as high as she did. Her dedication to the job and each individual case is why she got where she is now. She was one of the good ones. Honest, loyal and persistent. He trusted her and had all the faith in her abilities. Whatever this case was had her stumped enough to reach out beyond her comfort zone to ask for help. It had to be something more than a simple murder. He leaned back in the chair and said. "Well, not that it matters much to me, or that I could help, but tell me what you know."

Her eyes lifted from the coffee in her hands and a small twinge of delight appeared at the corners.

CHAPTER 11

Vincent rolled out of bed exactly 5 minutes before the alarm went off as he did every day. He trained his body to respond to his will alone and not subject to any external stimulus to control him. With the efficiency of a military recruit, he made his bed tight enough to flip a coin on it and immediately began his daily morning workout without hesitation or drowsiness. After donning his swim trunks, Vincent jumped from the stern of his boat into the frigid Puget Sound and swam the lanes of the harbor. There were 5 rows of docks with 40 boats moored along each of them. It was a 2 mile swim in total and would take Vincent no more than one hour to complete. After the swim he would finish his workout with 100 sit-ups and 100 pushups. He never used music or any warm up routine or equipment. He focused on what he wanted to do and did it. Vincent believed that his body was just as important as his mind and he took meticulous care of both.

With the exercise ritual completed he began his systematic routine of morning hygiene. Shower for a full 30 minutes scrubbing his body twice and shaving from head to toe in the hottest temperature he could stand. Over the years he has been able to increase the water to a degree that would send most people running for ice. It was one more thing that he did to master complete control of himself as well as becoming more effective and evolved than anyone around him. After the shower was complete he would make breakfast consisting of a 4 egg omelet, only the whites, very little cheese, onions and tomatoes with no salt or pepper. Two pieces of dry toast, half a cantaloupe and a glass of orange juice would accompany it. He did not require coffee or any other stimulate to assist him.

With the dishes cleaned and put away, dirty clothes in the wash and bathroom freshly bleached he donned a fresh costume. Vincent locked the door and walked down the pier. Today he was a middle aged, long haired man with glasses wearing blue jeans a flannel shirt over a white t-shirt with a brown jacket. The entire outfit was purchased a few weeks ago from the local good will store. It was more of a grunge look that was fitting to the North West.

His first stop today was the public library 24 blocks away. There was a library closer to the harbor but he had used it once already and did not want to risk any kind of a pattern. He would walk the distance and not use a taxi. The path he was taking was 48 blocks in total to avoid high traffic areas this time of the morning. He would arrive at the library by 0930. They opened at 0800, but he never wanted to be the first one there or the last one out. People tend to remember the first and last person they see during a day, but a plane nobody, walking in an hour after they have opened would go un-noticed among the mases.

Vincent walked at a normal pace. Not fast enough to draw attention as a man in a hurry, but never so slow to interfere with others and their commutes also resulting in a possibly memorable experience. His situational awareness was honed fine and sharp. He never walked in front of an ATM machine and avoided Traffic lights with his head down or facing the opposite direction. Large groups of people using phones to snap photos would be avoided as well as storefronts with windows. He knew that cameras and the digital world was swarming this age and everything was recorded. It would take dedication and diligence to remain invisible. Other than the fact that he was a living breathing human walking on the sidewalk, the rest of the world was oblivious to him and his presence. He blended into everything around him and nothing he did stood out as peculiar or necessary to dedicate to memory.

Even if he did, by chance, slip up and make a mistake by getting a photo taken, he doubted anyone would notice him or remember why he was there. Today's people were engrossed in their technology. Almost every person he saw had a phone to their ear talking as they walked. If they weren't talking they were busy looking at the screen as they went past. The sky could be red with falling monkeys and they wouldn't notice. The world was flooded with technology connecting everyone to each other on a global scale but in reality it pulled them farther apart than ever before. Human interaction was a thing of the past. If you couldn't text, tweet, or email someone, they didn't exist. It was the perfect camouflage for him and his work. He embraced it.

Arriving at the Library at exactly 0930, Vincent grinned to himself for his ability to plan. He wasn't surprised, just pleased. It was who he was and how he operated. In control all the time.

This particular library had two entrances. The main doors were located on the front side of the building facing the street. They were double glass swinging doors with huge brass handles that opened to a large entry way covered in marble tile. A small metal desk was situated off to the right side against the back wall in the entryway. Behind it sat an overweight red headed woman wearing glasses in a green dress one size to small. A medium sized plant in a pot rested atop a file cabinet behind her. A fern, possibly a gift from someone but most likely it wasn't. Upon closer inspection Vincent saw that it was a fake. The name plate on the desk read Patricia Stewart. Patty, he figured was what her friends called her. She wasn't wearing a ring and by the size of her purse sitting on the other side of the desk, Vincent could tell she had no plans to leave the Library for lunch. Obviously Patty brought her own food to work because there was no man in her life to share a meal with.

Patty was the receptionist to the library. They no longer used a librarian, it was now all digital. So the need to interact with a human being wasn't needed. He figured her main purpose for being there was to tell people not to bring in food or drink and answer phone calls. What a pathetic life.

To the left were two doors against the wall indicating sexes for bathroom use. This was the most used and busy way in and out of the library and because of this, it was the one he chose. The other entrance was on the side of the building, closer to an alley. It was also open to the public but was watched by a camera to those entering and exiting. Vincent knew he could blend in and be forgotten easily by the fat red head, but a camera could record him. He chose the main entrance and waited until he could fall in with a group just getting off the bus to proceed inside.

Once in he made his way through the library to the back room that had individual work stations with computers located at each. He kept at a steady pace and avoided eye contact as much as possible with his head down. He knew there was a fine line to take when trying to be invisible. If you avoided people too much, you would be noticed. If you blended in and made conversation when necessary, people would forget you were even there. But too much and they might remember something.

The library was old but had recently undergone a remodeling to bring it into the new era. The walls of book shelves sitting back to back still remained along the perimeter of the room lined with volumes but instead of multiple tables filling the empty spaces between them with reading lamps for the patrons to use while selecting a title, they were covered with monitors and keyboards. The public library system needed to embrace the world of technology if they were to survive and the Seattle public city system was doing the best they could. The tables looked new and computers looked unused. Each of the screens had the iconic windows logo floating across it awaiting use. Where no monitor sat was a small internet/power port with people already plugged in and using the free service with their own devices.

Vincent scanned the room for a station that was as secluded as possible, but unfortunately most of them were already taken. The World Wide Web that was designed to connect everyone and bring them closer had done the complete opposite. Now people wanted as much space between each other as possible so they could log onto the web and connect with people. He grinned at the hypocrisy and lunacy of it all. Vincent walked around the tables selecting a station to use and could see the screens of multiple laptops and library provided monitors as he passed. None of them had books or literature of any kind on them. Everything from a cat playing the piano to what he suspected was borderline kiddie porn was being viewed. The book shelves around the perimeter of the room were void of anyone and stood untouched. The hundreds or thousands of books sat unattended. A world of knowledge was only feet away from all these people. Free for the taking and they willingly chose to surf the internet for useless and redundant forms of entertainment that would only increase their ignorance and inability to function in this world. Vincent smiled as he walked.

He found a spot near the center of the room in between an adolescent boy no more than 14 and an older man pushing 60. From what he could see the young boy was looking at sport highlights on you tube or the cheerleaders of the teams to be more specific, while the older man seemed to be browsing lingerie being worn by women half his age or younger. It never failed to surprise Vincent on what people deemed valuable. Every computer in the library searching the net was being used for something it was never intended. He smiled at the ignorance and weak nature of the sheep around him. The more he wandered through this world the more clear his path and purpose became to him.

The man and the boy didn't look up from their screens when he pulled out the chair and sat down next to them. If anything they turned away even further to hide from their sins. Yet again, another reason he could go unnoticed in this world. The man didn't seem to care or even notice when Vincent turned the small camera attached to the computer with a cord directly toward him as he sat. Vincent knew that the right person with the correct knowledge could remotely access any camera in the Library and see the user. He would not take such a chance.

With a swipe of the mouse on the pad next to the computer, the screen came to life. An image of a lighthouse, probably in Maine, filled the background. It was a colorful photo. Full of beauty and the peaceful solitude one might expect from such a place. This picture was as close as any person in the library would ever get to such a site he thought to himself. They were all predisposed with the world in the box and had made it the center of all their lives refusing to test it limits or step out of it.

Vincent moved the mouse to the google tab and clicked. Once the search engine produced a search window he moved the keyboard to a comfortable position in front of him. With the precision of a surgeon he began to type. He was filled with anticipation while he clicked away on the keys. Soon, he thought to himself, soon he would travel again. The joy of the hunt was upon him and he loved it.

CHAPTER 12

"Why do you think these cases are connected?"
Jack asked while getting up to refill his cup.

He had heard the whole story from her. Starting
with the Atlanta case that involved a family in a small
quiet suburban home killed with a knife out of their own
kitchen to the college girls sharing a room in Colorado
that had been drowned in a tub and smothered with a
pillow. She ended her story on the old couple in Oregon
that were bludgeoned to death with a hammer belonging
to them in their home in the country. He didn't say a
thing or ask a question during her brief. He listened to
her and took everything in. He knew Cathy and could
hear the frustration in her voice about the cases. He felt
her loss of direction in them and the fact that she was
sitting in his house made her conviction all the more
concrete. Now that she was done talking, Jack wanted to
know what she thought, not what Allen thought or the
FBI answer on it.

"At first I didn't think they were connected." She
said. "They appear to be different MO's in every sense.
But it's the lack of similarity that is bringing me around."

"So you think Allen is right about the connection?"
Jack asked.

"Yeah Jack, I do. I think somehow these three
scenes are related. I don't know how, but my gut tells me

these three are connected and worse, there could be more that we don't know about yet."

"Ok, let's dig in a little." Jack said while sitting back down. "Was anything taken from any of the homes?"

She looked at him sitting in the worn chair that she was certain he had spent many an evening in. With the fireplace behind him and the snowy backdrop through the windows. He was exactly where he had always wanted to be she thought. He fit in here like the color on the walls, but he still had that way about him when it came to a case. He could shift gears and his focus faster than most people changed their mind.

"Nothing that has been reported by family or friends was found missing from any of the homes. It seems that theft or robbery were not in the least bit important." She answered him quickly, while snapping back to the files in her hands.

"Means of entry?"

"Same as the selections of the people. Different at each place. The home in Atlanta had no signs of forced entry. No broken windows or jimmied locks. Just a dead husband, wife and 4 year old."

"The Colorado place?"

"Broken bathroom window in the alley to the north of the home. It appears to be the way they got in." She said.

"And the Oregon home?"

"Same as Atlanta. Nothing, no visible sign of forced entry anywhere on or around the home." She answered.

"Could it be possible that this guy is just a good lock man and left no trace?" Jack asked while throwing a piece of wood into the fire.

"We went over every lock, window and door jam on the exterior of the home. If the guy used anything other than the key for the house, we couldn't find any trace of it." She said.

"If that's the case and these are connected, why do you think he broke a window in the Colorado home to get in? Why not pick the lock like the others? Were the locks for a couple college girls that much more secure than a family in Atlanta?"

Cathy leaned back and answered him. "That's just it, the window he broke was one of the small high bathroom windows. The thing is 8 feet off the ground and tiny. The kind you normally use to vent out a room. If he did use it to get in, we found no tracks on the side of the home he used to climb up. No scuff marks on the window sill. Nothing. He would have to be an acrobat just to fit through it."

"So why do you think it's the same guy?" Jack asked.

"The mode of death and lack of evidence between them all." She said. "This guy uses whatever is at the home to kill them. Whatever is there at his immediate disposal becomes the weapon of choice. He doesn't steal anything from the house and appears to bring nothing in with him to assist. No signs of a struggle or fight and nothing is disturbed in any of the homes. Then there is the complete polar opposites of the victims. A family in the suburbs, two young coeds in a duplex and an elderly couple in the country spread across the United States almost 2000 miles between them. I know that nothing usually means nothing, but if you have a lot of nothing on all three, that might add up to something." She said with a half desperate tone in her voice.

Max came into the room from the kitchen. Jack must have a pet door located on the other side of the house she thought. The dogs back was covered in fresh snow and he did his best to share the wet outside weather with Cathy as he pushed up against her and sat down on the couch. She instinctively pulled away from the large wet dog.

"You allow him up on the couch?" She asked while leaning away from the wet dog.

"No" Jack said grinning at the scene "But he is allowing you on his couch."

"Ha Ha" Cathy smirked at him. "Seriously, what do you think?"

"I think he likes you."

"No, Ass, what do you think about the case?"

"Sounds like you got your hands full with a lot more questions than you do answers. Not sure what it is you expect me to do?"

"This guy's a ghost Jack. I am running out of directions to look here. If the timetable means anything, this guy is upping his game and should be selecting another victim any day. " Cathy said with a slight inflection in her voice.

"And you think I can give you something to go on?" Jack asked.

"I was hoping a fresh set of eyes would pop up a clue or give me anything at all to go on, yeah."

"You're a good agent girl. One of the best I ever worked with. If there was something to find or connect these three cases you would have found it by now. It may be possible that these are not related at all. Just three random acts of violence." Jack said.

"I don't think so and neither does Allen." Cathy shot back at him while trying to regain her spot on the couch that Max so busily and effectively was taking from her.

Jack had only worked with Cathy on a couple cases during his time with the FBI. One of which was his last case, and it didn't end well for either of them. Seeing her now sitting on his couch brought back the memory of that hot summer day in Missouri. That dark basement filled with horror and pain. He knew she was extremely talented then and he had no doubt that she had only improved over the years. For her to take the time to find him and ask for his help must mean it was something she was very determined about or stumped on. He got up and stretched his arms over his head while walking back to the kitchen. "You bring any files or photos on the cases with you?" He asked while walking away from her.

"Yep!" She said almost jumping off the couch. "I have the complete reports on all three with all related photos. There on my laptop in the car. I'll be right back."

Max and Jack both watched as she left the room and out the door. The dog looked at Jack and cocked his head to the side as dogs do, while wagging his tail.

"Don't worry bud, she'll be back." He said to the lab as he put his cup in the sink and looked out at the falling snow in the mountains beyond the glass. He began to have the feeling in his gut that he used to while on a case. The twinge of adrenaline and investigative curiosity that made him good at what he did was surfacing with Cathy's unexpected visit. Her smell still floated through his home opening boxes in his memory he had closed up so long ago. She needed his help in more ways than one.

He was a good agent, but that was years ago and the last case he had ended in a bad way. He wanted to help Cathy but wasn't sure if he had it in him anymore.

He wasn't sure what an old, behind the times, agent could do in this world of technology and youth but Cathy needed his help and who was he to not give her a hand.

Vincent grinned at the screen and waited while the computer did its work. He enjoyed this part almost as much as what was to come. The anticipation of waiting filled him with the untold reward he would have. It was like fishing he supposed. He had never actually gone fishing but had read about in many books. He had no doubt that if he were to go he would be a remarkable fisherman. He had read what kind of bait would work the best for each species. He knew what time of year was best to catch them and where to do it. He could identify hundreds of fish by pictures alone and would never forget a single one. This, he supposed, was like that. He knew what to use as bait and where to fish for them. He knew the best way to do it and once he had a bite, it was a matter of reeling it in and admiring your trophy. This he knew how to do oh so well. The only difference he supposed was that he wasn't doing this for sport or sustenance. He was doing it because he could. Because he was the top of the food chain and understood more than they did or ever would. He was the reason the human food chain existed and reveled in the fact that he alone kept order in it all.

The screen blipped up a message and Vincent smiled wide and deep as he read it. He hit the button and opened another search screen and began typing. After fifteen minutes Vincent closed the search browser, deleted all the recent activity in the history and typed in a code used to clear computers and reset them to factory settings.

It wouldn't disable the thing or draw unwanted attention, it was simply a way to wipe any trace away. He left the library at 1100 and began the walk back to the harbor. Vincent was happy. He had another task to complete and it filled him with excitement. In the fishing world, he had a bite!

CHAPTER 13

"Hey Sam, you want to join us for a couple drinks after work?" Came a voice from the desk across from hers.

Samantha Adams or Sam as everyone at work and most of the people in her life referred to her as, didn't want to join them for a drink now or anytime. She didn't want to be around most of them even when at work, but was forced to at times for mandatory meetings or group functions. All she wanted to do was her job, get paid and go home. She didn't have much of a life outside of work that involved other people. She liked that and wanted no change in it or her routine.

Sam didn't consider herself homely or unfriendly in any way. She worked out regularly, ate right, dressed appropriate to the situation and applied the recommended amount of makeup to fit in but not look like a street walker. She really didn't have strong political views one way or the other and as far as religion went she didn't see the harm in it if you believed or not, just don't push it on anyone. Compared to most of the women at work, she felt to be in the top 20% of attractiveness, maybe more. But, she didn't go out with anyone at work. Did not socialize with them after hours and really didn't care to know any of their family's names, history or stories. She was never rude or short to any of them and always said she was sorry or to catch her again when she turned down offers for afterhours activities. To Sam, this was nothing more than a necessity to pay the bills. The fact that she was good at her job and it came naturally to her it made it easier.

"No thank you Jimmy. I got a ton to catch up on here and was going to work through it all and head home early for the weekend. Thank you for the invite. Maybe next time." She answered with an apologetic smile on her face while lying through her teeth.

"You sure? They got the 2 for 20 deal at TGI Friday's right now and if we get there soon enough we can make happy hour."

She looked up from her keyboard and put on her best regretful and sorrowful face. "I am sorry Jim, but I have to get this done before the weekend. Can you give me a rain check on that?"

"You bet. Have a good weekend. Workaholic." Jimmy said while walking away toward the elevators.

Sam watched him walk away and out of sight with the rest of the Reps from the Insurance firm. He seemed like a nice enough person. Younger than her by a couple years she supposed. Maybe 26 or 28. He seemed to be healthy and active with a very boyish charm about him that she was sure a lot of women fell for, but she knew from past experiences that looks could be very deceiving. More than likely, Jim wanted to take her out just to get into her pants as most men wanted to do. She turned back to her computer and pulled up the screen she had minimized before Jim asked her to go out and interrupted her. She clicked the resume icon at the bottom of the screen.

Since she started at the firm, 2 years ago after moving from South Dakota up here to Billings Montana, she had been given a raise every year due to her performance and dedication to work. The work ethics she learned from working the farm with her parents had carried over to her career in the insurance business. It seemed like hard work was a dying trait nowadays and the tiniest amount of dedication to your job went along way. Sam took full advantage of that.

Crunching numbers and reviewing policies on spreadsheets came very easy for her and it didn't take much to impress the boss. It was some of the simplest work she had ever done and yet it impressed so many people at the speed she could do it. She had no doubt that within the next year or so she would be given her own office and pulled out of the "Bull Pen" with all the other minions. An office would be nice for the privacy it would provide her more than anything else. Once she had a door separating her from the others, her name would most likely be forgotten and she would no longer be bothered with questions like the one just asked.

Glancing down at her watch she realized it was only 3 pm and they were already leaving for the day. No wonder she was the one getting a raises and upcoming promotions she thought to herself as she moved the mouse across the screen and replaced the headset over her ears.

The truth was, she had finished her work an hour ago and was busy with her real life. It was her online life and she immersed herself in it. In this Second Life world she was a supermodel with more money than she knew what to do with. She surrounded herself with virtual friends and would travel the world on vacations doing whatever she wanted whenever the urge would grab her. Here anything was possible and her friends were in the hundreds if not thousands. She would use the high speed internet at work for a few more hours before calling it a day. It wasn't completely wrong to take advantage of work resources like this because her job was complete. She just used a little more electricity is all. She would make sure to not clock in any overtime for the internet use as that would be stealing.

In Second Live, her avatars' name was Victoria. She was an extremely buxom and athletic woman with fire red hair that dressed more provocatively than Sam would ever dress. It was the complete opposite of Sam and how she lived her life. In the virtual world she could do and be whoever she wanted. Today she, Victoria, was boarding her private jet that was painted purple and decorated inside to look like a dance club. She was taking a trip with 50 other people to Paris where they would BASE jump off the Eiffel Tower together. Maybe they would make a side trip somewhere during the flight and go exploring. Maybe she would hook up with a guy on this trip. She normally did. It was safe here. No worries of what they thought, or cares of them knowing your real world. They got what she gave and no strings were ever attached.

With the headset on she was talking with a tall man dressed in a tuxedo that was sipping a green drink on the jet. He had gotten her attention earlier before Jimmy interrupted her. She started to make her move on him when a small audible bell was heard in the background. It was a notification of an incoming mail or post. Sam minimized the screen again and pulled up another without thinking. After all, she was still at work and if it was important she would take care of it right away. She was careful to never let her virtual world interfere with work.

It was on her Facebook account where the sound came from. During any given time of the day Sam would have her work email, private email, Face book and Twitter account routed through her iPhone to the computer as well as Second Life running. She could multitask better than anyone she knew.

Her Facebook did not have a lot of private information on it like so many other people had. It did have a photo of her. It was old, maybe 8 years ago taken on the farm back home, but not much else. She primarily used the service to see posts and videos that others added to her timeline and comment on what she liked or disliked. At this time she had 224 friends and the small flashing icon for new Friend Request was on her screen at the top right.

She clicked it and read about the person wanting to be her new friend. Apparently she was an architect in the Houston area that enjoyed virtual reality as well as animated cartoons. Without granting her request, Sam couldn't see much more, but the photo of an attractive enough woman in her mid-40s was who the request was coming from. She looked nice.

Sam clicked accept.

CHAPTER 14

Jack stared at the photos on the laptop. He scrolled through each one while Cathy read from the paperwork explaining the image he was viewing at the time. Most of the time she didn't require the reports she had in her hands to give the background on the pictures. Cathy had been on this case long enough to have devoted most of it to memory. Jack understood, he had done the same thing when on a hard case. It would become his world and nothing would intervene until he solved it. Cathy wasn't any different. This kind of dedication was great for the job and helped in cracking down on the crime, but played hell on your personal life.

He was done with the Atlanta case and was on the home in Colorado. He didn't ask any questions while studying the pictures of the poor coeds lifeless and dull in their home. He just absorbed everything he saw and heard. Picture after picture and syllable after syllable he took it all in. There was nothing in the images he had not seen before and to his surprise it didn't bother him too much even with him being out of the game for so long. Stopping only to get another cup of coffee or adjust his position at the counter he and Cathy went through everything.

After the last photo had clicked past and Cathy ended her briefing, Jack stood upright and stretched. She watched him like a pet watches an owner hoping for a treat. Jack knew she wanted him to give her some profound clue or direction that she may have missed to help catch this guy, but truth was he didn't have anything like that. The only thing he could see, she wouldn't like. But she did drive all this way for his help, so he told what he thought.

"Well girl, I think you got a serial on your hands." Jack said.

"You think they are connected? You think it's the same guy?" Cathy asked immediately without hesitation. "Why, what did you see?"

"It's what I didn't see that makes me believe these are connected." Jack said as he moved back into the living room to stand by the fire.

Cathy followed him into the room and sat back down on the couch next to Max. The dog gave her a small grunt when she moved his rear end slightly to sit but didn't bother to move any more than necessary.

Jack stared at the flames flickering around the fresh log he deposited in the fire place. He watched as they licked their way up and around the wood embracing it like it was hungry for it. Soon the crackle and pop would follow the colorful show and the heat would poor into the room.

"So, is that it? Can you elaborate for me on your conclusion of a connection between them?" She asked again while he stood looking into the fireplace.

Jack moved away from the fire and settled back into his chair. He looked at her and took a deep breath. He could feel himself thinking like an agent again. He was already mapping out the routes to the murders based on the address given in each of the files. He was flipping through the images in his mind he just saw from her laptop and assembling a 3D model of the homes from memory. Every window, door and hallway was placed where it should be. The décor of the homes would be precise in his mind's eye. Every detail in the photos would be transported to his mental picture and he could walk through them at his leisure any time he needed. The names of the victims, age and sex was as concrete in his mind as his own now. This was how he operated before and it was coming back to him again.

He wasn't so sure he wanted to do this again. He had spent so much of his life in this world of death it had almost killed him. He had a good life up here. Just him and Max. It was a simple life and peaceful. The most he worried about was the power going out or not getting in enough fire wood. He didn't stress the crime of the city. The pollution and overpopulation wasn't a thought to him. He had worked so hard to get to where he was now that it seemed almost a waste to dive back into it. The rest of the world could fall away and he wouldn't mind too much. At least that's what he used to think before Cathy pulled into his driveway and back into his life.

Now he had seen the victims. He was given the opportunity to think about the killer and who he may go after next. He knew he couldn't sit by and let it go. He knew he had the ability to make a change or help. If he never knew about it was one thing. He could continue on with life without giving it a second look and nobody would blame him. But not now. Not now that he saw them, knew the names and was given the ability to help. If he turned her down and put his head in the sand he would be no better than the man doing the killing. If you're not part of the solution, you're part of the problem and Jack took this to heart.

He also knew Cathy was reaching out beyond her comfort zone to come to him. It was not in her nature to ask for help. She was the most independent person he knew and extremely capable at her job. For her to express this much vulnerability to him and he simply shrug it off would put him at the top of list for Ass Hole of the year award.

"Ok." Jack said leaning back in the chair. "Let's go over the last murder first and work through it to the beginning."

"Alright." Cathy said sitting a little more comfortably on the couch. She eased back, crossed her legs and rested her left arm on Max's butt. The dog didn't move in reaction to her touch for good or bad. He was asleep and would remain there until someone got up and headed for the door or the food dish.

Cathy's initial opinion of the dog must have changed, Jack thought as he watched her get comfortable. He could sense the relief in her. She was no longer uptight and on edge wondering if the long journey up to see him was worth it. Just him agreeing to go over the cases made her relax a little. Whether or not he could help her solve this would give her and himself the satisfaction that he tried and didn't look the other way.

"The couple in Oregon." Jack said from memory. "Tom and Aggie Anderson. They were a retired couple from Klamath Falls where they had lived and worked their entire lives. I would bet the two of them were high school sweethearts and have stuck together ever since. According to the local Sheriff they were liked by everyone in the community and from what I read, there are virtually no crimes of that nature ever in the area. At least for the past 50 years or so. The home had no sign of forced entry on any windows or doors which would suggest the victims knew the killer and let him in the home. But we already agree on the fact that nobody in the Klamath Falls area would want to do the Andersons any harm. So that means they didn't know him first hand. Maybe a delivery man, UPS, or FedEx?"

"No on the delivery man route. I contacted every carrier that delivers in that area. They all know the Andersons and according to dispatch records backed up by GPS's on the vehicles, no deliveries have been made or even past the home for a week." Cathy said while inadvertently stroking the dog's fur.

"Ok, so not a delivery man, maybe a salesman. They still do that sort of thing in Oregon don't they? Maybe it is a traveling salesman. Vacuum, cleaning products, Mary Kay cosmetics or whatever. That would put more explanation to the vast distance between the crimes."

"I looked into that as well. Apparently the Klamath Falls area only tolerates one sort of door to door salesperson and that is the spreading of the Good Word. One church in the local area is allowed to do it. They happily gave me the routes and names of people on them for the time frame of the murders. Turns out the Andersons were pulled off the route because they would tie up too much of the door knocker's time inviting them in for lunch and visiting. I guess the Good Word is on a time crunch and can't afford to be burdened with a social visit for too long. So nobody has been ringing that bell for the last 6 months."

"Well that leaves the human factor." Jack said. "These were nice people living in a safe place. They don't know crime and the evil that is in this world first hand. It's very possible that they would open the door to anyone that knocked. I bet a beating at the door in the middle of the night would be answered with the same, how ya doing, as someone in the middle of the day. Hell, I bet they didn't lock the door at night. So we could be looking for a complete stranger or drifter. However if that is the case and the guy is rolling from place to place, why not steal something? Why not take at least cash or jewelry? Are you sure that nothing was taken from the homes?"

"Nothing." Cathy answered. "Even the murder weapon that belonged to the Andersons was left. Same at the Atlanta home and Denver."

"Ok, let's look at that." Jack said leaning forward in the chair. "The killer used a hammer belonging to the Andersons. Did you find out where it was kept? Did Tom keep it in the home or the garage? Was it something that would be laying out in the open or possibly in a place that a person would have to know where it was to find and use it?"

"Mr. Anderson was a handy man for most of the people in the area." Cathy answered him. "He did everything from restoring or building new front porches on homes to installing a new hot water heater. From what the Sheriff told me, he'd only work for the cost of materials and maybe a home cooked meal. There was a tool belt in the bed of his pickup truck parked in front of the house with the hammer missing. The Sheriff confirmed that it was his hammer and the back of his truck was its normal place along with his other construction related items."

"So it was a weapon of opportunity." Jack said. "Except that it was out front of the home. He would have had to leave the home, go out to the truck to get it, and re-enter to use it in the crime. Which means, he grabbed it on the way in. He knew what he was going to do when he arrived at the home. Which implies this guy came to the home with one reason. To kill them. He had every intention of doing it and had no intention of bringing his own weapon with him to do so." Jack said, looking back into the fire.

"So you're saying it was a hit? Who would put a hit out on an old retired couple from a God fearing community in Oregon?" Cathy asked.

"Did you check their financials? Do they have any dirty secrets? Have you talked to everyone in the area?" Jack could hear his voice as he threw the questions at Cathy.

Normally she would respond to this kind of questioning with a raised guard and a little more attitude if it was anyone but Jack, but she knew he didn't mean anything by it. He was going over all the avenues, just as she had done.

"Yes, we canvassed the area and could turn up nothing close to a dirty little secret. The Andersons financials were squeaky clean. They lived on a simple budget of his retirement and social security checks. The only crime I found dated back 18 years to an unpaid parking ticket up in Eugene. Chances are the thing blew off their car and they never knew they received it."

"What about kids or relatives? Could any of them be in some kind of trouble that could bring the heat down on their loved ones?"

"I checked into the children." Cathy answered him without attitude. "They had 4 kids. Three girls and one boy. All of them are married with families of their own. Two of the girls live in Klamath Falls only a few miles from the murders. The other two live in separate states. One in California and the other in Arizona. All of the children's financials check out and we could find no criminal charges except for a couple speeding tickets on any of them. Two are school teachers. One is a dental assistant and the other runs a small at home business. I don't think this was connected through the family."

"So this guy, whoever he is, drives out to some rural home on the way to nowhere. He grabs a hammer out of a tool belt in the back of the truck parked in the drive way and walks right through the front door like he lives there. He goes directly upstairs and kills the man first while asleep in bed. Then he kills the wife and drops the hammer at the scene and leaves without stealing or touching a thing? This makes no sense. "

"Thank you." Cathy said raising her arms over her head like she was signaling for a touchdown. Max raised his head at the sudden movement and groaned then laid his head back down.

"Alright, let's walk through the next one." Jack said heading back to the kitchen counter and grabbing the next file. He found himself more interested in the cases than he should be or at least more than he thought he would be. He thought he had eft this life behind. He never imagined he could feel this way again. It was thrilling in its own sick and twisted way. His life was great. He wasn't wanting or needing anything he didn't have and yet the desire to open the folder in his hands and dive into it in search of this murderer was saturating his mind.

He returned to the living room and set the folder on the table before Cathy. Jack tossed another log into the fire and sat back down picking up the file as he did. She could see the look on his face. She had seen it before. He was into the case and wanted to know more. He was on her side and if Jack agreed to something, he would be in it to the end. Her hopes of finding this guy were increasing.

The minutes turned to hours and blurred on into the night. Neither of them realized how late it was until Max rose from the couch and started nuzzling Jack against his leg. It was past the dogs feeding time and Max was making sure he knew it.

"Yeah, Yeah, I know you spoiled mutt." Jack said rubbing the dog's ears. "Sorry girl, gotta feed the pup. His clock is more accurate than any Timex I have seen. It's getting late. Maybe we should call it a night. Did you get set up with a place in town?"

"What town?" She asked.

"Metaline Falls." Jack stated, leaving the files on the coffee table and filling a bowl from an enormous sack of dog food in the kitchen. "There's a little motel just off Main Street. Nice place, family owned and operated for years. Beds are soft and rooms are clean. Not sure what the rates are, but defiantly cheaper than the rooms in the big city."

"Well, I never made it as far as town." She said with a grin. "Matter of fact I wasn't planning on staying this long. It was a 50/50 chance I could even find you and from there an even longer shot that you would help me."

Jack finished up with the dogs food and set it down for Max. The pup eagerly put his head in the bowl and started in on it without hesitation. Jack walked to the front windows of the cabin beside the fireplace and peered into the night. The stars were out in force with the moon glowing through the trees. The snow covered ground was illuminating with the stars and moon shining from the ground up. The place was heaven on earth for him. But with no clouds and the darkness falling over the mountains he knew it was going to get cold tonight and it was getting there fast.

He couldn't let Cathy drive out looking for the town and the motel at this hour. It wasn't that hard to find but with the long day she already had, the weather outside and her lack of knowledge in these conditions it didn't seem like the smartest of ideas.

"I have a guest room. Why don't you stay and we can hit the rest of this first thing in the morning. I can whip up some breakfast and you can hit the road. What do ya say?"

"Don't worry about it Jack. I appreciate the offer, but I will head into town." It felt strange the thought of staying in his house. This place wall all Jack. From the wooden steps coming up the front porch to the coffee stained mugs he drank out of. She doubted a women had been in the house since he retired. At least not for any length of time.

"Cathy, the temperature outside has dropped 15 degrees since you arrived and will continue to drop well below freezing before you get into town. I would feel a lot better if you crashed here for the night. These roads can get pretty hairy when the weather is against ya. Don't think you should take the chance."

She didn't like imposing any more than she already had on Jack. Her showing up unexpected went better than anticipated and she didn't want to push her luck any more. But she wasn't an idiot and knew that he was correct about the weather outside and she had to assume he knew the roads up here better than she did.

"Well, I need to check in with Allen and let him know my progress. I have a flight out tomorrow evening. He only gave me 48 hours to find you and get your help, then I need to get back down to Oregon and assist with our team on the house." Cathy told him while pulling out her phone. She remembered after a couple swipes on the screen that she had lost service before she got to Jacks house.

He watched her on the phone trying to make a call without success and the frustration in her face when she realized he didn't have service.

"You can use my land line if you need."

"I can't believe you don't have cell coverage up here Jack." She half questioned and barked at him while replacing the phone into her pocket and taking the cordless phone he was handing to her. "It doesn't bother you that nobody can reach you?"

"Hell no. That's one of the biggest perks living out here." He said, while walking down the hall beyond the stairs. "I will get your room squared away. Just a warning tho, Max will probably be in early to say hi. He likes sleeping on the spare bed."

CHAPTER 15

The weekend flew by for Sam. They all seemed to anymore. Since she had discovered Second Life, most of her spare time was filled with the virtual world. After work on Friday she stayed at the office another 3 hours past her scheduled shift exploring her fantasy world. Everyone had gone home, leaving the place all to herself. Her supervisor didn't mind her doing this as long as she locked up when done and didn't log in any overtime.

Sam was an honest person and didn't cheat any more than the next did she supposed. Her parents brought her up right and she took pride in her daily actions proving her convictions were true.

She only left the office when she did because the busses stopped running her route at 8 o'clock. If she missed it, she would need to get a cab to take her home and she couldn't afford that. Billings Montana wasn't a large metropolis like New York or LA, with millions of people on top of each other scrambling for a place to live. It was spread out and open. The public transit system was much more sporadic than in a major city with not a ton of options. If you didn't have a vehicle, you would need to use it to get anywhere. Walking from place to place was almost impossible and definitely so in the winter. Sam had been saving for a car, but didn't have enough cash built up yet to do so. Unfortunately for her, she kept dipping into her moneys to upgrade her computer and gaming software so the freedom of her own vehicle was steadily getting farther away.

Second Life was the one vice she had but figured it could be worse. She didn't smoke, didn't drink and was not very materialistic when it came to fashion or what was the in thing. She spent her hard earned money on the necessities of life, bills and what was important to her and Second Life was at the top of her list.

Tonight, she was in a swimming pool on the roof of a skyscraper in some futuristic looking city with no site of the ground below her. Only clouds could be seen as far as you looked. Her avatar was wearing a tiny black bikini that in real life would get you arrested or at the least kicked out of a public pool. From the time she arrived home Friday evening to now she had only slept 8 hours in total. It didn't bother her to be shut in all weekend. She would sleep well tonight and hit work Monday morning refreshed and ready to survive another week of the mundane job.

At times she felt bad turning down offers to hang out or go someplace with co-workers, but the truth of it was, she enjoyed her time alone more than with anyone else. Sporadically through the weekend she would take a break and run on her treadmill or take a shower to get refreshed and rejuvenated. She wasn't one of these obese nerd shut-ins that ate pizza pockets, drank Jolt cola and hid from the sun. She was active enough and ate right. She didn't have the look of the addicted online gamer types. The simple fact was that she loved her alternate reality world more than the real one but knew what she had to do to in order to succeed.

Fitting in with society was important. She knew this and did what needed to be done to accomplish it and not stand out more than necessary. It felt like a game at times for Sam. The days would blur by in chaotic nonsense of deadlines and reports, all of which seemed so vital at the time but in reality were just as fictitious as Second Life was.

It was 9 o'clock Sunday evening and getting close to her bed time if a solid nights rest was to be had before work in the morning. Being refreshed and performing well was a must for Sam so ample sleep would be needed after a binge weekend of Second Life. She prided herself in the ability to stop when she chose and not let the game control her life completely. It was difficult at times, but so far the battle was hers.

The rooftop pool party she was in was beginning to get boring anyway, so leaving before it was over didn't bother her much. The acquaintances she made in this world were just as important as in real life. Maybe even a little more. She said her goodbyes to the normal friends and her new ones as she made her way out of the pool. One of the nice things about this world was she could leave whenever from wherever she wanted and be home instantly. There was no travel time, traffic or other issues. Then, when she wanted to go back, it was click of the mouse and she would be there.

At 9:15 she logged out of Second Life. The virtual world closed and her email filled the screen in its place. She gave it a quick look for any new messages and minimized it. Her Facebook account that was always open replaced the email and she scrolled through the new updates and photos posted from friends and family during her time spent in the virtual world. This never took her long and she seldom added anything to it. Just a thumbs up or thumbs down on something she liked or didn't and moved on. The new request she had accepted a Friday afternoon at work still had not posted anything on her account and it didn't bother her. If the woman in Houston was anything like her, only a comment once a week or so would be the extent of the communication between them.

Closing her computer, she stood up and stretched her arms high over her head, flexing her fingers and back. Long hours at the computer tightened up her muscles and joints. She would make sure to hit the gym this week more than she had been. She didn't want to end up fat, single and nerdy. That would be too much. It was too late to eat because anything after 7 would go straight to her hips. At least that's what all the fitness models say and she was too tired to take a shower. That would have to be done in the morning before work. Sleep was important right now.

Sam left the tiny office that she had converted from a good portion of her living room and picked up the dirty dishes that had accumulated at her desk while in Second Life weekend. In the kitchen, she rinsed out the cup and bowls then placed them upside down in the sink for later. There wasn't enough to fill a sink with soapy water and wash them. Besides, it was late and she was ready for sleep. She left the kitchen and went down the small hallway to her bedroom and bumped into a man who was standing in her room, filling the doorway.

He was taller than her by more than a foot and easily twice as wide. He wasn't yelling or reaching for her. He had a pleasant smile on his face and didn't look like a burglar should. He looked like any other guy you would see on the street but being here shocked her and she opened her mouth. Her scream was cut off low in her throat when the blade opened it from one side to the other. She never saw what it was in his hand. Or what he used or even saw it move. It was a blur of motion and surprise. Sam didn't feel any pain but instinctively put her hands to her neck when the crimson spray covered the wall beside the man as she jerked away from the shock of him touching her. She fell backwards, trying to get away and gain distance but tripped instead landing on the floor of the hallway. The man stood above her watching her go down. He wasn't talking or screaming or reaching for her. He just stood motionless watching her try to hold in her precious fluid that was so rapidly pumping from her body.

Sam couldn't think of anything but stopping the blood. She wanted to scream, but all the air coming from her lungs was exiting her throat before it made it to her mouth from the new opening the man had made. On the ground looking up, the man seemed huge and massive in her rapidly blurring vision. The walls of the hallway began to grow dark and close in around her losing focus and clarity of the pictures and shapes on them. The light behind the man silhouetted him in an eerie shadow, like the light had no effect on him and he would have no face if he was standing in the direct sun.

The shadows circled her vision now seeping inward like a tunnel screwing closed at the end. The man's image fell farther away to the end of the tunnel and the darkness came in closer. Sam felt a shiver cover her body, like being dunked in a cold bath and the lights went out.

She heard the thumps of steps on the ground and heard her door shut. Then the world of silence joined the blackness and Sam floated away in the abyss.

Vincent stepped over the girl, shutting the door on his way out.

CHAPTER 16

Jack was right about the dog. He came in around midnight and took up half the bed while Cathy slept. The animal became dead weight on the covers and she had a hard time moving him to gain more ground when the cold from winter night outside seeped into the room. Other than the intrusion, she slept well and hard. The flight up and long drive must have taken more out of her than she realized because she was asleep within minutes of her head hitting the pillow.

Once awake, she instinctively rolled to her side and checked her phone for new messages that was sitting on the nightstand next to the bed. She had forgotten that Jacks place had no service and wondered again at how a person could live like that. Instead of looking for the messages that would never come, she checked the time and threw her legs out of bed when she saw it was after 8. Pulling her jeans up and throwing the shirt over her head she fumbled with the lights for a second before finding them and illuminating the room. The Dog looked up from the bed and groaned at the interruption to his sleep but did nothing more and laid back down.

Cathy hadn't slept past 6 AM in 10 years. She didn't know if it was the mountain air, fatigue of the trip or the mental exhaustion caused by this case, but her body must have needed it. She took a quick minute making up the bed as much as she could. The dog refused to move much so just a flattening of the covers was all that was achieved. She threw her dirty clothes inside her roller bag and zipped it shut. After brushing her teeth and splashing water on her face she took slightly longer than she normally did in the mirror before opening the door and stepping out.

The smell of fresh coffee and bacon filled the air when she entered the hallway. She could hear the crackle of the fire and feel the warmth of the home the closer she got to the living room. For a moment it didn't feel like a stranger's house or any reason that she was here. It felt like a home. Like someplace so common to her that if fit like a shoe.

Rounding the corner of the stairs, into the kitchen she saw Jack at the stove. He was dressed in blue jeans and a checkered flannel shirt tucked in with a worn brown leather belt. He still looked good for a man in his 50's she thought to herself. His salt and pepper hair was combed back from his forehead as he always wore it and was neatly trimmed. He looked like he had been up for hours already and she was sure this was the case with the site of the dining room table.

Spread across the table were the remaining files they had not gotten to last night. Apparently he had gone through them while she was asleep. Either after she went to bed, or early this morning he had looked through every page it appeared and done so with scrutiny. There was an orange highlighter lying on top of the papers and she could see where parts of the reports had the bright highlighted ink on them. Maybe it was something he had found that they missed or just grammatical errors in the paperwork. Either way, she was pleased to see he still cared enough to look through it all without more of her coaxing.

"Morning Girl." Jack said. "Coffee?"

"Yes please." Cathy answered him stepping to the counter and sitting down on one of the wooden stools that looked like it came from an old west bar in the early 1800s.

"Did Max bother you much?"

"I didn't know he was there until I needed more covers." She said. "That dog is heavy."

"Yeah, he is kind of a bed hog when he wants to be. Normally he takes the whole bed as that room is rarely used. He thinks it's his own personal doggy retreat."

Cathy took the cup from him and sipped at the black brew. It was good and strong. He always had a thing with coffee and she could tell he hadn't lost the touch. "I see you looked through the rest of the files. Find anything interesting?"

"Oh, I don't know, maybe. Probably nothing, but thought I could go over it with you after breakfast. How do you like your eggs?"

"Cooked." Cathy replied and moved to the table eager to see what he had discovered. Jack could always find what wasn't there to find. He had a knack for seeing what others never could.

She started going through the paperwork by looking at the highlighted segment's first. She scanned them quickly, catching the phrases Jack had deemed important enough to mark.

Twitter.
FaceTime.
Snapchat.
Linkedin
Tumblr
Flickr.
Pinterest.
Instagram.

The phrases didn't seem to make sense to her as to why he would highlight them. "Ok, I'll bite, why did you highlight this stuff?" She asked.

He was busy pulling toast from the toaster and covering one side of each with a healthy portion of butter. "Oh, yeah, some of those things I assume were typos and a couple I just wasn't real sure about. So, I figured you could enlighten me on them and maybe this thing will open up a little more."

Cathy looked at the list of words he had highlighted again and could find no spelling errors. She stared back at him in the kitchen while he finished prepping the breakfast.

"Jack, none of these words are spelled wrong. They are just different apps that each of the victims had either on their Smart phones, tablets or PC's. We went through them all and found no connections."

"What apps?" Jack asked scooting the papers to the side allowing room for the plates. "Here, eat up. I am starved. Normally had my breakfast 2 hours ago and would be outside, knee-deep in a project by now, but I figured it wouldn't be very hospitable of me to eat without ya."

She scooted the papers away allowing the breakfast room. The plate was full. Two eggs cooked sunny side up sat perfectly on one side. A small mound of chopped potatoes grilled crispy with onions and green peppers rested opposite them. Three thick cut slices of bacon separated the items on the plate. He added a glass of orange juice and a small plate with two pieces of buttered wheat toast cut diagonally to the meal. Cathy didn't eat this well at home and definitely not in these proportions. How Jack remained fit was a mystery to her if he ate like this daily.

Max appeared from the bedroom wagging his tail all the way into the kitchen. He must have smelled breakfast cooking as she did. The dog didn't beg or get near the table. He laid down a short distance away at the mouth of the kitchen and watched. Cathy figured he would be getting the leftovers and knew not to beg for them.

After a couple forkfuls of the meal, Cathy wiped her mouth with the napkin and started her questions again. "So what about the words do you not understand Jack?"

"Well, basically, what are they? If there is no spelling errors involved, what is a Twitter, Linkedin or Pinterest?"

Cathy had to remember that it had been 4 years since Jack was with the Bureau and he fought technology the last few years he was active. Living where he did now with no service she doubted Jack had a computer and no way had he owned a Smartphone. I guess it was possible he had never heard of these things and she was sure it would be difficult to explain it to him. But she had to try if they were to move on with the case and any real hopes of finding any leads.

"Basically, they are online social media sites. They are used for people to stay in touch with each other and reconnected with lost friends all around the world. They are very common nowadays Jack. Almost everyone has at least a FaceBook account and Twitter, maybe more."

"And Pinterest?" Jack asked.

"It's another way to post pictures, videos and messages to your friends so everyone can see them at the same time. It's like mailing 100 letters to 100 different people all over the place and they all get them at the exact same time. Instantly."

"All the victims had these Apps?" Jack asked.

"Well, yes some of them. Not all of them had everything, but yes they all had at least a Facebook account and email. But we checked through them and besides the hundreds of regular posts, likes, dislikes and news feeds, there is no real suspect or connection between them. Of the 100s of friends they had, none of them were connected. Everyone checked out."

"What do you mean hundreds of friends?" Jack asked. "You mean that old couple murdered in Oregon had Hundreds of friends?"

"Yes, on their account, we pulled up 273 friends on the woman's Facebook and they also still had a MySpace account with half that many. Of course not many people use that anymore."

"You gotta be kidding me. Who has that many friends? " Jack said while finishing a piece of bacon.

"Well, Jack, the world is a little different now. People communicate a lot more than they used to and it's much easier to stay in contact than it was in the past. I have 300 friends on my account and I am a bit of a loner when it comes to social media."

"300 huh?" Jack said leaning back in his chair with a cup of coffee. "Name them."

"What?" Cathy asked looking at him while he stared at her with those icy blue/grey eyes.

"Name them. Give me the names of your 300 friends and where they live right now."

Cathy felt like a young recruit again. She felt like her supervisor was inspecting her and she was nervous about failing some test. Jack sat across from the table, silent waiting for her answer.
"I can't name them and where they all live right now, I would have to look at my phone." She replied.

"Ok, forget about where they live. Just give me the names. Hell, I will take first name only." Jack said.

Cathy could see what he was getting at. She could see his way of thinking and how he rated people in his life. Jack lived simple and easy. He didn't get bogged down with world events or friend drama. There was no way she could explain to him the need for social media and the difference between his definition of a friend and hers.

"Jack, I can't name them." She said, giving up the battle.

"If you can't name them, how can they be called friends?"

"It's just a title that the site gives them. But, I wouldn't call them enemies. I know them and they know me. That doesn't mean we get together on the weekends for drinks, but we are acquainted through other friends and people we know." Cathy said to him, slightly annoyed.

He could see that he had struck a nerve with Cathy but didn't care too much. He didn't understand the social media thing she was explaining to him or the need for it which she obviously believed she needed.

"Alright, let's say all the victims had this Facebook thing and that they all had hundreds of friends, like you do. Is it possible that one of the friends on these lists is the same on all of them? That could be your connection."

"No, we cross-referenced them all and none of them were the same. It's actually regular protocol now with the bureau to do that. Searches on phone records, bank records and computer history are standard practice to find any links. We turned up nothing that held a common link with the three."

Jack got up to put his dishes in the kitchen when the phone rang. He snatched it up on the way past the counter heading for the sink. "Hello?"

He listened for a minute not saying more than yep, nope and uh huh then handed the phone to Cathy. "Looks like you need to get going." He said. "There's been another murder."

CHAPTER 17

This was the first time Vincent had been to Montana. It was big, open and barren. The state stretched 545 miles from Idaho on the west to the Dakotas on the East with Interstate highways spanning across like arteries in a body. The speed limits had recently been raised from 70 MPH to 80 MPH and made the trip faster than most he had taken. The state was ranked 4th largest in the nation but only the 44th in population. It made his desire to go unnoticed all the simpler. They were correct in naming it Big Sky country, it seemed to never end around him.

Vincent drove at exactly 80 and watched the huge ranch land pass by while he thought about the girl he had just visited. Her home was so easy to gain access to. People just didn't lock doors anymore when they were home. Maybe it was some false sense of security they had. Maybe they thought, as long as they were home, nobody would come in and they were safe. Why would you think that? That is the best time to enter a home. A family could be distracted doing any number of things and you can walk right in like you belong there. People don't set alarms when they are home doing their pathetic mundane tasks they feel are required by life. They leave back doors open and windows to allow the breezes. It's funny when you think about it. The time of day with the most traffic, people and noises and you leave yourself vulnerable. Nobody would give a second glance to a person walking down the street in broad daylight and knocking on a door but you would surely remember someone at 2 am, doing the same thing.

The girl was pretty, he supposed. At least by the standards of society she would be held in the top 10 to 20 percentile for attractiveness and fitness that was deemed important. If he ever had the desire for female interaction he supposed it would be someone who looked like her. His hunts were beginning to get easier and faster than before. It seemed like he only needed to look for a short time and his new prey would volunteer themselves. This last time it only took a few hours and he got the invitation. This of course didn't bother him any as he was ready for the challenge. Nothing would make him happier than be given the opportunity to do his work every day.

The look on the girls face when he opened her neck with the box cutter was permanently imprinted in his mind. It was confusion, shock, pain and fear all rolled up into an expression that perfectly painted it all for his memory. He was thankful for that. He couldn't think of a more memorable gift she could've left him with.

The method he chose to rid the world of these people was the one thing that Vincent left to fate. Every other detail of his trip was planned out and memorized down to the ¼ gallon of fuel he would need and where to get it. His routes, disguise, ID and stops along the way if he needed them were all preplanned and nothing would change that. He took into account the weather and time of year just as much as he did the local law enforcement and history of state traffic violations, rules and regulations. Vincent had no doubt that he knew more about the places he was traveling to and from than those that lived in them. Just another reason he did what he did and why. If you were so naive to not gain the necessary knowledge of your surroundings, why should you be allowed to remain here to dwell in them?

For some reason, and Vincent could only assume it was a higher power granting him the ability, he was always given a method of ending them at the homes when he arrived. Whether it be bludgeoning, strangling, cutting or drowning, he never had to plan for it. They were sheep, all of them, and needed to be removed. He relived the moment at the girls house in his mind as he drove.

After walking in the girl's home he was given his implement of destruction only two steps through the door. A small table was set off to the left of the entryway with a small bowl atop it. In the bowl was some loose change, a half used roll of black tape and a disposable box cutter with a retractable blade. It was like she had purchased the thing that was painted in a bright pink color, just for him to use when he arrived and left it right where he would need it. The set up was so serene that Vincent didn't even close the door when he entered. He picked up the pink weapon, stepped down the hall until it opened into a living room and kitchen area. There she was. Sitting with her back to him on the computer clicking away on the keyboard, oblivious to anything going on around her. Vincent watched the screen in front of her as the computer animated people moved about in absurd clothing. They were doing things he would never do and he didn't recognize where they were, but the girl was enveloped in it.

After 20 minutes of observing her ignorant life, Vincent decided to leave her to the fictional world and wait in her bedroom. He didn't want to take her at the computer for fear of a camera being on at the time or her screaming into the headset she was wearing, possibly alerting whoever she was talking to. It was a risk he wouldn't take. He could wait, he was good at waiting. Besides it made the thrill of the hunt all the more intense.

He looked through her room while he waited. All the while being mindful of the sound of keys clicking on the keyboard to reassure him of her location in the tiny home. Not that it would matter too much if she did surprise him during his snooping about. But he did not like being interrupted. It would be better for her and quicker if she remained where she was until he finished his looking around.

Her bedroom had the look of a single person. There were no photos of a boyfriend or children on the walls. Only store bought images of fantasy world creatures and unobtainable goals decorated the tiny space. A unicorn surrounded by floating fairy's in some mythical world of false dreams hung behind her bed. On the nightstand was a small photo in a frame of her as a child. He assumed the people standing next to her were her parents. The back ground in the photo was green with a large barn in the corner. Sam must have lived on a farm as a child and gave up that world when she got older. How sad for her, he thought.

The bed, dresser and small vanity were made of cheap materials. Nothing was true wood or had any devotion to history or craftsmanship. The entire room could be purchased for under 800 dollars at any of the large super chain stores across the country. The more Vincent looked through her things the more the girl's reason for existing vexed him. This was a perfect example of why he did what he was called on to do. What could she possibly add to this world? What good does she do? She is a waste, a leach. Nothing more than the fill between cracks of the better people trying to make the world great.

The clank of dishes and water running ended his inspection of her room and he returned to the doorway to wait.

The mile marker drifted past on his right side as a large suburban filled with people passed him on the left. By his calculations he had another 300 miles before he would hit the Seattle city limits. Vincent had been driving for 8 hours now and had another 6 or 7 to go before he would get home. He checked the fuel gauge to ensure he had enough to make the distance. He knew he did, but it was a subconscious thing to do as you drove. MPH, temp, fuel, left mirror then right, back to the road and continue all over again. It kept him in full control of his surroundings.

Back in her room now, standing in the doorway awaiting her arrival, Vincent could feel his blood pump faster as he drove. He would relive the moment many times over but the fresher it was in his mind the more he enjoyed it. He remembered the smell in her room. It was a mix of sweat and cheap perfume masked over with the smell of instant food from the microwave and a fruity lingering scent of body wash coming from her bathroom. In any other circumstance, the stench would be sickening to his senses but now, it only enhanced his recollection.

He listened as she placed dishes in the sink. A cup and bowl, he thought. Those were what he saw on the desk in front of her as she typed. He saw her in his mind's eye as she rinsed them out and set them aside for later. She was too lazy to clean them properly. Lazy and worthless he thought.

The sound of her sock covered feet were muffled on the carpet as she left the room. He saw the light go out in the main room and heard the flick of the switch a millisecond later. Then she was there. Right in front of him. He felt her bump against his chest. A deep waft of her hair filled his nostrils. It was like watermelon and pine needles. Strange he thought. People picked the most insane fragrance's to bathe in.

She didn't scream at his sight. She was in shock. Horror and fear paralyzed her. The animal instincts of survival and fighting to survive obviously eluded her. He struck.

Vincent clinched the steering wheel tighter with his right hand as the memory of the kill flooded over him. He could sense the slight resistance her epidermal layer of skin gave when the blade first made contact. Then the sensation of a knife through a tomato came as he pulled through her throat, and out the other side.

Vincent tingled in the seat. He looked down and pulled up on his foot because he had accelerated during his memories by accident. The look on her face was frozen in disbelief. She must have thought she had so much more time on this earth. So much more she would accomplish and it was being taken from her. He soaked it in while she stumbled back and fell in the tiny hallway. Her blood sprayed across the walls and on him. He didn't care. The clothes would be disposed of three states away. He didn't bother to move from the path of the spray. He wanted to take it all in and he did.

It was over so fast, but the image he will have forever. Vincent threw the box cutter to the floor next to her. He took one last look at her as the last of her blood stopped pumping out and she laid still. It amazed him at how quickly a person could bleed out. The human adult body contained 4 to 5 liters of blood depending on size. He assumed the girl had no more than 4. The heart was capable of pumping multiple liters per minute. With the Carotid Artery severed as hers was, she had less than a minute. So little time to enjoy.

Vincent focused back to the road and adjusted himself in the seat. He had another 6 hours to replay Samantha's death in his mind and he would do it all the way home.

CHAPTER 18

Cathy thought the Spokane Airport was small, but the Billings Airport didn't even hold the International title as Spokane did. They were still stuck with "Regional" before the name, making it more of a bus stop for propeller driven aircraft than an airport. Like Spokane, it was clean and organized with smiles on the faces of most the people working there or traveling through. It must be something in the water up here she thought to herself. Why else would everyone seem happy all the time? Was life really this simple to make everyone appear to be in a constant state of satisfaction?

The flight was short out of Spokane but bumpy and loud. The flight attendants on the plane did their best to accommodate the passengers but it almost seemed like a waste of time as the plane was only in the air 45 minutes and they were beginning the decent and preparing for landing.

At the baggage claim area, Cathy checked her phone and began answering messages she received while in flight. Two were from Director Allen confirming her reservations at the hotel and updates on the crime scene. The other was from the Billings Sheriff department informing her that a car would be waiting for them at the airport upon their arrival. Normally she didn't check any luggage, but due to the extremely small aircraft, even her carry-on bag had to be checked.

"You want some coffee?" Jack asked producing a cup.

"Thanks." She said taking it from him and juggling her phone with her other hand. She was glad that Allen approved Jack to tag along as an advisor and even more pleased that he agreed to come. For some reason things seemed to flow smoother with him along. Nothing was hurried or chaotic when Jack was around. Instead of standing next to the conveyor belt waiting for the luggage, he sat down in a rocking chair supplied by the airport for those in standby status. He sipped his coffee and watched the people around him coming and going. He looked out of place in the airport but perfectly set in the chair. Cathy smiled at him and was more thankful for him being here than she realized. Jack made the world slow down to a speed you could enjoy and everything seemed to work out.

The glass doors to the street directly behind the baggage area slid open and a Police officer, wearing a brown cowboy hat walked in. He made a bee line directly for Cathy.

"Ma'am" he said, tipping his head down slightly. "I am Deputy Chad Thomas of the Billings Sheriff department. Sheriff Storm, informed me that you FBI folks would need a ride into town."

Cathy looked the man over. He appeared to be in his early 30's, well built with a slight bulge around the mid-section. Nothing a moderate diet couldn't fix. He was married by the ring on his finger and his uniform looked very presentable. So far these police were better than Klamath Falls, at least in appearance, she thought.

"Thank you, I am Special Agent Chambers." She said giving him a return nod, but not a hand to shake as she was still scrolling through her phone for messages. "How did you know I am with the Bureau?" She asked.

"Not too difficult Ma'am." He said, "We don't get a lot of suits up here and no offense, but you do stand out from the locals."

Cathy looked around and began to notice what Deputy Thomas meant. She was the only person besides him that was not wearing flannel, a Carhart Jacket or cowboy boots. She turned to look at jack, leaning back in the chair taking it all in. He rolled his eyes and smiled at her. She knew what he was thinking and yes, she did stand out a little.

"Ok, Deputy, as soon as the bags come out, we can go."

"Yes Ma'am. I was told there would be two of you?"

"That's my partner over there." She said pointing at Jack rocking lazily in the chair.

Jack gave a two finger salute/wave to the officer and went back to his coffee and people watching.

The home of the latest victim was set in a small apartment building two stories high. It was on the ground floor and shared the building with 3 other units. As before, the door was locked when the first officers arrived on scene and no signs of forced entry were found. A chalk outline of the girl, in her mid to late 20s was on the floor in the hallway only a few steps from the door. According to the report, her throat had been cut and the weapon was found lying next to her. With no other signs of theft or struggle. It was the reason Allen had sent her to the place.

It had been a long time since Jack had seen an actual crime scene but he didn't miss a step at fitting in. After doing it for so long, it was something that you wouldn't forget. The place was swarming with people. Each had a jacket with different letters across the back. Some were FBI, some said CSI. Others said Sheriff. The apartment was barely large enough for one girl to live in and now you had at least 15 people passing through. Jack could see that if there was evidence left by the killer, it was gone now or virtually impossible to find.

Cathy could see what Jack was thinking. The scene was compromised and she needed to preserve what she could.

"Ladies and Gentlemen, excuse me, I need everyone to exit the building now." She said it loud enough to be heard from the other apartments. She could be authoritative if need be and executed it in a professional manner. The mass of people caught the inflection in her voice and didn't protest about her request. One by one they left the apartment and gathered around the vehicles outside to wait for permission to come back in. She assumed most were happy to leave. The scene was a bit to gruesome for these country folks to see, with or without a body.

Jack moved from the entry beyond the girl's outline on the floor into the small living room and kitchen area. The place was neat. Not spotless, but clean. Organized as much as a single woman living alone would have, he supposed. It was easy to see that she didn't entertain other people on a regular basis. The home was oriented around a single individual's needs. A single cup and bowl sat in the sink. No other dishes were seen around the kitchen.

A small couch with room for two people if you were very friendly sat in the small living room. Only one coaster sat on the end table and no other seating arrangements were present for guests as well as no television. From the looks of the small home it was obvious the girl spent most of her time alone.

The remaining space left over in the living room was filled by a large desk covered with two monitors and a keyboard. Additional electronics sat on shelves above the work station that Jack did not recognize. Some looked like smaller versions of laptops he had used when he was with the FBI. Others appeared to be something out of a Sci-Fi novel. He stood in the small area and stared at the desk. To him, it looked foreign in a home. It belonged in an office building or on the bridge of the Star Ship Enterprise. So many different styles of electronics, all of them with wires coming out and connecting others.

"What did this girl do for a living?" Jack asked.

Cathy opened a folder she had been carrying that was waiting for them when they arrived and flipped through it. "She was an Insurance administrator." She answered.

"Do Insurance administrators need this kind of computer stuff?" Jack asked while inspecting the work station.

Cathy looked at it and shrugged. He could tell she was not as intrigued by the wall of technology as he was.

"Boyfriend?" Jack asked.

"No, single."

"New to the city?" Jack asked looking at the island of technology, still trying to figure out what some of it was.

"Fairly new. According to this, she moved here two years ago. Family is from South Dakota. No relatives in Montana. "

"Rich Parents?" Jack asked looking at the items on the desk and trying to figure out what they were all used for. One of them appeared to be a flat piece of glass no thicker than a magazine. It had finger print smudges all over the surface like someone was touching the glass.

"Farmers." Cathy said. "Generations of them. Apparently she didn't want to follow in the family's steps."

"Did she work from home?"

"She worked downtown Billings at a large Insurance firm. Nothing in the files here state that she worked from home."

"So what's the deal with the computer lab thing she has going on here?" Jack asked moving over the items on the desk.

"She was probably an online gamer." Cathy answered him not looking up from the report. "It's a normal thing for kids nowadays. They tend to spend a lot of their free time online and not in the real world."

"Were any of the other cases, online gamer people?" Jack asked.

Cathy moved to the desk and looked at the monitors, headset and keyboard. "Well, yes, but none of them were set up quite like this. They all had some sort of online game going on with a profile, but this girl seemed to take it a little more seriously."

"You're saying that old retired couple had online gaming stuff like this?"

"No." Cathy answered back. "Not like this, but yes they did have an online profile." She flipped through her phone looking for a specific message. "Here it is. He played World at War, it's an online game you play with other people."

"Is that what this girl did?"

Cathy looked at the file again and answered. "No, she was into Second life. Completely different and from the looks of her home, it was her priority."

"But, you said they all had Twitters, LinkedIn, Facebook, and whatever else, right?" Jack asked moving around the items on the desk with a pen.

"Yeah, Jack, but so do I and pretty much everyone I know. It's a standard thing to be a part of social media and like I said, we crosschecked them all and found no names to connect them."

Jack looked at the station and then back to the room. The place wasn't tossed and no sign of struggle was seen. Just a simple home for a simple girl. It made no sense for someone to kill a person with no reason. No theft, no rape and apparently no money involved. He turned back to the desk and using his pen, opened the laptop and tapped the space bar. Both screens came to life illuminating him and Cathy with an eerie blue glow.

The screen on the left produced a login box floating in front of a mountain range. It appeared to be somewhere in Canada he assumed or maybe the Himalayans. The screen on the right was a page titled Facebook with a picture of the victim in the top left corner. She looked young, healthy and happy. It appeared to be an older photo. Possibly one taken when she was still at home a few years ago judging by the horses behind her in a stable. The screen had multiple pictures of other people across the top and down the left side. The middle of it was filled with video links and cartoons. It was a busy image for Jack to take in. So many things covered it and all of them seemed to be of some importance or of none at all. Some were flashing, others were moving and one of them was fading in and out with a small number on it like a countdown clock.

"So this is Facebook, I assume?" Jack asked, looking at the chaotic jumble of sentences and statements surrounded by photos and pictures of people.

"Yep, this must be her account. Makes sense it wouldn't be locked if she lived alone." Cathy said, donning a pair of gloves and stepping beside Jack to use the keyboard. She scrolled up and down on the screen. "Looks like the last thing she was doing was checking her new friend accounts."

"New friends?" Jack asked, "Like who?"

"Well, she accepted a new friend on Friday at 1530. A woman in Houston Texas, apparently."

"What does that mean, Accepted a new Friend?" Jack asked.

"It just means that someone who knows her or knows a person she knows, has asked to be her friend on social media and she accepted it."

"Ok, again, what does that mean?" Jack asked.

Cathy had to remember that he had no idea about any of this and she would be starting from ground zero trying to explain it. She took a breath and stood up from the computer facing him. "Basically, it means that this lady from Houston can now view the things that Sam puts on her web page. Pictures, cartoons, video clips, whatever. If Sam adds it, she can see it and she can comment on them. Same with all the other friends she has. Likewise, Sam can view her posts and comment back on them along with all her friends. It's a way for them to stay connected and share stories or happenings in their lives instantly over thousands of miles of separation."

"But she is a new friend, right? Means this girl didn't know her? Or she was getting to know her?" Jack asked.

"Yes, a new friend means she would begin to communicate. But it's possible she already knew her from her past, or through another friend and they were just reconnecting."

"How many friends does she have?" Jack asked.

Cathy scrolled the mouse up the screen and responded. "345 it looks like."

"Holy shit, 345 Friends! Is that possible?"

"That's not that bad Jack, and again, they are not friends like you think they are. They are simply acquaintances she knows or a friend of hers knows. It's a harmless way to share your likes, dislikes or feelings and stay connected."

"Ok, so on her profile thing, it says she is single and living in Billings." Jack said leaning over her shoulder reading her profile info that Cathy had opened.

"Yes, it posts her information or at least, the info that she wants her friends to see."

Jack couldn't understand the website or the need for it. But he did understand that now 345 people knew that Sam was a young woman, living alone in Billings where she moved 2 years ago. They could see that she worked at an Insurance firm 5 days a week and didn't own a car or a pet and she liked rainy days more than sunny ones. She preferred Chocolate ice cream, not vanilla and liked cartoons more than dramas. Apparently she was not in a relationship and was happy today.

"So are you investigating all the people on her friend thing?" Jack asked

"No." Cathy replied, "Our IT people will cross check her profile with the other victims. If any of the people are the same, then we will dig deeper. Other than that, there appears to be nothing in common with the sites."

"So, aside from the lack of evidence, mode of entry and no obvious reason for the crime or difference in mode of death, there is nothing solid that connects the cases?" Jack asked her.

"That's right. It just like the others. Nothing taken, murder weapon belonged to the victims and left behind. No signs of forced entry. The selection for these people seems to be as random as the weather." Cathy answered him.

Jack walked through the apartment and stopped at the kitchen. "It seems to me, the one common link to all these is this social media thing. I know you think it's as normal as finding a gallon of milk in the fridge, but to me it's not girl. Isn't that why you asked me to help? Give you a fresh set of eyes?"

Cathy listened to him and felt like she was being briefed by a supervisor not so much talking with a co-worker and friend. Maybe he had a point, maybe she was looking at it wrong and the thing that she was looking for was something right in front of her. Something she took for granted as a way of life and norm. Maybe this guy was using social media to choose his victims. If he was, how were none of them connected? They had scrubbed the lists of the past victims but came up empty handed with no similarities on any of them.

"Let's assume, you're right Jack. Let say, this guy is using these sites to pick a victim. Why can't we find any connection through the friends to any of the other victim's?"

"Can you delete your profile?" Jack asked. "Maybe he does that after they become his friend and he has made the decision to kill them. Maybe he is covering his tracks."

"No, we can see who has been deleted in the history of the accounts. Our Intel department can scrub her hard drives entire history. There isn't a keystroke we can't recover, and none of the people are the same."

"What about the new friends, the ones she most recently added? Are any of them the same?" Jack asked.

"No, they had no connection as well. Same as the others."

"Did all the victims have new friend requests?" Jack asked.

"Yes." Cathy answered. "But, again, none of them were the same, no connections."

"Yes, but connected or not, each of the victims did have new friends accepted on their accounts?" Jack asked.

Cathy thought about what he said. It was possible she supposed but a long shot to say the least. "Yes, Jack, they all had recent new friends on Facebook."

"Recent, like within the last couple days recent?" Jack asked

"Yes, they all did, but none of them are the same." Cathy said again.

"So how different are they? I mean is it possible for a person to make up an account completely? Can you do that? Can you make up a fake name, picture, and background and fool the web site enough to post on it?"

"I don't know off the top of my head about the new requests, but there was nothing that jumped out all Ted Bundy like. They all seemed to be legitimate people living normal lives. It would take months to do follow up checks on all of them. Not to mention the legal, privacy hoops we would have to jump through to track them all down. But, yes, it would be possible to make up a fake account. Not sure why, the purpose of social media is to connect with friends." She said.

"But if this is how a guy was choosing a target, how would you go about tracking him down?" Jack asked.

"If that is the case, and it's a big if, it would be easy." Cathy answered him, moving away from the desk. "If we found one that we were suspicious on, our people would use the IP address of the computer to track the user's location and time. But again, you are talking about hundreds of people, maybe thousands. Each person has friends, and those friends have friends. The entire world is connected now Jack. We would need to pick one person."

"I wouldn't worry about all the friends in her account already. I would focus on the new request that they all had. Even if they are different people. This girl had one sent to her on Friday afternoon. 2 days later she is found dead. Does that timeline correspond with any of the other victims?"

Cathy dug into her mental files about the other cases. She remembered the girls in Colorado had just accepted a new friend 3 days before their murder. The couple in Atlanta had as well, but it seemed like it was a week before the killings. It could be a possibility she thought to herself, but she would need the get the rest of the files to confirm Jacks suspicion.

"Well, it seems to me like the only real connection we have between the cases is this Facebook thing. I would suggest starting with the newest friends accepted by the victims and work back." Jack said interrupting her thought train.

She didn't know if Jack was teasing about his lack of knowledge or he was just a good damn agent, but it was the best lead she had that connected the cases so far. She was slightly upset at herself for not seeing it by now.

"Ok." She said walking past him. "Let's start with this lady in Houston."

CHAPTER 19

It felt good to be home. Vincent loved the privacy and solitude of his boat. The drive back from Montana gave him plenty of time to replay his visit to the girl over and over in his mind. It made the miles fly past reliving the moment as many times as he wanted. The sounds and smells of her and the apartment saturated his mind. It filled him more completely than any meal ever could.

This was his second trip in less than a month. His work was increasing but it didn't bother him. He didn't feel fatigued and not at all worried about being caught or discovered. For reasons he could only assume were justifiably from a higher power, he was being given more opportunities to show the world how incompetent they were and he reveled in the possibilities to come.

The car was finished and tucked back into its auto cocoon. It was cleaned to the same degree as before and would remain until he needed it again. He went to work unpacking his bag and restoring himself back to his routine and the quest for knowledge. After all, without constant improvement one becomes stagnant and useless.

After a shower and dinner consisting of roasted turkey breast, asparagus and a small potato with garlic butter, Vincent settled down with his newest book and began to read. He picked it up the last time he was shopping at goodwill for clothes. It was a book of the greatest Serial Killers of the 20th century and how they were tracked down and caught by the FBI or local Law Enforcement. Sometimes he would dream of being in one of these books, but that would mean he had been caught and that would never happen.

He would read until he fell asleep and start the morning off with a swim. Maybe he would go back to the library and try another hunt. The thought instantly filled him with anticipation for the morning to come. The same feeling he had as a child when he slept that night. The night that he decided to change his life forever. He remembered the rain outside his windows trying to get in. The sound it made was like tiny fingernails tapping in hundreds of individual rhythms on the glass. Each of them fighting for his attention. Vincent recalled the complete feeling of satisfaction he had as he laid in bed that night listening to the rain and silence of his home.

He remembered Arthur's voice waking him the morning after with a sense of urgency. It was fun to play the game of victim and surprise when the man rushed him out of the house and into the police cruiser waiting outside. He remembered forcing out tears as he heard the news of his parents fate that night while he slept and how they feared the person could still be in the home or would come back for him later. It wasn't the attention that thrilled him as much as the stupidity of them all. They were looking for a man that didn't exist. They were wasting hundreds of hours and thousands of dollars in assets for what? They were dead, anything they did from this point on would not bring them back but they continued the search. It amazed Vincent at how long they looked and searched for the man that would never be found.

The years that followed his self-resurrection played out exactly how he planned them to. His father's brother and wife moved into the home and took over his father's affairs and company. They tried to be his new parents. Vincent continued in school, passing their pathetic and elementary exams while expanding his own knowledge and passions after the mandatory days were finished by reading and studying at home. By the end of high school he had read every book in the library and was starting again. He was never a bother to his uncle and would randomly have an emotional breakdown about his parents to continue his charade of a heart broken child.

On his 18th birthday, Vincent inherited the entire family estate and business as per his father's will. By this time he had been accepted into Yale and would continue with his college until complete. He would allow his uncle and Aunt to get fat on his father's hard work while Arthur leached more from his family while he was away at school. He was allowed a very impressive allowance from the company and lived well below what he could afford. Vincent didn't mind going away to school. It was easier to fit in there than anywhere else and he still had so much to learn.

College was easy. All you needed to do was pass the exams and not cause problems and the professors would leave you alone. If the school got paid they could care less how you chose to spend your time. Most of the time, Vincent was one of the few that attended class daily. The bottom line was, nobody cared. It was a scam. The entire Higher Education bit was nothing more than a money pit for the rich.

He avoided all clubs and social events but maintained enough public presence to not draw suspicion to himself or be labeled as a weirdo or outcast. He could feel the need rising in him while in school. The need to rid the world of the worthless and moronic people that dwelled in it. They were all around him. Wastes of oxygen, all of them. But he had a plan and would stick to it without deviation. He couldn't begin his true path until he was ready. The world of technology had flooded his generation and everyone was busy now on phones or laptops. Each of them scrambling from Wi-Fi signal to Wi-Fi signal. It made Vincent sick the more he saw it.

Graduating as the Valedictorian from Yale could have been easy for him, but that would be too memorable for the life he had chosen to live after this, so Vincent simply went through the paces and walked the stage as the rest of them did with a 3.0 average. Again, not too impressive, but nothing to raise concern.

As he knew they would, his Uncle and Aunt were there, making a show of how proud they were of the young man who had overcome so much tragedy in his life. All the while oblivious to his real desires and plans, but they would know soon enough.

After he returned home, he took over the business as the sole heir and shareholder. Within a week of running the company, Vincent sold it off. His uncle tried to dissuade him of the sale, but being the primary holder in the company, nothing could stop it. He didn't care about the hundreds of employee's that would be out of work or the fact that so many people had devoted their lives to the company to make it the success it was. Vincent had a plan and liquidating the estate was the first step. The home, the land and everything in it went to the first bidder. He didn't care about the price he sold it off at or waiting for a higher one. Everything needed to go and the sooner the better. It was a whirlwind of events that even the massive and overpaid group of lawyers hired by his uncle could not stop. Within a year, it was all gone and the family name was no longer a part of the elite crowd of the wealthy in America. After a few more years it would be forgotten entirely leaving Vincent to blend into the folds of the world and be forgotten.

History would reflect the events as a spoiled child pissed away all that his family had worked for over the generations and had no remorse of doing it. Vincent took the money and disappeared.

At the age of 25 he purchased his boat that would begin his new life and be the base for all operations. It was a cash sale from an old couple living in the Puget Sound area. He had made contact with the couple a year ago and had stayed in communication with them until all the funds had cleared. The 1957 Criss Craft wooden Cabin Cruiser had been meticulously cared for by the couple over generations of ownership. It measured 58 ft from bow to stern and had two staterooms, a galley, three bathrooms along with crew quarters and an engine room for twin diesel caterpillar engines that were new to the vessel. Vincent had always wanted a boat. The freedom of movement and lack of tracking made it the perfect selection for him.

Since he wasn't a materialistic robot like the rest of the world, the size didn't matter. He needed no more room than the ship provided. Mental rewards along with physical was what he searched for and achieved. These were worth more than anything else.

The slip that moored the craft in the harbor was included in the package deal and Vincent paid cash for all of it along with 10 years moorage fees in advance for a total price of 750 K. He had the money transferred from his account to theirs immediately and took up residence on the boat the next day. Soon after he was situated, Vincent drained the remaining funds of his accounts into cash assets and closed them all. He would live on a cash basis preventing any tracking of his movements from this day forward. If he held himself to the budget that he had allotted, the 4 million in the safe on his boat would easily last him the rest of his life.

Finishing the book on Serial Killers, Vincent retired for the night. He had decided that tomorrow would begin another hunt for him. Maybe he was proceeding faster than needed, but it was so easy anymore. People were so eager to share their lives with a complete stranger and have no reservations about doing it. He had heard nothing of the murders in the news or if law enforcement had even connected them. He seriously doubted they would connect them. They were fumbling buffoons and incapable of operating at the same level he was. He would find another tomorrow and hopefully, within the next week he would be reminiscing of his most recent kill.

Vincent slept.

CHAPTER 20

"Ok, thank you." Cathy said after hanging up the phone. "Here is what we have on the newest friend contact with our latest victim. The lady from Houston is an account created in Seattle Washington. It has no pictures and no other friends associated with it. From what my IT guys tell me, it appears to be a fake account. The name was fake, and photo was pulled off the internet. Just a random photo someone posted of a middle aged woman. The name crosschecked with a lady that died 24 years ago. Not sure if there is a connection to that or if it is coincidence. Our guys are looking into it as well. Bottom line is, the entire account is false and is now closed with no further activity coming from it."

"Meaning?" Jack asked.

"Meaning, you may be right about them." Cathy answered him.

"So the other victims had this Lady from Houston as a friend as well?" Jack asked

"No, only the girl from Montana received a request from her, but the other victims also had new friends that were accepted very close to their times of death that also lead to fake accounts. All of which originated from Seattle."

"Seattle? That's a long ways from Atlanta or Colorado. I can see possibly the Oregon case or this one here being the same guy, but all the way across the Continental USA is a long way to go just to kill a few people." Jack said moving to the window looking down at the street. "Can your computer nerds tell you anything else about the person that created the account?"

"Unfortunately, no. Facebook accounts are relatively free to the public to create so there is no real record of payment. The information put in is all on the user. It could all be completely fake and nobody would know. Your pictures that were posted, history, location, likes and dislikes can be false. There is no way to confirm it unless you knew the person that did it." Cathy said.

"So these people, accept a person that they have no idea about and let them view their life and personal information? That's crazy! Why would you allow that to happen? It's like inviting a complete stranger into your home and leaving them alone to roam about your house while you're gone. Aren't there privacy issues with doing that stuff?" Jack asked, turning back from the window.

Cathy could see that he didn't understand it and her trying to explain the need for it would fall on deaf ears. He was old school. A phone was for calling, not texting or messaging. A computer was used for reports or looking something up to gather information on that report. She knew he didn't understand but it was his lack of understanding that gave them the one and only lead they had and it was looking like a solid one.

"Let's say for instance I wanted to create an account." Jack said. "Could you show me how to do it? I mean is it something that requires knowledge of a computer or is it a thing anybody can do?"

"It's very easy, Jack. All you need is an email account and you can get started."

"So this guy has an email account attached to the Facebook account? Can you track him through that?" Jack popped back to her.

"The email accounts originated and terminated from the same IP addresses as the Facebook accounts did. Totally fake." Cathy answered him. "You can create an email account and be just as fake as anything else, but, what we do know, is all of them have come from the Seattle area. Our people determined that the four fake accounts were created and deleted within a few hours of opening them and all were done from public libraries located in the same area of the Pacific Northwest."

"Can your people close in on the dates and times this happened?" Jack asked, genuinely curious.

"Yep, they can, and not only that, they can take us to the exact computer used."

Jack could hear the inflection in her voice and felt the same spark she did. They had a lead. All they needed to do was go to one of the libraries in mention. Pull the footage from the cctv cameras that were in all of them now. Pick the date/time and they should get a good view of their suspect.

"If this is the same guy, it's safe to assume that he is living in Seattle. That could explain the lack of time between the killings. How long from the murders in Atlanta to Denver?" Jack asked.

Cathy answered without looking. "30 days from the family in Atlanta to the coeds in Denver."

"And the old couple in Oregon?"

"Two weeks." Cathy said.

"And it's been four days since you came to see me on this Montana girl. It all fits if the guy is based in Seattle. Driving time alone would be longer for Atlanta or Denver. Oregon and Montana are close." Jack said.

"Well, that's saying the guy drove. He could've flown. He doesn't need to bring any weapons with him remember. We are already checking flights in and out of the airport a week before."

"You're wasting your time with that." Jack told her. "This guy is smart. He leaves nothing to trace him at the scenes and takes nothing that could ID him. He makes up fake accounts then deletes them as soon as he finds a target and never uses the same one twice. He would never use public transportation especially an airline. Too easy to track."

Cathy put her paperwork down and moved around the small office. She was tired. She had been moving since Denver nonstop without much of a break. The Sheriff's Dept. was nice enough to give them an office to use while her IT people dug into the computer history of the girl. She and Jack were spending the time going over the other cases trying to find more connections.

"Jack, how far is it from Washington to Georgia?" She asked stretching her arms and looking out at the winter weather through the window.

"Oh, I suppose you are looking at 2000 to 2500 miles, depending on the route a person took."

"How long would that take you to drive?"

"Well, on a good day, with the weather allowing it, I can cover 600 to 700 miles without feeling like complete shit when I'm done."

"That would mean it took this guy 3 to 4 days drive time to get there. He murdered them and drove 3 to 4 days back. Who would spend 8 days on the road to kill a family he doesn't know?" Cathy asked, looking at the snow fall outside.

Jack sensed her frustration. He knew Cathy was a good agent and persistent as anything when she was on a case. But, she was relying too much on why the guy did what he did. "Listen girl, remember the guy I chased across the country? It was the last case I was on?"

"How could I forget Jack? The guy almost killed you and me. I will never forget."

"True, he tried, but he didn't. You know why he raped and murdered all those women?"

"No, why?"

"I don't know. Nobody does and never will. He was a freak, a psycho. Maybe he did it for thrill, maybe an invisible friend told him. Maybe God was talking to him or he saw it in a vision while eating his oatmeal. None of that matters. I know you want to try and understand. You think it might help you catch the guy, but the bottom line is some people are just born bad. Some people you can't understand and never will. This guy may be killing these people because it's a Friday not Saturday. It doesn't matter, what you need to do is focus on what we have. We know he uses Facebook to select his victims by creating a fake account. We know he is in the Seattle area. It's a real good chance that the guy drives to his victims in his own car to prevent a trail. We know he is smart enough to elude all your state of the art forensics and keep you guessing for a long time."

"Great. Thanks Jack. Anything else you want to tell me!" Cathy didn't need to be reminded of how far behind she was on the case.

"But, it also means that somewhere between the west coast and Georgia he had to buy gas, stop for a piss or purchase food. Somebody in that 2000 mile stretch of road has seen him girl. That is something."

"You're right, but that is a long stretch of road to cover." Cathy said turning from the window with a spark of hope in her voice.

"Maybe he got a speeding ticket. Driving all that distance he may have been pulled over. I could check with the state patrol and look at all tickets issued in a specific window on the main routes."

"I seriously doubt this guy would make a mistake like that. He is so careful about everything he does, speeding wouldn't be the thing that he slips up on. I would be willing to bet he chooses routes that keep him away from largely populated areas. Less chance of cameras at stoplights and gas stations. Less law enforcement. He would take the longer routes on state highways and county roads to avoid the Interstates."

"Well, that makes me feel better about us finding him." She said with a hint of sarcasm in her voice.

"Smaller roads and rural areas may mean lack of cameras or law enforcement, so your digital means of tracking may be limited, but it does mean smaller towns and down to earth people. The more rural the area, the fewer strangers pass by. You have a better shot at someone remembering a person from out of town passing through a small place like that than you do a busy truck stop on the freeway with hundreds of cars an hour pulling in an out."

Cathy sat down opening her laptop. Her fingers flew across the keyboard in a flurry of motion and clicks. She pulled up MapQuest and punched in directions from Seattle Washington to Billings Montana. A route appeared on the screen. It was almost a straight line between the two points stretching across the middle of Washington and half way through Montana. The blue line highlighting the route dipped down once it crossed the panhandle of Idaho then shot straight across the state to Billings.

"Jack, come look at this." She said, excited about what she was looking at.

Pointing at the screen and moving along the route she started talking. "Look, if the guy left from Seattle, there are only a couple routes he could take to cross Washington without dipping all the way down into Oregon then back up. But that wouldn't give him enough time. This girl was murdered 4 days ago. The couple in Oregon were killed 8 days prior. Which means he had to take this route if our thought about him driving is correct. There just isn't enough time to do it any other way."

"How far is that?" Jack asked.

"820 miles." She answered after clicking on the line.

"That's just over a day's drive for someone dedicated to what they're doing, maybe less. It's possible someone along that route may remember something out of the ordinary if this guy passed through within the last couple days." Jack said pulling on his jacket. "Let's go girl. Daylight's wasting."

He was on the move and Cathy knew if she was going with him she needed to keep up. Jack wasn't much for waiting around to see what a bunch of computer geeks could pull up. He was old school and driving the same route the murderer just did was the best thing he could do right now. She didn't think driving across two states in a rental car during the winter would be the optimal use of their time, but it was the way Jack operated and he was leaving.

She dialed her phone on the way out the door. "Allen, its Chambers. We have a lead. I sent you the Intel we gathered and need a team at the location the accounts originated from in Seattle to look for any trace evidence and check camera footage. Get ahold of the field office there and let them know we will be arriving in a day or two to go over what they have found."

She was done talking by the time she reached the car. Jack had it started and was pulling on his seat belt. "Allen good with this?" He asked.

"No, he's not, but what choice does he have. He will send a team to the location of the fake accounts inception and go over camera footage. They will wait for us to get there."

"Sounds good. Buckle up girl, we got 800 miles to go and no time to waste."

CHAPTER 21

Vincent enjoyed driving. His father always had someone drive him and his mother around. Even with the collection of automobiles he had, Vincent couldn't remember a single time he saw his father behind the wheel. Maybe it was because he was a poor driver or because he had so much money that he felt the need to impress people around him with his frivolous spending. Personally he figured it was just laziness. Why would anyone give up the freedom of sitting behind the wheel? It made no sense to him. He was in control of everything while he drove. He would never let anyone have that kind of power over him.

This was the first time Vincent had turned around so quickly from one hunt to another. Only a day of rest at home and he was back on the road. It was getting so easy to find them anymore. People were so eager to let someone into their lives. It wouldn't matter who he was or where he was from. Yesterday only took 45 minutes of hunting and he found one. People were so eager to share their pathetic lives with anyone that would listen to them. It didn't matter who they were. This world of technology, designed to bring everyone closer together did just the opposite. Maybe on an electronic scale or by some measurement taken in a university somewhere it made sense, but in the real world of flesh and blood the streaming world was creating walls between people you couldn't climb and severing the need for human interaction all together. He saw it on a daily basis. Everywhere from driving a car to eating in a restaurant. Everyone had their faces glued to a screen of some kind. Mothers and fathers with children were oblivious to anyone around them while they swiped and typed on what truly mattered in their life. All the while the real world passed by them like a wraith.

Perhaps it was a sign and he was being tested by being given so many opportunity's so quickly. Maybe his work was only going to increase and he would be challenged constantly to maintain the order of the world. This was a course that he reveled in. He would gladly spread his work as much and as far as needed. Vincent was stronger and more capable than anyone. He had trained and prepared his entire life for this, both physically and mentally. He would be up for the chance to prove to the world how inept they were and the road they were traveling on would lead to certain destruction. Soon, they would see the error in their ways and understand that what he was doing was right, just and long overdue.

This hunt was closer to home than he had ever had before. It was only a 3 hour drive to the small town of Ellensburg just over the mountains from Seattle, but it didn't matter. His method of selecting his next one would not change, no matter how far or close they were. This was the one random act that Vincent allowed in his life. He left their inevitable fate in the hands of his victims. They had the power to choose whether or not to let him in and after it was done, there was no turning back. The people were ripe for the picking and Vincent would harvest all that were given to him.

The home was larger than any he had been to in the past. It stood alone in a spread out rural community with the closest neighbor about a quarter of a mile away across a densely treed stretch of land. Each home seemed to be on large acre lots. Possible 10 or 20 each. You couldn't see the next house from the driveway of this home so it made his approach all the easier. Vincent drove directly up to the front of the home and parked. For some reason, a stranger in a car approaching a home was less scary than a stranger on foot. He didn't understand this thinking since they were so eager to let strangers into all the vast secrets of their life without care on the internet, but a random person knocking on the door aroused suspicion.

The house was older, maybe built in the 50s when homes were constructed for use, not so much for appearance. It was a simple square two story home with a tiny one car garage attached to the side. The home was a faded blue color with a clean white picket fence surrounding a small yard directly in front. The sidewalk was covered with freshly fallen snow but had been recently shoveled off. Most likely in the last hour or so. He was sure that underneath the white powder was either a brickwork path or poured concrete walkway. The front porch had firewood stacked up against the outside wall with a bucket full of smaller pieces and ax sitting in a block used for splitting off kindling for fire starting. The whole thing was covered with a roof that protruded off the front of the home about 12 feet. It appeared to be added later as the paint wasn't as faded as the rest of the home. Perhaps it had just been painted within the last year. The door had a weathered look, but seemed to be structurally sound enough. Overall, the exterior of the place seemed well kept, at least as much as he could see with the snow piled up around it.

With no doorbell on the outside of the home, Vincent knocked. Nothing hard and fast or that would cause alarm. Just a simple three knock jingle that stated someone was here that wanted to talk or visit. From inside he could hear a woman's voice yell out something that sounded like, I will be right there. Beyond it, was the sound of a dog barking and two other voices. Possibly kids he thought, young, maybe girls. This didn't bother him, neither did the dog. Movies put so much faith into dogs. They make them out to be some sort of impenetrable defense to a home when in reality, they worked more to his advantage. People cared for pets more than their own lives. They would risk so much to save a stupid animal even if it cost them their own life.

He could hear the footsteps approaching the door. The home must have hardwood floors, he thought. It would fit with the age. The knob turned and the door squeaked on poorly oiled hinges swinging open. The woman was older than her profile picture appeared. Possibly in her mid to late 40s. It didn't surprise him that she had lied, most people did. She was wearing red sweat pants and a grey baggy t-shirt that had stains on it. Her hair was a mess and from the look of her she had been busy cleaning or cooking or both. Her eyes were blue, just like her photo on face book, but her appearance was definitely worse than the one she posted and much more aged. Most of the people he went to meet posted photos that did not truly show what they looked like. Perhaps it was vanity or self-consciousness, but he had yet to find one photo that was taken within 6 months of his targets when he met them.

Vincent smiled at the woman as she met his eyes with hers. She grinned back slightly and opened her mouth but was cut off before speaking when he brought the hatchet down hard. The tool used for chopping the kindling was surprisingly light, making his swing significantly faster than anticipated. It sank deep right where he aimed it. He could feel the crunch of her skull separating as it passed through the bone into the soft tissue beneath that it failed to protect. The axe vibrated in his hand that gripped the handle.

From behind the woman a small girl no more than 8 years rounded the corner asking who was here. She was wearing what looked like a pink princess costume. Maybe they were playing make believe and he interrupted. Perhaps it was a snow day and they were home from school. Her little eyes took in the scene and she froze in place. Her mouth opened preparing to scream when the dog jumped from behind the girl.

It was a large dog, maybe a German Shepard or cross breed with something like that. The dog leaped for Vincent snarling and snapping his jaws as it came. The hatchet was stuck in the woman and wouldn't come out in time. With the dog now in midair and only seconds away from sinking its teeth into him, Vincent dodged to the right and the dog landed on the front porch sliding across the frozen deck. Vincent slammed the door shut after kicking the lifeless legs of the woman out of the way, locking the barking dog outside.

He walked into the home following the little girl that ran around the corner screaming. He could hear the dog barking outside and smiled at the stupidity of the animal. The dog would bark until Vincent came back out and then he would silence it for good. A door slammed from ahead of him and he could hear another small voice.

They wanted to play hide and seek. That was fine with him, Vincent loved games. He always won.

At the end of the hall was the kitchen and the counters were covered with flour. Cupcake tins and bowls with batter were spread about in separate places. Small containers of icing and sprinkle were opened and he could see where they were being applied before he knocked on the door. Apparently it was a snow a day and they were making some treats.

Vincent heard a door slam upstairs. He picked up the rolling pin laying in the flour and took the stairs two at a time. He wasn't sure if the young girl had a phone upstairs, but he wasn't going to risk a call being made.

Kicking in the door to the room was easy as most homes only have a simple knob lock on interior doors. Once inside the two girls sat huddled at the far end of their bed hugging each other. Neither had a phone.

Vincent raised the rolling pin as walked across the room.

CHAPTER 22

"I am not so sure this is the best way to be using our time Jack. Driving 800 miles when we could just fly seems to be a bit on the wasteful side, don't you think?"

Jack looked out the window then back over to Cathy sitting in the passenger seat. She was tapping on the screen of her smart phone and clicking her laptop at the same time. "Why do you think it's a waste of time?"

"Well, it's gonna take at least 14 hours to drive when we could be there in less than 5 if we flew for starters."

"Ok, and what would you do if you got there in 5 hours? You think the guy will be waiting at the library for you with a sign around his neck?"

"No, but I would be able to assist with the tech teams to pull camera footage and go over the workstation that was used for starters." She answered him while still reading emails. "If we find the right station he used we could possibly get prints or DNA. That would be a start."

Jack didn't look away from the road. "Oh, so you are an IT Guru/CSI now? I didn't know the FBI sent you to nerd camp to learn all that hacker stuff and pull DNA. I thought you were a special agent assigned a possible serial killer case?"

She could see what he was getting at and he was right. There was nothing she could add to the team that would be arriving at the library in the next hour. In fact, she would most likely end up getting in the way as they dusted for prints and gathered evidence. Jack knew this and that's why he took the road route. They had a better chance of running into someone at a gas station or rest stop that might remember an out of state car or something that peaked their curiosity more than fumbling around the library with a bunch of lab geeks. Besides, if they did get a print or DNA from the library, they would need something to compare it to. So far, they had nothing.

"You have an idea of where you might make your first stop?" She asked, giving up on her phone because of the lack of Wi-Fi on the prairies of Montana.

"At least another 100 miles before we start looking for an older, more run down gas station and start asking questions is what I was going for."

"Why another 100 miles? Why so far? We have already been driving for at least a 100 miles now. I know I gotta pee, this guy would to, don't ya think?"

"This guy is smart girl. My guess is he would stop as far away from his final destination and scene of the crime as he could and fill his tank. That way he could leave and know how far he could go without stopping on the way back. I bet the guy has his mileage figured out down to the ounce used. Granted we have no idea what kind of car he is driving but it is safe to assume it gets reasonable fuel economy. If this guy drove all the way to Atlanta Georgia from Seattle, it would be a must otherwise he would be stopping every couple hundred miles to fuel up. Each stop is a risk he would take to being seen and later recognized. Also, I doubt we're looking for a tiny little rice burner of a car that gets amazing mileage. They are too uncomfortable on a long trip and impossible to sleep in. I doubt he would use a hotel and risk a record of his location as well. That means he would need a car large enough to stretch out in if needed to get some rest. Somewhere between a Geo Metro and a Suburban I would guess.

"Oh, well that makes the search so much easier." She said listing to him play out the killer's mode of transport.

"We will be looking for a gas station that is older. Not a big chain place like all the ones we are passing full of lights and trucks but a smaller mom and pop type station. If there is a camera outside, forget it and move on. He wouldn't risk a recording of his route. I would think there is enough little places around that with research he could pick his way across the country and not be seen."

Cathy had forgotten how good of an agent Jack was. He hadn't let much go during his retirement the last few years. She could see the wheels moving behind his eyes. The man was on the hunt and fitting back into the groove without missing a beat. He was thinking like the guy and that was good.

"Ok, I'll buy all that." She said. "His vehicle wouldn't stand out in any way. It wouldn't be a bright color. Nothing easily dedicated to memory. Maybe tan, or beige or white. Also, the make would be plain and common. Nothing foreign or exotic." She said, adding to his theory.

"Right." Jack stated. "Count out BMW, Mercedes, Volvo and any other luxury cars. It's probably safe to rule out any kind of a pick-up or truck as well. In order to sleep in the back he would need a camper and that would not only stand out, but would get shit for mileage. We will be looking for a four door sedan or station wagon.

Not new but not too old. Something built within the last 15 years. It would be a very well maintained car, but nothing too impressive to look at."

"With Washington plates." She added.

"Yep." Jack said. "If Seattle is his home base, he wouldn't have fake plates on a car. No way would he risk that random check by a State Patrol. I bet he is completely legit. His insurance will be up to date, no traffic violations or citations, everything on the car would work, giving no reason for the police to pull him over or give him a second look. Beside these killings, I bet the guy is a law abiding citizen."

"That might be the first thing we ask." Cathy said, looking at her phone again for service. "See if anyone has noticed a Washington plate in the last 3-4 days. Don't you think that might stand out in the middle of Montana?" Still no service, she put it back down.

"Couldn't hurt to ask, but in reality, it's not that far from the border so a Washington plate wouldn't be too far out of the norm to see. However, cash will be his primary method of payment I am sure. No doubt he has credit cards, but he wouldn't use them on these trips. No way would he risk any record of him being within 500 miles of a murder scene by a credit card receipt for a few gallons of gas. If he is stopping as little as possible to get fuel, it means when he does, he will be purchasing at least ¾ of a tank at a time or more. With gas prices the way they are, the guy may be floating out 100 dollar bills. That would be something these small town folks would remember long before a plain car with out of state plates. I doubt they see many Benjamin's at these small places."

"How would a guy like this have the money to do what he's doing? Or why?" She asked herself out loud more than pointing the question to Jack.

"That I don't know. Maybe he is independently wealthy and doesn't need to work. If he had a regular 9-5 job he couldn't afford a week or longer road trip every other month to go kill people. We could be looking for a trust fund baby or a guy that has recently sold everything and gone off the deep end on a killing spree." He said to her, answering her vague question.

"I suppose we could run checks on Trust fund recipients in the Seattle area. I already know the list will be huge. It's a very popular place for people to retire or the rich to have homes."

"Yeah." Jack said. "That's a definite needle in a stack of needles there. Better off going door to door than finding a connection valuable enough to move on with those search parameters. But, it does get me to thinking. If this guy is as careful and smart as we think he is and he has a car, he must park it somewhere and that somewhere would almost certainly be out of sight."

"So a home with a garage?" Cathy said.

"Well, not necessarily." Jack answered, adjusting in his seat a bit. "This wouldn't be his primary mode of transportation. He wouldn't risk it being seen every day for that one in a million, just in case, time that someone came around asking about a vehicle of the same description. He would store it somewhere out of sight or away from where he lived and use another mode of transportation on a daily basis. Hell, for that matter, the guy may maintain a lifestyle that describes him as a person with no car at all. That way it wouldn't be connected to him directly by people that knew him."

"Wow, you are giving this guy a lot of credit Jack."

"Think about it girl. He has killed at least 10 people that we know of in different states within the last 4 months and left zero evidence for you to go on. His victims have been selected at random, and until just recently we have determined Facebook to be the common link. Other than that he is a ghost. This guy is methodical and disciplined in his methods. No trace, no fingerprints and no signature weapon of choice. Hell, the guy is a ghost, we need to think like one."

"Ok. Let's say you are right. Why start now? Why just all of a sudden, start killing people using new Friend Requests on Facebook as your death lottery?" She asked.

"Maybe he was preparing beforehand. Maybe something in his life snapped and he went off the deep end. It's possible we're looking for a recently divorced guy or someone that has lost a loved one recently."

"That's a smaller search." She said. "I could look at deaths involving family's leaving only the husband within the last 6 months to a year. Then crosscheck with DMV records."

"Yeah, that might turn up something but I doubt it. I got a feeling this guy has been at it awhile and we never connected the cases, or he is just getting started and he isn't making choices based on bad strokes of luck. He is picking these people and planning it all out, being prepared with military type precision. He doesn't think he will get caught." Jack said, looking through the windshield at the falling snow. He hit the wipers and eased up on the accelerator.

Cathy looked at the snow falling and felt the car's speed diminish slightly. She wasn't worried about Jack's ability to drive in the snow. He lived in this environment, but regardless, she double-checked her seatbelt.

"50 miles girl." He said to her without looking over her direction.

"50 miles what?"

"That's where we start looking for a station off the main drag and out of the direct thoroughfare of traffic. We start this side of Missoula then to the west side. It's as good a place as any to start. We find someone that remembers something like the vehicle we are looking for within the timeframe we have or someone floating large bills within the last couple days and we might have a shot at a face or vehicle."

Pounding the ground was something she had given up years ago when she got promoted. It was what young agents were for. Her time was better spent managing people and putting the pieces together that had been found to close a case. Jack didn't think that way. He was a boots on the ground, getting your hands dirty kind of guy and she was along for the ride. She could see an exit approaching with a blue sign identifying fuel and a hotel at the next exit. Jack didn't slow down or turn on the blinker.

"Why not here?" She asked pointing out the sign.

"Too big. Hotels mean restaurant's, which means gas stations and more traffic. Usually means at least one traffic light as well. Traffic lights have cameras and hotels usually do too. Not here. We keep going."

She knew he was right but it did get annoying at times. "How far are you planning on getting today? It will be dark in about 5 hours."

"Should make Spokane tonight. From there it's an easy drive to Seattle. Depending on how many stops and how long we spend at each we should arrive in the early afternoon tomorrow."

"Ok" she said, "Let's go over it again from the top." As she opened the files.

CHAPTER 25

Once when Vincent was young, his parents took him to a video arcade. It was the only time he can remember his parents ever doing anything with him or together as a family. It wasn't until later in his life that he realized the purpose for the trip was business for his father more than a family outing. It turned out that his farther purchased the entire mall complex a couple weeks after the visit and had it refurbished into another one of his factories.

The arcade was full of machines and kids at each of them pumping in quarters. The lights and sounds of the flashing electronic ships and cars filled the area. It was sensory overload especially for Vincent that lived in a life of books and knowledge. This place was chaos. He didn't enjoy it and wanted to leave moments after arriving.

Against the back wall were older games that did not involve a lot of electronics. One of them had a ball and a runway with a ramp on the end with holes in it. The object was to roll a wooden ball down the runway, up the ramp and land it in one of the holes. It was tolerable for him to do. Another game involved a hammer and 8 holes on a board. At random, ground hogs poked their heads up out of holes. The object was simple. Hit the heads as they popped up as fast as you could and repeat.

The thought of the Ground Hog whacking game reminded him of the little girls in the upstairs bedroom. Vincent played the whacking game until the little heads no longer popped up.

After finishing up in the house, he left through the rear door as the dog was still barking out in the front yard. Vincent determined he had been in the home roughly 8 minutes. He typically didn't like to exceed 10. A roughly shoveled path led around the back of the home to the rear of the garage. Vincent took the path and entered the garage by a service door at the back. Normally he would have already left and been miles away by now, but the dog was between him and his car. Without anything to subdue the animal he didn't want to risk being bit, and possible DNA left at the scene. Not that he was in any data base, but he wouldn't want to give the authorities anything to connect him or a starting point. So far he was a mystery to whoever was investigating his work. He had read nothing about a case being built or suspects being looked at. He knew they were in no way onto him. He was too smart for that.

The interior of the garage was a cluttered mess of boxes and tools. It looked like the organization that was so carefully sought after in the home stopped there. This area seemed like a catch all for anything they didn't want or didn't know what to do with inside the home. Piles of Christmas decoration along with other holiday décor was sticking out of the tops of boxes everywhere he looked. Some had been sealed up but others were opened and left that way. Clothes, books and toys that were no longer used, or needed, were stacked everywhere filling spaces and gaps between the boxes. Sitting in the middle of the piles of boxes and unwanted miscellaneous crap was an old Ford Mustang. Maybe a 1960 or 65. It sat on four flat tires and was missing the front windshield. Vincent highly doubted that the vehicle ran or ever would again. If it was a project car, the project had been long since abandoned and no sign of recent restoration could be seen. He was happy to rid the people of this world.

A tiny walkway, just large enough to squeeze through carved a path around the car to the other side through the junk piles. Vincent walked around the car, careful not to make any noise to draw the dog's attention outside to the garage. On the far side of the car was a wheel barrel with various hand tools lying inside. Vincent selected a long handled spade shovel. The tool gave him distance from the animal and would work if he needed to use it. He wasn't a bad person and felt no need to kill the animal unless it was necessary. The dog had no control of its owners and their pathetic existence. It just did what it needed to do to survive. It was a lot like him. He did what was needed.

The garage had an automatic door opener with the button on the back wall near the door he used to operate it. Pushing the button and quickly scooting along the path at the back of the car to the other side, he ducked down out of sight and waited. Just like he knew would happen, the animal shot into the garage and straight out the rear door he left open to the back of the home at a full run. Vincent took the chance and ran from the other side of the mustang out to his car. He started the engine and turned out of the driveway. It didn't bother him that he let the dog live. The animal couldn't choose its owners and it would find another home. Of course killing the animal would be of no issue if it came to that, but the dog wasn't his target.

Snow had been falling since he was inside. An inch of accumulation was on the windshield by the time he was back to the car. Usually, he spent as little time as possible in the homes, but the two children made it more difficult to finish his task and increased his time more than he was comfortable with inside. Even with the time wasted, Vincent knew the hazards of driving in the snow and would be careful on the county road he used leaving the home. He wouldn't allow something as foolish as getting stuck in the ditch bring an end to his work.

The house's driveway was no more than 100 yards from the main road. Pulling out and turning, Vincent saw a car coming the opposite direction. It was large with a flashing light on top. At first, for only a short moment, he thought it was the police, but the closer it got, he realized it was a plow truck. The state or county must maintain these roads during the winter and plowing them was a normal occurrence. The issue he had was that his car was not a normal vehicle seen here. In a small community like this, a stranger would be remembered when the bodies were discovered and questions started being asked about traffic in the area during that time. This was something Vincent wouldn't risk.

Once on the road, he turned on his emergency flashers and flashed his headlights at the oncoming plow truck. Like most country folks, the plow slowed to a crawl coming to a stop beside Vincent in the opposite lane of the barren road. Checking his rearview mirror for any more traffic and giving a final glance up the road beyond the truck he could see the road was clear. Vincent pulled his hat down over his ears and zipped his jacket up to the top. Getting out of the car, the winter wind hit him and found his exposed skin.

The plow driver rolled his window down and shouted out to him. "Everything ok buddy?"

Vincent didn't answer him, instead he walked to the driver's side door and stepped up on the running boards using the mirror and handle against the cab for support. From this height, he was looking the driver in the face. He was an older man, maybe 50 or 60. He wore an old John Deer hat with long grey hair sticking out from under it in all directions. He was a good 40 pounds overweight and his face was pocked with a red rash on the nose and cheeks. Alcoholism did that to a person if you spent your lifetime in a bottle, he thought to himself in disgust while looking at him.

"You ok fella?" The man asked him again.

Vincent smiled at him pulling the revolver from his pocket. He pressed the muzzle of the 38 caliber Smith and Wesson against his temple and squeezed. The shot rang out, bouncing inside the small confines of the cab in waves of echoes. The man fell to the passenger side with his brains splashed against the opposite window.

Vincent didn't like using a gun, but in this situation it fit his need more than anything else. They were quick and effective. He opened the door and rubbed the pistol against the man's coat sleeve then placed his dead fingers all over the cold steel of the gun before dropping it to the floorboard at his feet. He rolled up the window and shut the door, leaving the truck idling on the road in the falling snow.

Back in his car again, he made for the interstate and then West back to Seattle. Killing the truck driver was not part of the plan. He didn't like it when things didn't go as planned. He wasn't worried that it would be traced back to him but regardless it was a change in his itinerary and possibly could affect his destiny. Vincent prided himself in staying in control of everything that happened to him. The truck driver had interrupted his organized and peaceful life. This upset him.

Leaving the gun wasn't a concern. He acquired it from a crack head he had rid the world of almost a year ago. The druggie thought that Vincent looked like an easy target when he was walking home one day from shopping and using side streets as he always did to avoid the public eye. Unfortunately for the doper he realized that he was in all actuality the prey and Vincent was every bit the predator on the top of the food chain that night. He left his lifeless body in the alley where the man attempted to rob him, but kept the gun. He had been carrying it with him on his trips ever since for instances, just like this.

By the time the truck driver would be found, most likely within an hour or two, the police would immediately assume suicide. The serial number on the gun would be run through a search as that was standard practice now. He didn't know who the owner might be, but he didn't care. It wouldn't be him. If anything they would assume the over the hill, alcoholic truck driver finally gave up any reason to live and finished himself off with a gun he bought at a gun show some time in the past and never bothered to register it. With a lot of luck it would draw attention away from the house a quarter mile away and the dead family would go unnoticed even longer, giving him even more time to get home before anyone found out.

Vincent turned onto the freeway heading west. Once no traffic could be seen, he rolled down his window and tossed the gloves outside that he was wearing when he shot the man. Gun Shot Residue or GSR, was a very unique and incriminating method to identify a shooter. He would have none of it on his body or clothing by the time he got home. His jacket would be discarded at the next rest stop then his shirt. He would take a couple extra stops to get back but nothing would be left to connect him to a gun shot or the killings by the time he arrived home.

Planning out his return trip filled his mind as he drove. The thoughts of the women and two children flipped through his memories like a slide show. He was beginning to love his work. He could feel the anticipation of returning home and finding another. He had to fight back the urge to drive faster than the speed limit and stay in control and with the plan. Maybe he would park the car and walk to the library when he got back instead of going directly home just to see if there would be any easy targets awaiting his request. Maybe just for a quick 30 minutes.

That thought made him smile and he pressed the accelerator down a little more. He wasn't speeding per say, but traveling faster than he had in the past or that he normally drove. A little bit of speed wouldn't ruin him. He had earned the right to do it. He wanted another hunt and he wanted it now.

The flashing lights in his rear view mirror brought his attention back to the moment and the police cruiser behind him.

CHAPTER 26

Cathy woke to the sound of the key hitting the lock on the motel room door. She half jumped up to a sitting position and scrambled for her sidearm sitting on the nightstand next to her. It took a second to remember where she was and that it was Jack at the door, not an intruder. Her internal clock was scrambled as well as her sense of location. More than 4 months now she had been in hotels, field offices, airplanes and now somewhere between Montana and the Pacific Ocean in a small motel along the freeway with Jack. A man that for the last 5 years had been nothing but a memory and now they were sharing a room somewhere west of Americas Heartland. The last 72 hours were a blur in her mind.

The door opened and Jack came in holding a small brown bag and carrying a tray with two large to-go cups of coffee. The white background behind him through the open door told her the weather was still cold and filled with snow. Jack looked just like he did when she saw him for the first time 4 days ago. He didn't look tired or fatigued from the road trip the day before. He looked like he had been up for at least an hour now and was ready to go.

"If you're gonna shoot, do me the honor of at least getting out of bed" he said, setting the bag and cups down on the tiny coffee table supplied by the hotel.

"What is wrong with you Jack? Its only 6am, when did you get up?"

"Oh around 4 or so. Got a little stir crazy sitting around the room so I went out and got some breakfast and brought you back a bagel, a maple bar and sausage/egg biscuit. Wasn't sure what the new FBI ate nowadays so figured I would cover the bases. If you were up earlier, you could've had steak and eggs with me at the restaurant. Pretty good. You missed out. Don't worry, I saved the receipts so you can have Allen file it with your expense report."

"I forgot what it was like working a case with you Jack." She said, rubbing the sleep from her face and swinging her legs off the side of the bed. "Thanks for the coffee, you can keep the rest. What's the plan for today?"

Jack sat down in the retro looking easy chair that he assumed every room in the hotel had. He looked at Cathy and her morning ensemble. She was wearing a pair of blue jogging shorts with an old V-neck white t-shirt. Her hair was a mess, but she was still an attractive woman. He remembered the first time he met her years ago on the case in Missouri. She was younger then and a little more wild but her beauty had only increased over the years. Even after being promoted to Special Agent she obviously made time for the gym and stayed in shape. She had always been attractive to him and the way she looked in the morning didn't hurt her standing any. "I say we head to Seattle. Straight shot. No real reason to stop along the way."

"Why not? We made at least 8 stops yesterday, questioned every person we could find." She said reaching for the coffee and lifting the lid to get a smell of the caffeinated ingredients.

"Yeah, I know, but from here to Billings is just over 500 miles. I don't know a car made that can make that trip on one tank of gas except for maybe one of those new hybrid things and I doubt this guy is using one of them. They stand out too much in this area. That means he filled up at one of the places we stopped at and nobody remembered him. It's also possible he took another route, something longer that was even more off the grid than I anticipated, or he has some sort of modified tank in his car that allows him to make epic road trips without the need to refuel. If that's the case this guy is more prepared than I thought. It means he has altered his life to do just what he is doing. It means this guy has no other purpose but to kill and he has adjusted his world to accommodate this as a profession."

"Or he is a truck driver. That would explain the distance between his kills and the ability to go so far without fuel. Those truck have massive tanks on them don't they?" Cathy answered him while sipping her coffee.

"No." Jack said quickly. "A semi-truck would be something remembered at one or two of the murder scenes at least, if not all of them. It would be a simple solution to the difference in locations and I am sure Allen would want to pursue that route but it would be wrong. A large truck wouldn't fit in without somebody remembering seeing it sitting at the old couple's house in Oregon. Or the fact that nobody in Atlanta remembers seeing a semi in the cul-de-sac of the suburban house that a family was murdered in. Besides, weren't the two girls in Denver murdered in a duplex? That was downtown right? No way this guy drove a big rig down town Denver to park outside a duplex to murder two girls and left without someone noticing. Nope, this guy has either figured out a way to wipe people's memory clean of his existence or he has modified his car with a huge ass fuel tank allowing him to go as far as he wants."

"But a guy has to go to the bathroom right? He would have to stop somewhere and take a leak. Nobody can drive that far without a break. Could they?" Cathy asked.

"Not necessarily. Truck drivers use water bottles to piss in when they are driving long distances to save time from pulling off and stopping on a long haul. It's possible this guy does the same and honestly, it wouldn't surprise me any."

"So where does that leave us? And by the way, gross." She said.

"We continue on to Seattle. No sense in stopping anywhere to ask questions until we get to the library and meet up with your team. I am sure your nerd herd has scrubbed the area and turned up nothing that will seal the case but it would be good to get a look at the place. Maybe from there we can find another direction to start looking."

Cathy stood up and stretched. She moved over to the chair opposite his and sat down with the coffee. She opened the laptop and punched some keys. The screen came to life revealing her email with 10 new messages. Half of them had attachments sent to her from the team at the library. The others varied from Allen's daily report requests and the team in Oregon. She sipped her coffee and started opening files and reading. Jack got up and paced the small room stopping at the window to look outside for a minute or two then continued pacing. She knew this sitting around was killing him and he wanted to get out on the road but ultimately the decision to leave, and when, was up to her.

The lack of leads they got on the trip over bothered him. He was usually spot on when it came to profiling a suspect and gaining ground on a case but it seemed like he just wasted a full day on a hunch that didn't pan out. Jack looked out the window and went over the drive again in his mind. The long stretches of road through Montana that he had just been on with no other places to stop that he could remember. If this guy was what he thought he was and doing what he was doing, he was beginning to worry about how much help he would be to Cathy or the FBI on catching him.

She could see that the lack of evidence of this guy was starting to weigh on Jack.

"The lab boys sent the report from the library Jack. They found the computers that were used to create the accounts. Looks like the guy used 3 different ones in total, all at the same library covering a 4 month window. That corresponds with the murders. According to the report, he uploaded some sort of reset virus that wiped the hardrives clean and sent them back to factory settings."

"What's that mean?" He asked, stopping at the window again and looking outside.

"It means your idea that he is using FaceBook is correct for one. And that we have a hell of a good place to start looking as well. But, it also means he is smart. Smart enough to not only, leave no trace evidence at the scene either by fingerprints or getting caught on camera, but also, he is tech savvy enough to understand how to wipe a public hardrive clean without setting off any kind of alarm with the library's internal IT systems and firewalls."

"Where is the library located?" Jack asked facing the window and not recognizing her compliment about the guy.

"Downtown Seattle."

"So it's a big place?"

"Well, yeah, I suppose. It's one of the major ones in the Seattle Tacoma area. Pretty big I would assume."

"It's been awhile since I was in Seattle, but I don't remember a lot of parking in the downtown area. It's pretty congested. If that's where the library is, it would mean he would have to walk or take public transit and I doubt he uses the latter. Which means he lives within walking distance." Jack said.

"Not necessarily." She responded to him. "He could drive to one of the many large parking garages in the area around downtown and use it, then walk."

"I doubt it." Jack said. "He wouldn't risk a parking ticket or a fender bender. This guy is anal about everything he does and being seen. Living off the grid in the shadows is what he does. He wouldn't pay to park. Most of those things don't take cash anymore anyway. They are all electronic with card swipes nowadays. Not to mention every garage will have CCTV's installed. No, this guy walks."

She could see that discussing it with him was no longer a winnable venture so she went back to her email and clicked another message. She jumped up while reading the screen. "Jack, look at this!"

Moving around the side of the chair and looking at the laptop he recognized the FBI logo on the top of the message. It was a standard BOLO update sent out to all field offices in the area that were in involving recent major crimes. State and county police departments used it when serious incidents occurred in their jurisdiction and were more intense than a department could handle. Normally it was observed more as a SPAM kind of thing when he was in the FBI. Cathy must have it routed to her email since they were going to be in the area. She was smart. A good agent. Jack read through the message.

"What do you think?" She asked.

"I think Ellensburg is only 2 hours from here. Get dressed."

CHAPTER 27

It was a Washing State Patrol vehicle behind him. He looked down at the speedometer and saw that he was going 68 mph in a 65 zone. It wasn't fast enough to notice or pull him over. He had been passed by other vehicles since he hit the highway traveling at much greater speeds. Why was the cop behind him? No possible way they could have connected him to the truck driver or the woman and kids in the house already. He doubted anyone had even called in the two incidents yet. Vincent cursed himself for allowing his mind to wander and slipping on his focus.

Vincent turned on his blinker and slowed the vehicle to let the patrol car know that he had been seen. The sooner this was over the better he thought. He continued traveling until he saw a wide spot along the highway that the plow trucks had cleared off and pulled over slowly to avoid sliding on the icy road. Keeping the engine running and cracking his window only slightly, he gathered all the information the cop would need and waited. He knew the officer would be running his plates and looking for any violations outstanding. He also knew it would all come out clean. What he didn't know was, why he was being pulled over or how he was going to get out of this if a record of him being pulled over was being made.

The cop didn't wait around long behind him like they normally did. Within seconds of being stopped he was out of his car and approaching the window.

"Can I help you officer?" Vincent asked politely looking up at him through the half open window.

"Yes sir, would you mind showing me your license and registration along with a proof of insurance please?"

"Of course." Vincent replied to him, handing over the documents he already had waiting for him. "May I ask what the problem is officer?"

"Did you know there's an 800.00 dollar fine for littering in the state of Washington Mr. Vincent Holbrook?" The officer asked, reading the ID he was given.

"Yes actually, I was aware of that, but what does that have to do with me officer?" Of course he knew that, he knew more about the state than most the people living in it. What the hell kind of a question was that?

"Well Mr. Holbrook, I watched this pair of leather gloves fly out of your vehicle about 4 miles back." The policeman said, producing the gloves that he had so recently tossed out the window. "I would've caught up with you sooner, but I had to stop and collect them."

Vincent was furious with himself and his inept laziness. Why did he throw the gloves out the window? Why did he do it and risk so much? Maybe he was getting sloppy. Maybe his mission was coming to an end? Maybe he was no longer needed to show the world the error of their ways. No, that wasn't possible. He had worked so hard and dedicated so much of his life to this purpose. It wasn't feasible that it was supposed to end it all here. He had so much more to do and so many other plans. A simple road cop would not be the end to his purpose. It was just a mistake. A simple test at his abilities to recover from it. Yes, that was it. He was being tested.

"Thank you officer. Yes those are my gloves, but I didn't throw them out the window. I must have forgotten them back at the gas station. I put them on the roof while I fueled up left them when I drove off. I have lost more gloves and sunglasses that way." Vincent said to him trying to lighten the mood and get out of this without any record of him being here, besides the memory of a Highway cop.

"Umm, no sir, I am pretty sure I watched you toss them out the window. It was right beyond the on-ramp to the freeway coming out of second exit to Ellensburg. I was sitting off to the right below the on-ramp wall and watched you toss them out after you got onto the freeway."

Vincent could feel his heart in his chest. He was fairly certain the cop had already ran his plates but wasn't sure. With the snow and slush on the roads, it was possible his rear plate was obscured and he only reported the make and model of the car when he was initially pulled over. That might explain why he was so quick to approach his window after stopping. Maybe he didn't have any information yet to even place a call. He had already been caught in a lie about littering and anything else he said would only delay him getting distance between him and the inevitable discovery waiting back in Ellensburg. He had to get back on the road but the cop had his gloves that had a good amount of GSR on them and he had seen his face. If he did get away now with only a citation for littering, even a stupid highway cop would be able to put two and two together and figure out that this is the guy responsible for the murders or at least be one hell of a good suspect to start with when the investigation kicked off.

The stretch of road was long in both directions running out of site into the white landscape. The winter weather had started to drop more snow making visibility worse than before. Vincent knew that killing a police officer was something he needed to avoid as it seemed that everyone got worked up when that happened more than usual. You could kill as many homeless or poor people you wanted and it didn't matter, but one cop got murdered and it was on the front page for weeks. He didn't understand this and it made little difference to him in the big picture. But it did raise a lot of questions when one of them were killed.

Unfortunately he didn't have much choice. If he played the game out and left with the ticket, it would be a matter of days before they would be knocking at his door and questioning him on his reasons for being in the area at that time. He would need to give them alibis that he didn't have. That would put an end to his mission and he wasn't ready for that to happen. If he decided to end the cop here, then he had the problem of his car and the recording device that he was sure to be attached to the front windshield of the police cruiser, recording the entire event in real time. He was fairly certain that the cameras on the Washington State Patrol cars only recorded to an internal hardrive somewhere in the car. Probably in the trunk. But he was sure it didn't stream back to the station house automatically for storage. Each one would have to be manually uploaded to put them on file or view for court purposes, which means if his plate was covered and all the cop got was a description of the car reported back via radio when he was pulled over, Vincent had a chance to make this all go away. Right now he had to worry about the situation at hand and how to rid himself of the cop.

"Yes sir, those are my gloves. I am sorry." Vincent said to him looking up through the window. "I spilled my coffee on them getting on the freeway. I figured they were ruined and it really frustrated me so I threw them out the window. I do apologize for it sir. I normally don't do anything like that."

"Yes, I know they are your gloves MR. Holbrook. That's why I pulled you over and that's why you will be receiving a ticket for littering. Now if you please wait here a minute sir I need to run your information. I will be right back."

The cop handed the gloves to Vincent and turned to leave. The fact that he needed to run the license confirmed to Vincent that he had not seen his plate yet and probably hadn't called in the stop or at least no name was given. The window of opportunity was open to him and he wouldn't let the limited time go to waste. Vincent checked his mirror and saw the road behind the cruiser was clear. For the moment no traffic was coming his way as well. The cop was at the rear of his vehicle now, moving to his own car. The highway in front was void of traffic as well through the windshield. Vincent felt the power in him grow with the absence of cars and opportunity he was given. He would not waste it. This must be another test for him. Just another way to show that he would be the one to survive and carry on. Vincent pulled the screwdriver from his door panel pocket.

In one fast and controlled movement, he opened the door and jumped out in a full on sprint toward the cop. The patrolman heard the door open and turned but was too slow to do anything other than let out a half command to stop, half scream before Vincent was on him. He held the officers right hand against his chest that gripped all of his information preventing it from flying away in the wind and not allowing access to his sidearm. He thrust the screwdriver up to the handle through the cops chin. Judging by the twitching displayed in his limbs Vincent figured the top inch of the long 9 inch tool was buried in the frontal lobe of the cop's brain. It would only take a second or two before the twitching stopped and the lifeless lump of flesh would collapse to the wet, snow covered highway.

Vincent moved fast. Another car could come around the corner into view any moment and he had a lot to do.

CHAPTER 28

"Argghh! The Fucking cell service out here sucks!" Cathy yelled at her phone as another call to the Ellensburg Sherriff dropped without warning. "What is it with this part of the country? Why is your coverage such shit?"

Jack didn't answer.

"Seriously, what is the deal out here? You had no service at your place and we are on an interstate no more than 80 miles from Spokane, a pretty major city. I mean it has an international airport for Christ's sake and I have no service! Why is that Jack? How do you get anything done? It's like you people refuse to move forward with the advancement of technology or something."

"Let me ask you a question girl. Why do you need it? I mean does it really make your life that much easier? Jack asked, looking out the windshield.

She could see where he was going with the questions. He was the same way years ago when they worked together and he was forced to sign for the new smart phones they issued. Jack refused to accept technology and the way of the future. He fought it so much back then that when he retired he moved to the mountains where it wasn't even an option. She supposed he was partially correct about some of what he said, but without the access available on the net that she used daily, half the cases she had solved in the past would still be open. It was a necessary evil at times and to be honest, it seemed harder to live without it than just embracing it.

"Forget about it Jack. How much farther till we get there?" She asked swiping her phone again and redialing the call.

"Another 20 minutes. What did you get from the Sheriff?" Jack asked, doing as she asked and dropping the subject. Even he could tell when a good time would be to argue the faults of the advancement of society.

"Well, before the call was cut, he said there were 3 dead in a home just outside the town of Ellensburg. A mother and two children. Nothing more than the report I got this morning that we both read. It was a mystery to why they were killed. Nothing was taken and the home had not been vandalized. He also said there was a suicide a quarter mile from the house. Apparently some truck driver decided to shoot himself. He also said there was something else he wanted to tell me."

"A suicide? Really? That's weird. Only a quarter mile from the house? Sounds fishy. What is the something else he wanted to tell you?"

"That's what he said, suicide but I don't know any more because you have no service out here and I lost him!"

Her phone rang and she answered it immediately. "Sheriff?"

Jack drove and listened to her giving one word responses then replying with more questions about the home and who had been there and timelines. He heard exit markers and timeframes being repeated. She was running the gambit of standard procedures and questions that all agents did when responding to a fresh scene. The miles rolled by as she talked. Jack really didn't want the call to cut out again for fear of her freaking out and taking it out on him. It's not like he was in control of cellular communication in the North West or something.

"Ok Sheriff, we will be there in 10 minutes." She hung up and looked at Jack.

"What? You had service the whole time. Why are you looking at me like that?" He asked.

"A State patrol car was found 10 miles west of Ellensburg burned to the ground with the patrolman still inside Jack."

"This doesn't make any sense." Jack said walking around the plow truck. "I don't believe in coincidences and sure as hell not three of them in the same day. No way was this family was murdered, a snow plow driver decided to off himself half way through his shift and a highway patrolman spontaneously combusts while we are on the trail of a serial killer that happened to use this exact route, not happening."

The area was taped off and traffic was being routed to another road around the area preventing anyone unauthorized from getting in. There were two ambulances, 3 county police cruisers, a Highway Patrol car and a van from the Coroner's office. Red flares burned in the falling snow along the road identifying the closure ahead and slowing people down to eventually turn them around. Jack and Cathy were allowed through and parked along the road side in front of the home. They had decided to divide and conquer so she went to the house and Jack took the plow truck.

On first inspection of the scene to an untrained eye it seemed like a pretty simple suicide. Jack could smell alcohol from the inside of the truck when he opened the door and the man had the appearance of a seasoned drinker. But after a short examination he ruled out self-termination.

"Excuse me sir, Jack is it? Is there anything I can help you with?" Asked a young deputy that was apparently responsible for the truck scene.

"Yeah, just a couple questions." Jack asked hopping down from the truck.

The deputy was young, maybe 24 or 28 years of age. He had the wide eyed look of a person in over his head and inexperienced. He was sure the kid became a cop more for the ability to carry a gun than to fight crime. In a small town like this, the most action he would see would be a Friday night bar fight or a deer hitting a car. This was more than the kid wanted to see and Jack knew it.

"Did you know this guy?" He asked pointing at the truck.

"Yes sir, I did. Mr. Reynolds is his name. He has been running that truck since I was a kid. Same routes he had when I was riding the bus to school."

"Has he always been a drinker?" Jack asked.

The deputy seemed slightly shocked at the question, but answered him. "Yes sir he has, but it never affected his work."

"How long has he been married?" Jack asked

"As long as I can remember. He and his wife own a nice place about 20 miles from here. A small ranch with horses and a few cattle. They do sleigh rides in the winter for the local Elementary School. It's a Christmas thing for the community. It doesn't make any sense that he would commit suicide."

"Don't worry about that kid, he didn't kill himself. He was murdered." Jack said stepping past him and walking toward the house.

"What? Who would kill Mr. Reynolds and why?"

"That's why we're here. Don't worry, we'll find whoever did it. Do me a favor and keep everyone out of the truck until the FBI can get a team up here to go through it in detail. Might be the one thing we need to catch this guy is still inside that cab. Wouldn't want to lose it."

Inside, the house was grizzlier than the truck. The blood was still wet and sticky on the floor in the entryway. The woman had been taken out already to the van but the cold winter weather was preventing the crimson pools from drying. The door handle and wood frame was already covered in black powder used to take prints. People were snapping photos and moving about the house with notebooks and video units. Cathy was upstairs when Jack caught up to her.

She was kneeling over a large blood pool on the carpet. In what appeared to be a child's room. The walls were blue and yellow with pictures of horses and other barn animals hanging around. Two small beds sat next to each other with a window separating them. Each bed had a theme. One seemed to be of horses and the other was some sort of animated character shaped like a yellow square. It was a happy room on any other day.

A small outline of a child was attached to the pool Cathy was kneeling at, making it appear that a white stick figure was lying there with an oversized red circular head. Past the mess below Cathy on the other side of the room was a closet with the door knocked off its rails lying next to it. Inside was another image from a horror film. The interior walls of the small walk in were splattered with blood. Large holes had been knocked into the sheetrock walls leaving red sticky trace in each of them. The dents seemed to be created by something approximately the size of a volleyball, maybe smaller. Jack knew what he was looking at and didn't like thinking about it. He could see Cathy was having difficulty with the scene as he was.

"Any luck with the truck outside?" She asked looking at the carpet and the small outline of the child protruding from it.

"Guys name was Reynolds. He drove the truck most of his life. Wasn't suicide. He was murdered."

Cathy stood up and faced him. Her cheeks were red and she looked tense. Maybe from the cold, but he figured it was anger. She was taking this too personal. She was feeling like these deaths were her fault because she had failed to stop this guy sooner.

"Why not suicide?" She asked.

"The guy was happily married. Had a small farm not far from here with a wife and a good job. Enjoyed the bottle a little too much, but it was a way of life for him. Not to mention he was right handed and the gun shot was on his left temple with the revolver lying next to the driver's door on the floor. Without pulling GSR, to prove my point that he didn't fire the thing, I also noticed the truck was in Neutral with the emergency brake pulled. No self-respecting snow plow operator would pull the emergency brake unless it was only for a short time. This weather up here will freeze it in place in a matter of minutes. If he was really planning on going out and offing himself, he would've parked somewhere, finished a bottle then do it. Sitting on a high traffic road with the truck in neutral and the e-brake on only means he was stopped and talking to someone temporarily. It's very possible Mr. Reynolds got a face to face look with our guy."

"Why shoot him and kill the women and children the way he did? If he had a gun, why not use it here?" She asked.

Jack moved around the room so the opening to the closet was behind him and he didn't have to look at it any more. "If this is the same guy, which I believe it is, I think the Plow Truck driver was a matter of necessity and not part of the plan. I think he came here to kill the women and kids because one of them accepted a new friend on FaceBook. Have you checked that yet?"

"Already confirmed." She said. "Ms. Stevens here accepted a new request from a lady that lives in British Columbia. A school teacher apparently. I already have our IT department tracking down the validity of the account but I believe it will come back fake, like the others. She accepted it Yesterday afternoon at 1300. The call came in from the neighbor down the street about the truck driver at 0700 this morning after he stopped to visit with him alongside the road. Police arrived at the truck around 0730 and found the scene at the house an hour later when they went in to question her."

Jack looked at his watch. "That means we are less than 12 hours behind this guy."

"Yeah, 12 hours late!" She responded, obviously disappointed in herself and the FBI in general. "So, back to what you were saying about the Truck Driver, why do you think it was a necessity?"

"This guy came here to kill whoever was in this house. I'm sure he had an idea of the occupants but it's still a gamble on who will be here when he arrives. That's probably why he brings a gun. It's the unknown, the human factor that he can't control. He most likely had it with him on all the murders. Up until now he hasn't needed to use it. He has accomplished his agenda without issue, but something happened here that changed his plans."

"So you think the driver was an afterthought, or maybe he saw something?"

"Exactly" Jack said. "The driver was a necessity. After he finished here in the house, he left using the garage. Probably to avoid the dog that I saw when I came in. He wouldn't want to risk a bite or maybe he's got a soft spot for animals, I don't know. Regardless, when he was done here, he pulled onto the road planning to head back the same way he came when he saw the truck coming. It's been snowing a lot lately, the plow trucks are probably on a regular route when the weather is bad to keep the roads clear. Chances are the truck saw him leaving the driveway, otherwise he would've kept on driving. But, being as careful as this guy is he wouldn't risk a description of his vehicle being seen leaving a recent murder. In a small community like this, everyone knows each other and what they drive. No matter how plain the vehicle is, if it's not recognized as a norm, the Truck Driver might remember it. That's a risk this guy wouldn't take."

"So what, he just flags him down and shoots him? Why leave the gun? We can trace it." Cathy asked turning away from the scene in the closet as well.

"The gun won't belong to him girl. Probably stole it or purchased it at a gun show for cash. No paper trail will be attaching it to him. I'm sure you will find no prints on the thing that belong to him either, so don't waste your time. Staging the impromptu suicide made more sense than just leaving him lying there dead. It would give him a little more of a head start. Hell, these boys are still asking why Mr. Reynolds shot himself. They wouldn't have connected the two things if we weren't here. That's how this guy gets away with what he's been doing for so long."

She had been thinking the same thing and needed the confirmation from Jack to solidify her thought. "Ok, I have the team from Seattle on the way right now. They will be here within 2 hours depending on the roads. The house, truck and bodies will be turned over to them for processing. If it is the same guy, nothing will turn up, but we can always hope he made a mistake."

Looking down at the stains in the carpet and back to the closet and the lack of weapon anywhere to be seen, Jack assumed the children were beaten to death.

"Not that I want the answer, but what happened up here?"

Cathy looked down at the stain below her then back to the closet. "Two little girls. One 8 and the other 6. Both beaten to death. The older one here." She pointed at the stain in the carpet. "Had her head caved in with a rolling pin right here on the floor."

The scene was hard to take and the description Cathy was giving made it worse. She held up a stained wooden rolling pin that was splintered in the middle.

"He beat the older girl with this until it broke. He dropped and went to the closet and kicked it in. He used the walls to end the younger girl."

"With this much splatter, he had to get it all over himself during the assault." Jack said looking around the room.

He didn't need to go into it any farther than that and was certain Cathy didn't want to discuss it as well, but the woman downstairs cause of death eluded him.

"How as Ms. Stevens killed?" He asked.

"A hatchet." She answered. "It was hers and sat on the front porch for chopping kindling. Another weapon of opportunity. Coroner said it was a single blow to the head. She was dead before hitting the floor."

"I didn't see it around the scene at the door. Did they remove it already?" Jack asked.

"Yes, before we arrived with the body. It was stuck in the skull. These small town folks don't know the first thing about the integrity of a crime scene and how valuable each piece of evidence is. If we hadn't gotten here when we did the entire place would've been compromised within the hour."

"Jack left the small room upstairs that had been turned into a slaughter house and stood in the hall listening to her. He felt out of place in a way. Everyone had a title and a job and were busy performing it. "What now girl?"

She walked past him and down the hallway. "We need to go look at the State Patrol car out on the highway."

Jack was happy to agree and followed her out of the house.

CHAPTER 29

The Police cruiser had been extinguished by the Ellensburg Fire Dept. before they arrived. Only steam remained drifting up from the burned out carnage. The right lane of the freeway was shut down and a similar mass of vehicles were swarming the area as was at the home back in town. A large flatbed tow truck was positioning itself in front of the burned out car to begin its removal as they pulled up. Cathy flashed her badge and had a few words with the officer stopping them before they were allowed through the tape.

The Town of Ellensburg obviously only had the one Coroner van, because what was left of the patrolman was loaded into the back of a police van that was most likely used to move supplies and never intended for bodies. Jack took the car and Cathy went to the body.

A large man wearing an orange vest was directing the truck into position when Jack arrived. "Excuse me, can you answer a few questions for me?" He asked the man.

"Who are you?" He responded to Jacks question with a little more attitude than necessary.

"Special Agent Jack Lawson, FBI. I need to know where the body was found in the car when you arrived." Jack spat out fast before realizing it was all a lie. He had been running with Cathy for too long he supposed. Or they were so close to this guy that dealing with an overweight tow truck driver and whether or not he had the authority to be hear was something he didn't want to waste time with.

"Oh, sorry, Special Agent sir, yeah, they pulled the guy out of the passenger side over here." He said, pointing at the burned out window of the side door.

"He wasn't behind the wheel?" Jack asked.

"No sir, uh, agent. He was laying across the seat on the passenger side when I got here. He was all curled up. Like he was trying to sleep or something."

The inside of the vehicle was scorched beyond recognition. The windshield glass had melted inward creating puddles on the floor. The seats were gone along with all the interior material. Only the metal floor boards and roof remained. The shotgun, which he knew to be standard issue in all police cruisers was fused into the mounting bracket used to hold the weapon between the seats. A hole in the roof directly above the shotgun indicated that the round in the chamber had gone off during the fire. The lower magazine tube was torn open from the remaining rounds that exploded as well from the inferno. The fact that the gun was left confirmed his suspicion that it was the same guy and not some random cop killer. He wouldn't take the cops shotgun or sidearm. They could be used to connect him to the murder if used or found in possession of them. Any other punk or crack head that had a hard on for cops would've stripped the car of anything valuable before setting it ablaze.

"Any idea how the fire started?" Jack asked the man.

"No sir, I don't, but the Fire Chief. Might know." He said pointing to the vehicle sitting at the front of the line of cars with a large red helmet painted on the side and the words, FIRE CHIEF underneath it. "Can I continue getting the car on my truck or do you need more time agent?"

"Go ahead." Jack said leaving him to do his job and heading for the fire chief's vehicle. Before he got there he could see Cathy had finished with the body in the van and was already talking to him.

He got there in mid conversation, so he listened and didn't interrupt.

The Fire chief stopped briefly acknowledging his arrival with a nod when Cathy didn't object to Jacks presence and continued. "As I was saying ma, am, it appears that the fire was started in two different places. One in the trunk and the other in the passenger seat. We found two burned out road flares in both locations. "

"Why was the damage so severe? I have seen cars fires before, but there is always something left of the vehicle." She asked.

"An accelerant of some kind was used. Most likely gasoline, but we won't know for sure until we get it tested. By the degree of heat and speed it spread I would say that the officer himself was thoroughly doused as well as the interior of the car to include the trunk before it was ignited." The chief said.

Jack spoke up. "Torching the trunk makes sense, it contains the hardrive for the cameras the cars use to record all traffic stops. This guy knew he was on video and had to destroy the evidence. Probably why the cop was killed."

"Thank you Chief, my people will be in contact with you as soon as your investigation is complete. We will need the car to be released as soon as possible to the FBI."

"Yes ma, am."

"So you think it's the same guy?" She asked him when the Chief walked away.

"Absolutely" Jack said. "The cop was found in the passenger seat with his shotgun still in the car. My guess is he pulled our guy over for something completely random and got himself killed because of the possible connection being made so close to the crime scene. You get a look at the body? Any idea how he did it?"

"Couldn't tell, the body was charred beyond recognition. Your right about his gun though, it was melted into the holster still on his hip, but other than that, there wasn't a piece of skin left on the man. It will take a complete autopsy to determine the exact cause of death." She said.

"What now?" Jack asked.

"What do you think? We have the freshest scene at our fingertips right here. It's possible there is something he left behind that would identify him." Cathy said, moving slightly to block some of the wind from passing cars.

"I think we could spend a week in that house and come up with nothing more than what we already know. This guy doesn't leave anything behind. This cop and that Truck Driver are evidence enough of that."

"So?" She asked him desperately looking for a direction.

"I say we go to Seattle." Jack answered her in the most confident tone he could muster. "That's where this guy lives. Everything starts there. He will be lying low for a while after this one. Too many things went wrong altering his plans. He is probably going to regroup a bit before he tries again. That might give us time to get a lay of the land and come up with possible locations he lives or even lay in wait for him. You said your people are at the same Library he has been using, so we get to it and take a look around. It's better than standing around out here looking for something we will never find."

Cathy was in deep with the case. She was beginning to feel a bit over her head with the multiple scenes and the teams she had spread out on each of them. Running across the country chasing a suspect wasn't how she did things. It was Jacks M.O for sure, but hers was about crunching the evidence and coming up with leads to act on with substantial merit after a solid profile was developed. But up until she got him involved she was drawing nothing but questions. Now with him on board they at least had the method of his target selections, mode of travel and where he lived. "Ok Jack, You drive, I have some calls to make."

Vincent finished cleaning the car and pulled the door to the unit shut. He picked up the trash bags and started his walk home on the path he had pre-determined to take. It allowed him three separate places to dispose of the bags in large dumpsters used by my multiple offices or restaurants. The city's sanitation department would be by first thing in the morning to pick it up. Within 36 hours it would be in a land fill somewhere completely destroyed and wiped out.

While he walked he wondered why so many things had happened on his last hunt that he didn't plan on. He was aware that people were unpredictable, but this was a lot of random things all coinciding during one hunt. He played back each part of the last 12 hours through his mind to check for any holes or things he may have missed. Each step of the way was recorded forever in his memory. Every smell, sound and feeling he had sparked in his mind. From the woman and children in the home to the cop on the highway he covered it all and found nothing that would point to him. He was confident he got away without being identified but it still bothered him.

Perhaps it was a test to him and his ability. Maybe he was being tested on his endurance and capabilities to adapt. Could it be that he was getting lazy with his previous hunts and it was time for him to step up his game? He didn't believe he was moving too fast. He could handle anything. Today only proved the fact. The thought that he was selecting targets too fast was irrelevant to him. Time meant nothing. Only the outcome of what he did mattered. If they accepted his request, no matter where or when it happened, they had sealed their fate and he would act upon it.

After the third bag was disposed of on his route he turned to start the walk back to the marina. He would pass by the library on his way. Maybe he would go in and see if there were any more quick hunts to be made just to prove to himself that he was capable and prepared enough to do it. Perhaps he wouldn't even need to get home before he would need to go back out again. That would definitely show his amazing abilities to the world. Vincent was a hunter.

The thought made him happy. The feeling surging through his body confirmed that he was made for this work. He embraced his calling completely and was honored that he was given the power to do it. He felt like a child waiting for Christmas as he approached the front of the library.

Entering through the same entrance he always used, he moved past the red head at the desk, keeping his face down and blending in with all the people around him. Once in the computer lab area he looked for an open station when he noticed the men. They were out of place here. They didn't belong in the library as the other patrons did. These men were different. They wore ties or had on collared shirts with pressed pants. Each of them had a personal laptop open next to the computers he had used before with cables attaching them. He couldn't see any badges or law enforcement identification but they all appeared to be working together and on the same thing.

Vincent walked past them to a book shelf and browsed the volumes sitting on it. He selected one and flipped it over to read the back while he watched them and listened. He could hear things like, search history and hard drive scrubs coming out of their mouths to each other. A couple names were spoken loud enough to be heard. Houston, British Columbia and Montana. Chambers, Ellensburg and Special Agent floated through the library to his ears. These phrases stopped him cold. Could they be onto him? Could it be possible that somewhere he left a shred of evidence that connected his work to this place? Impossible? Vincent thought to himself. They were spread across the United States. No way could they be connected to him all the way back here. He was too careful. He had scrubbed all the hardrives and left nothing at the scenes.

One of the men's phone rang in his pocket. The muffled sound of a song he had heard once before but couldn't place echoed as the man withdrew it. Patrons around the library looked at him with stares of hatred as it was very taboo to use a phone here. The man answered it rudely without a care to the people around him. Vincent could hear him talking like he was speaking directly to him.

"Yes Agent Chambers, we have located the computer terminals and are sending the information you requested right now. No ma'am the account for the last request was fake as well. We did however locate the exact terminal and have dusted it and pulled the hardrive. We are processing the workstation to see if we can locate any evidence of the user as well, but as you know this is a public place so.... "

The man was cut off by whoever was on the other end and he listened for a minute before speaking. "Yesterday afternoon, yes ma'am, will do. Today? Ok, Yes Ma'am See you soon, we will have it ready for you, Thank you." And he hung up.

Vincent took the pieces of the call he could hear and put them together while he flipped through the book in his hands. They were onto him. They knew this was where he started the accounts. They didn't know who he was but they were trying to find any trace of him on the keyboards and internals of the computers. He knew they never would. He covered his tracks better than anyone could but somehow they made it here. It most likely means they knew he was using Facebook to select his hunts as he heard Houston and British Columbia spoken. Two of his fake accounts were from those places. He also heard a name. Agent Chambers. FBI, he thought. A woman, he thought. She must be the agent in charge of the case and the one leading their pathetic charge to find him. She was smart. Smarter than he thought they would be. Maybe she was a super-agent. The FBI's best. Vincent was pleased that he earned the best they had but it was a pleasure tainted sour. This Agent Chambers, whoever she was could be a major problem for his continued work. Perhaps taking a break from his regular hunting habits would be needed while he corrected this issue with the FBI.

CHAPTER 30

Cathy hung up the phone. "The team at the library said they located the terminal used for the account. It was fake, same as the rest. The computer was scrubbed clean as well. Same delete code as before. If there is something to find, no matter how small, my guys will find it. They are the top of the game with cyber-crime, but so far they are coming up empty."

"What about cameras in the library? Do they have anything like that? Maybe we could go through the footage and find someone that fits the profile?" Jack asked.

"Only at the back entrance. The main doors do not have CCTV as well as the interior of the building. The one receptionist at the main entrance was already questioned and doesn't recall any one person that stands out above the rest. She said the library has hundreds of people a day coming through the doors and using the work stations, maybe more and it's just her."

"Well, this guy is smart. He would pick a place that didn't have much recording capability and the fewer people that worked there the better to mitigate any chance of him being recognized." Jack said looking at his watch, then back to the road. They had about 6 hours of daylight left and if the roads held out, they would be in Seattle in less than 3.

"I have coordinated a place to stay with the team on the ground there. Our rooms will be ready when we arrive. With any luck, tomorrow we can get eyes on the library ourselves and the people coming and going and maybe, just maybe we will catch a break." She said, laying her head back against the seat.

They drove in silence for a while. Both of them were playing back the scenes in their heads and going over what they thought they knew about the cases. It was the kind of silence that was loud. They both knew the other was jumbling images and timelines in their heads trying to stumble upon the one clue that would point this guy out.

The mountains out the windows were covered in snow and the people passing by or being passed in cars were coming or going from somewhere happy in the world they lived in. None of them had any idea of the killer loose and how each of them could be a target simply by accepting some new friend on Social Media. The idea filled them both with the feeling of dread and impossibility. How could you stop it? Was it possible to tell people not to use social media? Could you ever have the ability to monitor all the accounts of all the millions of people using it and determine which one was fake or ever come close to tracking them all? They both knew the answer to the question and it was no. Not ever. The one shot they had at stopping this guy was to get him at the source. To find him in the act of creating the account. Even then, if they found him, how could they connect him to the other murders? He left nothing behind. It would never hold up in court. This guy was smart. He would be out within days of being arrested unless they had more evidence. That's if they ever did find him of course.

Jack broke the silence first. "You know, this pass is called Snoqualmie. It's named after the Snoqualmie Indians that used to reside in the flatlands of Washington to the East. It is the only divided highway to cross the Cascades through the state of Washington and actually includes three separate passes. Stevens, Snoqualmie and White.

She looked over at him and smiled.

After the men finished with the futile attempt in finding anything that could connect him they left the Library and Vincent followed. He remained distant enough to blend into the grunge of Seattle and not be seen but close enough to watch and listen to their conversations. The group of men walked to a garage close to the library where they all loaded into a white van and drove to the Hilton Hotel, located 10 blocks away. He followed, using a taxi he hailed when they went into the garage. Under normal circumstances he would never have used a cab, but the necessity outweighed the risk for him. These men were here tracking him and Vincent would not let it go unchecked. He would not be the hunted.

He watched them check in to the hotel and waited until they were out of sight. He assumed they would be getting separate rooms since they were Federal employees. The government didn't care how much money they spent. He paid the driver cash with a modest tip at the hotel, then returned to one of the other 26 branches of the public library system located in Seattle on foot and looked up all the information he could find on Special Agent Chambers of the FBI.

Vincent loved the internet. So much information available to anyone that wanted it. He had the ability to hack and search whatever he chose and it was free. People were so stupid he thought. Why would you put your life out there for anyone to see? Nothing was private. Nothing sacred. The world of social media made it a playground for the evil to do whatever they wanted, whenever and wherever they pleased. It was ridiculous. Just for fun he thought about Friend Requesting Cathy. He found her profile and looked at all he could without being a friend. Wouldn't it be fun to see if she accepted him? That would be icing on the cake he thought but it wouldn't be the direction he took.

The route from Ellensburg to Seattle would take her 3 hours to drive if the roads were good. Vincent figured that's where she was when the men in the library were speaking to her after hearing the source of the fake account that he had used, so she should be arriving at the hotel by 5 PM or around that time. Vincent decided that getting rid of her would be a very important step in his operation and it needed to be done. Somehow the FBI had located Seattle and connected the dots closer than he ever thought they would. Changing his plans would be inevitable, but he needed to tie up the ends here before moving on and Agent Chambers would be first on the list.

With all the printouts from the library placed inside a magazine he purchased from a street vendor on the way, Vincent sat in the large lobby of the hotel and waited. He looked like anyone else would, he supposed, sitting in one of the large overstuffed chairs provided by the hotel for people to wait. Just a guy sitting in the lobby area enjoying a magazine while he waited for someone. Maybe he was waiting for a wife or girlfriend that was still upstairs getting ready for a romantic evening out and he was an early kind of guy. Maybe he was a business man here in Seattle for a convention of some kind and was awaiting his partners to come down for a few drinks on the town. The reason didn't matter, what mattered to Vincent was that he was invisible in plain sight. Of the dozens of people that came and went in the hour he waited, not one of them looked his direction for more than a second.

Human interaction was a thing of the past. No matter who came in or left, whether it was a family, a couple or just a single person. They all had a phone in their hand and was busy looking at it, typing on it or talking into it. He could be sitting naked on the chair and he didn't think he would be noticed. This world was filled with zombies traveling through the world they knew like ants on a hill. Each one was incapable of doing anything alone and needed the recognition of others to feel they belonged. He loathed them all. Everyone he saw he hated more than the next. He wanted to go hunting and continue his work right here, right now! The images of them beaten and bleeding at his feet made him smile. Then he saw her.

She looked like she did on her profile and the photos he had found of her online and printed. Slightly older than the photos he pulled from the papers on her successful cases in the past during his internet search, but remarkably close to the posted pic on Facebook. She was blond, with crystal blue eyes that seemed to hold in a surprising amount of knowledge. Staying in good physical condition was important to her as her body showed the hours spent at the gym. The miles of road just driven was evident in her face and in her gait but overall the woman was a pleasing sight to him. She only had a small bag that was pulled with a handle behind her making her simple and efficient. He approved of this. From the time she walked through the sliding doors her gaze was up and down on the faces of every person around her. At one point she looked directly at him and grinned slightly then went back to scanning the room while she approached the desk. He could hear her voice as she spoke to the lady at the desk and it wasn't an annoying sound.

The simplicity and stature of the woman was impressive to him until her attention went from the hostess to her phone. Without a thought, she broke off conversation with the woman at the desk and rudely answered her phone. Before the electronic device took control of her and sealed her fate in Vincent's eyes, there was a moment of appreciation he had for Agent Chambers.

That night on the boat, Vincent studied the printouts. His table was covered with hundreds of pages he had printed. Each of them contained newspaper reports, headlines, public records and photos of Special Agent Cathy Chambers. Vincent read through them multiple times. He knew everything about her. He knew she was born May, 3, 1976 in the town of Hanson, Missouri. Her Father, Ben, was a metal worker and her mother was a house wife that sold Mary Kay products on the side for some time. Her Dad was killed in a drunk driving accident when she was 17 and her mother passed away 8 years later from kidney failure. Cathy received a scholarship to the state college based on her outstanding academic record in high school and graduated top of the state 4 years later.

She was accepted into the FBI academy at the age of 24 and started as an analyst assistant. She applied for the Special Agent program after 3 years as an analyst and was turned down 4 times before being given the chance. She graduated in the top 2% of the class securing the top gun award for shooting. Since she became an Agent she moved from robbery, to homicide and was responsible for quite a few major arrests to include the man 5 years ago that had murdered and raped more than 12 women across the country. Apparently there was a shooting at the end of her chase where an agent was severely injured as well as herself and a couple of police were killed along with the suspect.

It appeared to Vincent that Agent Chambers was the reason the men were at the library and she was to blame for interrupting his life's work. He set the paperwork down and stood to stretch his legs. He contemplated his moves for tomorrow and the next week. He needed to make sure nothing was overlooked and nothing would be left to chance. He was in control of everything around him and this woman would not be his end.

He rechecked the supplies laying on the couch one last time making sure he had not forgotten anything and retired to bed. He had an early morning and a very busy day tomorrow.

CHAPTER 31

The hotel was much nicer than the one they stayed at on the road from Billings. The rooms had more than one channel to choose from and the bathroom had more than one towel to use. It was definitely above Jacks standards and nothing he would've stayed at or could afford for that matter if he was on his own. A hotel was used for sleep and shelter away from your car when on a trip and that's about it. He never understood the need to spend a fortune for something you were going to be in for less than 12 hours. But, since the FBI was flipping the bill he wouldn't complain.

After the long drive, Jack was tired and dirty from the miles of road he had put away not to mention the desire to rid himself of the multiple crime scenes he had seen. It was nothing a hot shower and fresh clothes wouldn't change. He and Cathy agreed to getting cleaned up then meeting back downstairs for dinner in the restaurant after 45 minutes. The hotel apparently prided itself on having one of the best steak houses in the Puget Sound area. Jack seriously doubted the claim but he was hungry and didn't want to drive anymore.

Arriving at the steak house only 30 minutes after arriving to the hotel it crossed his mind that he must be hungrier than he thought until he saw Cathy. She was already at a booth in the back of the restaurant with two pints of beer sitting on the table in front of her.

"Damn girl." He said sliding in the booth opposite her. "You must be starving. I thought I was early."

"I figured you would be down here by now and a cold beer would be at the top of your list." She said to him with a smile.

The winter weather in Seattle meant rain more than it did snow and it was coming down hard beyond the glass. It was dark outside with only the light posts spaced in the parking lot to dimly illuminate the wet Puget Sound. Jack liked the Seattle area but never wanted to live in it because of the rain.

"You know this place gets an average of 120 days of rain a year." He said taking a long sip of the beer.

Cathy looked at him across the table. Her eyes seemed to glow in the poorly lit room. Her hair was still slightly damp from the shower she just took and her natural southern color had returned. She was a good looking woman he thought. When he met her for the first time so many years ago she had the young sexiness about her that many older men sought after. Jack never mixed that kind of thing when he was with the Bureau, but now, time seemed to add to her beauty in a deeper way. She was attractive on more levels than just the skin. She was smarter now, more capable and experienced. It brought out a beauty in her that he had not seen before.

"Thank you for that bit of local climatic history. What would I do without you?" She said smiling.

"Well, without me, I doubt we would be sitting here right now." Jack said with more than just confidence.

She set her glass down and swallowed. "That's true. And thank you for that. I should've gotten ahold of you sooner."

"Nah, you would've ended up here as well. You're smarter than this guy. You and I both know it."

"No, Jack, I don't. Without you profiling the guy the way you did or discovering his link with social media, we would still be dusting for prints and moving bodies. We would still have more question than answers. Now we know where he lives, at least the area, and where he operates out of. With any luck, this guy will be in our hands very soon and nobody else will get hurt."

"I hope so. Not too sure how much longer Max can make it without me being home."

"I thought your neighbor was checking on him for you?"

"Oh, yeah he is. I'm just kidding. Max loves having the house to himself. He's probably on my bed right now just because he can. That damn dog doesn't even know I'm gone. He will sleep all day and wake up when Chuck comes by to feed him. He will bounce around and look all lonely then go right back to sleep when he leaves. Trust me. He's fine."

Cathy pulled her phone out of her pocket and began to scroll through it. She clicked on some things and read others then moved on. Jack watched her and drank his beer. Seconds turned to minutes and he watched.

The waiter arrived and asked for their order. Jack ordered a 12 oz. Porterhouse, well done without looking at the menu and another beer. Cathy said the same, without looking away from her phone.

The man left and Jack watched her. She was engrossed in the devise. He looked around the restaurant and saw only 2 other couples at tables waiting for their meals. At the bar sat one man alone with a half empty highball glass in front of him. Everyone in the place had a phone in front of them. Even the couples at the tables were looking at a phone and not the other person sitting a foot away.

He turned back to Cathy. "So I'm thinking about donating my penis to science."

Her fingers stopped sliding on the screen and she looked up. "What?"

"You know, my Junk. I was going to lop it off and give it to a school for study. I'm sorry, did I interrupt you? Did you not want to talk about that?"

She looked at him then around the restaurant and back. She knew what he was getting at and set her phone down. "Ok, I get it. I am sorry."

"No, its fine, continue. I will keep running up the FBI's bill here at the bar one glass at a time and you can finish up with whatever you are doing. I really don't mind."

"Believe it or not Jack, a lot of stuff gets done on the internet. I can accomplish more right here at this table than you could've done in a whole day back when you were with the service."

"Girl, I have no doubt that is a handy little tool. I'm sure it makes your life lot easier and is filled with all kinds of things that you don't think you can live without."

"Of course I could live without it, but it does make things easier."

"Sure, sure." He said finishing his beer and setting the glass down for the waiter to replace with a full one. "Have you tried going a day without it? Or maybe a day using it only as a phone?"

"I do use it as a phone and no, I never tried that because what would be the purpose?" She answered finishing off her drink and placing the glass next to his.

"I don't know, just to see if you can. Do you think you could?"

"Of course I could, if I wasn't on this case and didn't need to have it."

"Oh, you mean having that thing glued to your hand will be what stops this guy from killing someone else?"

"No, I'm not saying that, but I am saying it keeps the IT teams in contact with me on any updates as well as the teams processing the other scenes. I can get real time photos and the latest reports right here and share them with everyone at the same time. That's how it will help to stop the guy."

"Ok, as long as you feel you need it." He said giving the waiter a nod and taking the new glass of beer from him. "I just wonder how in the world I managed to catch anybody back in the day."

"Funny Jack!"

"Do me a favor girl. Put it away. Not asking you to shut it off, but put on vibrate and set the damn thing down for the next 30 minutes. Let's enjoy a conversation, have a drink, eat some food and tell a joke or two. Would that be so bad?"

She smiled and set it on the seat next to her. The lack of any more protest told him she didn't care to argue anymore or she did partially agree with what he was saying. Either way, he was glad she did it and leaned back in the booth.

The rest of the evening went off well. The food was good but did not hold to the claim the restaurant had on the sign of the best, however it was worth the price. They both cleaned off the plates in front of them and ordered another beer when the dishes were taken away.

He was certain Cathy didn't drink the amount he did and was feeling the effects of the alcohol more than him. By the flushed look in her cheeks he was certain it wasn't from the cold. She was smiling more than he had seen in the last 4 days and much more talkative. They were talking about people they had worked with in the past and making jokes. Director Allen was the main focus of the humor and they both enjoyed it at his expense.

She picked up the check when the beer was done and they left. The elevator ride up to the fifth floor was filled with small talk and the comfortable vibe two people had with each other. Cathy may have been 10 years younger than him but he was still a man and she was every bit as attractive now as when he first met her.

"So, what's the plan?" He asked.

She wrapped her arms around his necked and pulled herself up to his lips kissing him.

CHAPTER 32

Vincent woke at 0155. His alarm was set to go off at 0200. As always, he was in control of the world around him, not the other way around. He had never needed the alarm to wake, but being a man of preparedness, he would not allow the chance to happen no matter how slim it may be. This morning would not allow the time for his regular workout, there was too much to do. He simply showered and donned his costume. There was a lot going on today and he had a feeling he would get ample exercise with the events that were planned.

After the supplies were checked one last time and placed into the black duffle, he left the boat and walked to his garage. The early morning of the harbor was peaceful and quiet. Even the birds that you heard squawking in the dawn of the day could not be heard at this hour. Only the slow rhythmic rocking of the boats, silently splashing up and down with the tides was cracking the silence. His boots on the docks below him echoed like a hollow box with every step. Vincent pictured the woman and his plans as he walked.

Cathy was up and dressed before Jack. She didn't want to wake him and felt slightly weird about last night. She wasn't upset with what happened between them. Quite the contrary, it was something she had thought about ever since she met him. It was however a very curious string of events that ended up bringing them together. His age didn't bother her in the slightest. Jack was the strongest man she knew and he was more honest and capable than anyone. He wouldn't try to play her or lie to her like the younger men in her life. What they shared last night was going to change her life and she knew it.

Double checking the power on her iPod and slipping the key card for the room in her pocket she closed the door behind her as quietly as possible. The day was going to be busy and she needed to get her head clear before it started. A good morning run would do the trick she thought. It had been almost a week since she was able to do any kind of exercise and being stuck in the car for the last day an a half was making her feel like a sloth. She hoped to be back before Jack woke and the two of them could take a shower to start the day off with a bang then enjoy breakfast together.

She took the stairs as a warm up before she began her run outside and surprised the desk clerk when she appeared out of the door to the stairwell at this hour in the morning.

"Good morning miss. Going for a jog?" The man asked after regaining his composure to her arriving when he was not expecting it.

He was an older gentleman, probably the night shift guy. Most likely retired from a previous career and did this to bring in a little extra money. She imagined he was getting ready to hand the desk over to the day crew who would be arriving in the next hour or so. He had a pleasant smile and she would've felt rude for not answering him.

"Yes I am and thank you." She responded, while pulling an ear bud out.

"You know there is a very nice walking path just behind the Hotel. It goes down through the city park and back up the other side. Not sure how far it is, but it would keep you off the streets. A lot of people run there."

"That's where I was planning on going. Thanks again." She put the earpiece back and left the lobby. Once outside she turned right toward the path and began a slow trot to warm up.

The cars sitting in the parking lot were covered with fresh morning dew. The area was lit with random lamps spaced a good distance apart throughout space. They allowed a pale yellow cone of light beneath each one. At this hour only service vehicles were moving about in the distance. Other than that, the place was quiet. The path started like the man said on the backside of the hotel with a small wooden sign designating the entrance to the park and a pirate style map carved into it. A 1 mile loop was the number resting in the center of it all identifying the length. She would run two or three laps depending on the time left over. Her normal jogging routine started at 4 miles, but she had gone as far as 10 once when she had an abundance of stuff on her mind. Hitting the volume on the iPod up two more notches she started out. She had always enjoyed running. It cleared her head and made her feel better about herself. At times it seemed like the only way she could catch a break on a case. Something about the physical exercise and letting everything go for a while and focus only on one thing led to leads she would normally not find.

The wind was cold coming off the sound and licking at her skin where it was uncovered. With every step she could feel her body warming from the inside.

She knew that by the time she was done she would want to lose the sweatshirt. The trail winded through the trees and up small inclines then back down again making a large loop. From the starting point you couldn't see it all which made the route pleasing to joggers. On the right she could see the skeletal structure of a children's jungle gym. Shadowy shapes appeared and came into focus the closer she got then faded away as she past. Some were city trash cans and others were bike racks or picnic tables. She figured it was an hour till the sun would peak over the horizon to the east and Jack would be up as soon as it did, if not earlier. That would give her enough time for at least 3 laps and if she hurried up a fourth if she was up for it. She increased her speed with the new song that was randomly playing through her play list and ran.

Vincent watched her from the trees entering the park. He knew the woman would go for a jog and he figured if she didn't use the gym supplied by the hotel and it was not raining, this would be where she went. He was of course prepared for any situation and if she had chosen the Hotel Gym he would've been ready as well.

She was attractive now, just like she was yesterday. Her hair was pulled back into a tight pony tail sticking off the back of her head that bobbed left and right with her running. Even in the low light of the morning her face and eyes shined. She wore black running shorts with a navy blue hoodie sweatshirt. He was impressed with the woman and her value of exercise. He didn't like the electronic device she had attached to her with a cord running up to her ears. He was hoping she had more self-control than that. But very few were as disciplined as he was and he knew it. He couldn't possibly expect this woman to be his equal or remotely close to it.

It was a one mile circular path through the park. Judging by her pace and focus as she passed him, she would run it two or three times. Possibly four, but he doubted it by her speed. Vincent calculated her to a 6.5 or 7 minute mile. That gave him approximately 6 minutes to get ready for her return.

The light reflected on her shoes as she passed and continued down the path. Small strips of reflective material were catching whatever light was available and shining like little flashlights on her feet. It was fun to watch her quick moving light show from the shadows. He waited until she was out of sight completely before moving. Surprise was the most important aspect of his hunt and the slightest thing could throw off his prey. This he would not allow.

Cathy's mind was filled with images of Jack. The run was working to clear her mind of work and things she didn't want to think about right now. Ellensburg, Billings, the cop on the highway and the past 5 months were blurring away with the run. The memory of last night replaced them all and replayed over and over. She was happy she and Jack finally hooked up. Ever since she last saw him in Missouri all those years ago it was something she wished they had done.

The morning wind had a smell of wetness to it that filled her nostrils and amplified her memories. The image of that dark basement filled with death all those years ago became clear again to her. The fall off the top of the stairs down to the cement floor arced in pain across her shoulders. She remembered the view from the ground. Her sidearm spinning out of reach when she hit the floor and the man standing only a few feet above her with the gun shooting in a violent rhythm up the stairs. She could feel the shockwaves from the weapon as it exploded round after round in the confined space. His voice was loud and piercing over the thunder of the weapon and the darkness was filled with the strobe effect pulsing in unison with the shots.

She remembered seeing Jack across the room in blinks of light moving in her direction. The crazy shooting stopped only for a second when the man realized she was there. The end of the weapon turned from the stairs in her direction. She couldn't move. She was frozen in fear without a weapon. She was going to die here today in this dark place.

In the distance more explosions were heard and the evil end of the man's gun stopped moving her way and bounced back toward the other end of the room. She could see Jack running her way shooting his weapon at the man. Then the roar of his gun ignited the space around her again and the man emptied his magazine into Jack. She watched the rounds hit him one after the other, but it didn't stop him. Jack kept moving forward shooting. Round after round hit him and he held his pace and weapon as he fired. It wasn't until the clatter of the man's gun above her hitting the ground filled her ears that she realized Jacks shots were on target and the man was dead, lying on the floor next to her.

Jack fell to the ground immediately after that from the wounds he suffered. He saved her life that day. She knew it. If he had not been there she would've been slaughtered at the feet of the madman.

As it always did when she ran, her feet began to move with the beat of the current song and she didn't feel fatigued or her energy lacking as she picked up the pace. The more she thought of Jack, the faster she started to go.

It didn't feel like a mistake with him. It almost seemed like it was something that finally happened, something that should happen. A little bit of her knew it would, but never exactly when. She was glad it had and smiled at the thoughts of the night.

Rounding her starting point she wondered if another lap was needed or if she should go upstairs and give him a more personal reason to wake up. She was happy. Maybe Jack and she were brought together for a reason. The small sign passed her on the left where she entered the path and she looked at it giving the thought to turn back one more chance when the man stepped out directly in front of her. He was holding something in his hand and pointing it at her. Before she could decide which direction to dodge to go around him, the front of the thing in his hand exploded open with a small flash.

The impact was felt only for a second before her body seized in an uncontrolled muscle spasm that happened when hit with a Taser. She recognized the pain and feeling of complete paralysis the weapon delivers immediately. It was standard in the FBI to get hit with the weapon in order to carry it and it was something you didn't easily forget. Unlike the training she went through, nobody was there to catch her when she got hit and the charge lasted much longer than the standard 5 second jolt given by Law Enforcement.

Cathy crashed into the path with her face making impact first. The Taser made it impossible to move her arms up to brace her fall and her vision filled with stars upon contact with the hard concrete path. She felt her bladder give way under the waves of currents shooting through her muscles as her body gave up control of the most basic abilities. Only small grunts were able to leave her because her mouth was seized shut during the assault.

Her vision was blurred from the impact with the ground and she couldn't focus on anything beside the pain. Blood pooled around her face on the path underneath from her nose. It must have taken the brunt of her fall and was now bleeding.

The man that stepped out in front was busy near her feet now. She watched him pass by her but couldn't move her head to see above his knees. She felt her legs being kicked and moved around but was unable to do anything. The jolting current continued to pump into her. She could see the ground moving around her. She was being dragged backwards she thought. Then her world went completely black.

CHAPTER 33

Jack woke when he heard the click of the door closing. He rolled over to an empty bed. After a quick inspection of the room he came to the conclusion that Cathy had gone for a run or swim in the pool. He knew she was into fitness and hoped that was the reason for her being gone without waking him. Maybe she needed the time to think about what happened last night. He hoped that wasn't the case. Last night was one of the best nights he'd had in his life. Cathy was special on so many levels. He had always wanted to take a chance with her and apparently she felt the same at least that was before he woke up alone. The last few days had been filled with a rollercoaster of events both on an emotional level as well as professional one for her. Maybe she just needed some time to clear her head before embarking on another day that was sure to involve unanswered questions and stress.

Regardless of how she felt, he knew how he did. She was amazing and even if the feeling wasn't mutual for her, he didn't regret anything that happened. He got up and showered, then went about tidying up the room. He would be here when she got back and the two of them would go have breakfast together. If she decided that his help wasn't needed any longer he would leave, but not before telling her how he felt.

The minutes turned to hours as he waited. The bed was made, room cleaned up and he even refolded her clothes and set them next her bag in boredom. Not that she would wear it, but an outfit was selected and laid out for her. He figured she would work out for 45 minutes, maybe an hour, then be back but it had already been at least that since he woke. Her phone, ID and weapon were still in the room so returning afterwards would be a must he thought. He didn't see her doing much of anything without the phone at least. During his cleaning and re-organizing of the small space he didn't come across a note of any kind and the phone was not blinking with a pending message. The second key card for the door sat in the small cardboard sleeve that was given to each of them upon check in with the room number written on the outside. Jack took it and left the room.

The lobby was as busy as you would expect a hotel to be at 0700 in the morning. Small groups gathered around the desk with credit cards in hand while looking over printed out receipts from the night before and debating charges. A steady stream of people were coming and going from the room apposite the front desk that supplied a Continental breakfast for guests. Maybe she was grabbing something to eat after her run, he thought and went to the breakfast room.

The area was small, maybe 6 tables in total with an L shaped bar hugging the wall on the far end. A basket of mini muffins with bowls of fruit of all kinds sat on one end. A cold cereal dispensing machine with stainless steel carafes of milk was next on the counter. What appeared to be some sort of a do it yourself waffle maker was on the other end and large platters of pastries, yogurts and misc. coffee making stations filled the open space. Seattle was definitely known for its coffee, he thought to himself.

Only half the tables had people sitting at them and none of them were Cathy. He recognized one couple from the restaurant last night but nobody else. The others people in the room were new to him. None of the patrons seemed to be FBI or affiliated with the agency in any way. They didn't have the look of Feds. Jack got a cup of coffee from one of the machines and left to check the business center. He doubted she would be there, since her claim that the phone she used could damn near do anything, he didn't see why see would need to use the computers supplied by the hotel, but if she wasn't eating or sitting in the lobby, where else could she be?

Cathy's head bounced up after a large jolt woke her slamming into something hard only inches above her when she jerked up out of the comatose state she had been put in. The pain shot through her head like a wave washing away any numbness she had and bringing the injuries she just sustained back to the surface. She opened her eyes but everything was dark. She could hear the sound of an engine and feel the movement of the vehicle. She was being transported somewhere in a vehicle. The tires hummed on the roadway beneath her, amplifying in the closed space and making her head ache even more.

Judging by the wetness she could feel on her face and the copper taste filling her mouth she was hit in the head with something causing an open wound and enough bleeding to taste it. It must have caused her to black out. She was sure that a mild concussion was the least of her worries. Her hands were restrained behind her back and from the feeling she got when trying to move they were somehow attached to her ankles which were also immobilized. She was tied into a reverse fetal position and placed into what she assumed was the trunk of a car and being moved somewhere.

She tried to recall everything she could before the blackout. The jog in the morning she remembered. Lying next to Jack in the bed and the night before she could recall without issue. The trail, the sign she passed on it and the park outside she remembered. Then the man in front of her. He was white, maybe 6 foot tall, plain and normal. He was wearing a hat over a long mess of shoulder length hair. It looked blond, maybe brown, the light wasn't the greatest at that part of the trail. He hit her with a Taser, but something he modified. Even a civilian model didn't produce a surge of electricity for that amount of time. Did he say anything? No, he didn't. Nothing, not a word. He just stepped out, shot her, tied her up, knocked her unconscious then put her in the car. Without being able to see her watch she had no idea how long she had been out.

The car slowed and came to a stop. She could hear the driver's door open, then what sounded like a gate being pulled open on rusty hinges. The vehicle swayed slightly when the person sat back down and the door shut again. Then the car moved. Not far this time and not fast. Only 30 seconds or less then it stopped again and the sounds of the noisy gate repeated. Wherever they were, it seemed like this was the stop and she would soon get a look at whoever it was. She pulled against the bonds holding her but accomplished nothing. It felt like rope and whoever tied it was a master knot maker. With all the straining she did trying to loosen them it was obvious that no ground was gained and it seemed like they had gotten tighter from her struggle.

The shut turned off and the light flooded in filling her small space when the lid was opened above her. It wasn't daylight, but fluorescent. She was in a garage of some kind. The man holding the lid open looked down at her and smiled.

"Good morning Special Agent Chambers. So good to finally meet you." The man said reaching down and dragging her out of the tiny space by her feet and hands. She was pulled off the back of the car and dropped to the concrete floor like a sack of flour. She felt the new pain in her shoulder when she hit the ground.

After his third re-fill from the coffee pot in the breakfast area, Jack began to get restless. He had already been around the parking lot to check on their rental and it was still there. The gym was empty as well as the business center. None of the people he talked to in the lobby had seen her this morning and she still wasn't in the room that he had been back to 4 times now. It wasn't like her to be MIA for so long especially without her phone. He was surprised she left the thing in the room. He could see her running with it in her hand. Jack went back to the front desk.

"Excuse me; were you on duty earlier this morning, say around 0500 or so?" He asked the young woman behind the counter.

Her name tag ready Theresa. She looked young, maybe 25. Her hair was the same color as Cathy's, but her eyes were brown, not the blue he had grown so much to like.

"No sir, I'm sorry. I come on at 0600, that's when we let the evening shift go for the day. It's usually before everyone starts checking out so it's not so busy. Is there something I can help you with?"

"I hope so. Is the person you took over for still here or did they already go home?"

"Ummm, let me seeeeee." She said, leaning over the left side of the desk, looking out the window. "Oh, yep, he is just leaving."

Jack turned to look out the front doors where she was pointing. He saw an elderly man walking with a small lunch pail in one hand and a cup of coffee in the other. He was heading toward a car at the far end of the lot. Employee parking, Jack thought.

"That would be Mr. Paul Jensen. He is our night shift guy, real sweetheart. He normally waits around to grab a few things out of the breakfast bar before he goes home. It's not a big deal really. I don't think the manager cares. If you hurry you may catch him."

"Thank you." Jack said cutting her off and left the desk making a bee line for the Mr. Jensen.

Jack found himself almost running out the door to the lobby and across the lot between the parked cars. He didn't know why he was, but it seemed the right thing to do at the time.

"Sir, Mr. Jensen. Could I talk to you for a minute?" He half shouted still a good 50 feet from him.

The man stopped and turned to look at Jack approaching. He didn't move or make any gesture for him to slow down or stay back. He just stood there sipping his coffee waiting for Jack to get closer.

"Yes?" He said when Jack arrived.

"Sorry to bother you sir, but the gal at the desk said you worked last night?"

"That's right. 2100 to 0600 4 nights a week. You need something?"

"Yes sir, I was wondering if you remember seeing a blonde woman this morning. Maybe around 0430 or 0500. I think she was going for a run."

"Yep, good looking gal. Your better half?" He asked Jack.

The question took him off guard slightly and he didn't know how to answer it. "Um, yeah, something like that. She is actually my partner and I was wondering if she might have told you where she was heading or if you saw where she went this morning?"

"Sure. She was going for a run on the park trail over behind the hotel. Not sure how long it is, but a lot of folks use it around here." He said pointing back at the hotel's right side.

"Was she alone this morning? Did you see anyone with her or following her to the park area to run?"

"No, she was alone. Didn't see anyone but her. She looked pretty motivated by the way she took off outa here. You got a good looking woman there. Keep an eye on her."

"Thank you." Was all he responded with. Jack was running by the time he reached the end of the parking lot and found the entrance to the trail. He stopped at a funny looking sign with a description of the trails route and scanned the area beyond. It appeared to be a mile loop and you could almost see all of it from where he was. It was a circular concrete path surrounded by thick trees on the outside. There was no movement anywhere in the area. No joggers or walkers were seen. No sign of Cathy.

He stepped onto the trail and started walking scanning to the left and right for her. There was very few places a woman running could be that he could not see from his location. Only a few steps later he saw the small pool of blood and what appeared to be drag marks leading off the trail into the trees to the left. His heart stopped.

CHAPTER 34

The place didn't smell like a normal garage would. The lingering effects of the exhaust were still in the air like you would typically expect, but the overpowering smell of bleach and cleaning detergents was the main aroma filling the space and not the oil and grime you would be waiting for. Her shoulder was aching from when he pulled her out of the car but the pain was bearable compared to the brass band playing in her head.

She was in a chair sitting against the wall now. How she got in the chair eluded her. She must have blacked out again when he removed her from the car. Her hands were tied around the back of it and she could feel her feet move every time she tested the restraints on her wrists confirming that she was tied to her own feet again behind the back of the chair. In front of her sat a Ford Taurus station wagon. It was light brown and looked exactly like Jack described the man's car would look like. The thought of him brought back the night before with him and how much she wished he was here right now. Movement caught her eye to the left in the garage and she turned.

At the rear of the space behind the car she could see a man working at a bench. He was busy packing things into a bag and the sound of metal being moved across the floor filled her ears. She was unable to focus clearly on him. Blurry shadows invaded the sides of her vision when she looked at one point for too long. The smack on the head he gave her earlier was already showing the signs of worse things to come, she thought.

The man looked in her direction and stopped whatever it was he was doing when he noticed her watching him. He approached her and leaned against the car directly in front. He was only a couple feet away now. She could smell him. He smelled clean.

"You surprise me Special Agent. I thought you would be able to withstand more than what I did to you. I figured you were stronger than most people, but to my dismay you proved me wrong. I am not normally wrong about things. But this isn't the first time you have done that is it? You seem to find joy in disproving me and my work. Why is that?"

Cathy opened her mouth to speak and found there wasn't enough saliva in her throat to utter more than a dry coughing hasp.

"Hang on a minute." He said and walked away. He returned a moment later with a plastic bottle of water and thrust it into her mouth before she had a chance to object. He squeezed it hard forcing a huge blast of water down her throat. She immediately choked and gasped, spitting most of it up. He repeated it, this time holding her head back preventing her from bending forward to cough it up and making her choke.

Jack touched the small pool of blood and found it still wet. It wasn't a huge amount, but enough to get his attention and definitely more than one should find this time of the morning with nobody around. It was cold, but hadn't had the chance to dry. It couldn't be more than an hour old. Everything inside him told him it was Cathy's blood. There was no proof to validate his thinking, but his gut was talking and it had never let him down in the past. He followed the drag marks off the path through the wet grass into the timber away from the trail. Once inside the wood line, the trail evaporated into the thick brush and foliage that the area is so well known for.

He searched the area in ever growing circles looking for anything that might give him a direction. Eventually his searching pressed through the trees emerging out the other side onto the edge of an overflow parking area, most likely reserved for big trucks or vehicles with trailers that were staying at the hotel. The drag marks re-appeared in the wet grass to his left outside of the trees continuing to the curbside of the parking area then vanished.

She was taken.

He flushed the water down her throat over and over again until the bottle was empty. Cathy coughed and spit trying to inhale over the flood of water. Her nose must've been broken when she fell because she was unable to get any air through it and battled the fluid filling her windpipe for oxygen. She tried to get a look at the man, but with her blurry vision and his constant onslaught of water, she couldn't hold still long enough to dedicate his features to memory.

Throwing the empty bottle to the floor he finally let her head go and stepped back to the side of the car again.

"I am sorry Special Agent, or is it Cathy? Would you prefer Cathy? You were trying to say something. What is it?"

The last time she tried to answer him he damn near drowned her. She may have been dumb to go for a jog without her piece or letting Jack know where she was going but she wasn't stupid enough to go down that road again. She knew this was the guy they had been tracking. She was seeing him face to face. What she didn't know was how he discovered they were on to him. How did he know where she was? They must've been closer than she thought to discover who he was and this was the only way he saw out of it. She looked at him silently without uttering a sound but recording every detail of his face.

"Ms. Chambers, allow me to introduce myself. My Name is Vincent. I believe you have been following my work for some time now. Normally that wouldn't bother me and would mean nothing. I mean, who doesn't enjoy a loyal fan base. However, because of your constant persistence resulting in the situation you find yourself in now, you have forced me to break my own protocols and that is very frustrating to me. You see I have a lot more to do before my time here is over and this interruption is causing me to alter my timelines and methods that I have so diligently maintained."

She listened to him and did her best to take in as much of the room around him while he talked. She had no idea where she was. The ambient temperature was still cool which meant she had only been out for around 20 minutes at the most when he was moving her. She had been out of the vehicle for 15 minutes now tied up to the chair so given traffic in the Seattle area in the morning she could be up to 10 miles away from the hotel at the most. The place was smaller than a garage and she could see no other door other than the main roll up one used to drive the car in. The walls were grey cinderblock and 4 double halogen lights hung from a 12 foot ceiling by chains, evenly spaced across the roof. On the other side of the car was a wall of shelves and each one had boxes and supplies neatly organized and stacked on them. It resembled an auto parts store with so many different sized items all on display but arranged in a meticulous order.

With no other way in or out she figured she was in some sort of storage unit and not a garage attached to a home. Jack was right again, she thought. This guy had an entire room designated to wiping away any trace of his movements.

"Oh, I see you are observing my place." Vincent said as he walked beside her grabbing the chair and tilting her back, dragging her to the rear of the garage. "Let me get you closer so you don't have to pretend to look interested while I speak. I don't mind if you see what I'm doing. What you hear or see today will have no change to your outcome Special Agent. I think you and I both know that. So please feel free to ask whatever you like of me and take it all in. I have some things to finish up with so don't be offended if I am working while we speak. I will give you my full attention, I assure you."

Jack bolted from the overflow parking lot back through the trees across the path and back to the hotel in a dead run. He played back the clock in his head of this morning's events. He was woke at 0415 when he heard the door close to the room. Assuming that it was Cathy heading out for a run that gave him a starting point. The downstairs night shift guy said he talked to a woman fitting her description between 0430 and 0500. Jack was leaning more toward 0430 if she left the room at 0415, it only takes a couple minutes to walk down the stairs and he was pretty sure she would use them before going on a run and avoid the elevator. He looked at his watch and it was now 0700. He had been outside for the last 30 minutes talking with the night shift guy and locating the trail. That leaves a window of 60 to 90 minutes for her to have be taken.

Hitting the doors to the main lobby at a run Jack headed for the stairs and ran the four flights to his room. Re-confirming that the room was empty and just as he left it, he snatched her phone, ID and pistol off the nightstand and grabbed the keys to the rental car on the way out the door. Taking the elevator down, he fumbled with her phone trying to get to her recent calls but other things kept popping up every time he touched the screen.

"Fucking phone!" He yelled at the device in his hand and his inability to use the thing.

The doors opened and he shot out, pushing through a young couple with bags waiting for their turn to go up. He didn't apologize or say anything to them as he bulled past them. Theresa was still at the desk typing on a keyboard that was below the top of the counter out of sight. She smiled at him the same way she did earlier when he got to the desk.

Not giving her a chance to speak, Jack handed the phone to her and asked her to pull up his most recent calls. The girl looked at him with a puzzled grin. "I am sorry sir, you want me to do what?"

Jack could see how it looked but didn't have time for a long discussion on his ignorance with technology or to even begin discussing the reality of the situation with her. He reached into his pocket and withdrew Cathy's ID. Holding his thumb and forefinger across her photo, he flipped it open on the counter.

"Theresa, I am Agent Lawson of the FBI. I need you to please pull up the most recent calls from this phone for me and I need it done now."

Her eyes grew looking at the badge and she didn't question its authenticity or reason. She scooped the phone up and started moving her thumbs around the screen. Seconds later she handed it back to him with a list of names and numbers next to them down the side. "Here you go Agent, is there anything else?"

Jack looked at it and started running the clock in his head again. This time from yesterday and their trip to from Ellensburg to the hotel. "Yes, I need you to pull up a call made from this phone to a number yesterday at 1600. Can you do that?"

"Sure." She said and started moving her fingers on the screen again.

It was the only thing Jack could think of right now. At 1600 yesterday she had contacted the IT guys that were at the library. They were staying at the same hotel, but he never got a name or room number of any. Maybe with their help he would have a chance to locate Cathy.

"Here you go sir." Theresa said handing back the phone with a name and number highlighted. "All you have to do is touch it with your finger sir and it will dial."

He took the phone, touched the name and waited.

It was answered on the third ring. "Good morning Agent Chambers, how can I help you?"

"This is Jack, Cathy is gone, where are you?"

CHAPTER 35

The man had a large metal frame on a work bench that he was busy assembling in the rear of the storage area. It had hinges on it with multiple angles and pieces made of black metal. She didn't know what it was and he didn't seem concerned about her watching him. From where she was sitting, the back end of the garage was visible and she could see no windows. It was a box made of concrete and there were probably hundreds of them in the area. Her watch was on her wrist behind her back and no clock could be seen anywhere. The blackout caused by the wrap on her head wouldn't have lasted more than 15 minutes. She had never been knocked unconscious before, but had seen it happen enough times to know it didn't last that long. At the most, she was no more than 20 minutes from the Hotel. That would place her near the waterline if he took her west or out of the city in one of the smaller towns at the base of the mountains to the east.

She saw no weapons hanging from hooks or instruments of torture in the unit. Just the car and shelves upon shelves of items stacked neatly organized. Besides the fact she was tied to a chair and the man working on the project in front of her was a psychotic killer, the place seemed like any other storage unit might.

Her vision was returning to her faster than she thought it would. Maybe she was getting used to the pain or the concussion wasn't as bad as she thought. She watched him assemble the metal box thing on the workbench. He was between his mid-30s to 40s. She was leaning more toward early 40s. He wore a ball cap over what appeared to be a clean shaved head. The man that hit her with the Taser had long curly hair she thought. A wig maybe. It's possible. If this was the guy, a wig wouldn't surprise her.

"What's your name?" She asked him forcing it out as clear as she could and risking another attack.

"Vincent." He answered not looking up from the project and not immediately assaulting her with water again.

"Vincent what?"

"Vincent Holbrook." He said.

Cathy knew the name. For some reason it sparked a memory to her. It wasn't a case she had worked on. Maybe an old one. Something she helped out on in her earlier years as an analyst. Maybe just a random name she saw on a report long ago and hearing it now popped it to front of her brain to recall. She thought about it while he worked. The thing on the table was beginning to take shape. It looked like a metal octagon with multiple hinged openings around it.

"Why?" She asked unable to come up with why she knew the name or what he was doing. But wanting more sound than the metal clanking on the table.

The man looked up from his project directly at her. He didn't look like a killer or a psychopath, of course most of them didn't. He looked like any other regular Joe walking down the street or sitting in a coffee shop waiting for his order. That fact that he seemed so plain and normal sent shivers across her shoulders. He must've seen it because he smiled and set down the socket wrench and pliers he was using to assemble the thing on the bench.

Stepping to the front of the car and half sitting down on the hood he was only 3 feet away now and devoting all his attention directly at her. His eyes were a pale brown, almost grey. They were lifeless but determined. He had the look of a man that was in complete control of his world but only with a paper thin grasp.

"What is it you would like to know Cathy?"

Jack arrived at the fourth floor room of the man that he had on the phone. Knocking hard three times, the door opened. Jack didn't wait to be invited in or bother identifying himself. He shot past him into the room.

"You are part of the Nerd Herd Cathy sent over here to look into the library computers right?"

The man was taken back by the stigma given to him from someone he had never met before and the fact that his space was just invaded, but answered him all the same.

"Yes I am. I and 3 others from the FBI were sent here on Agent Chambers request to go through the hard drives of the labs at the library and pull whatever footage we could from CCTVs. Is there a problem?"

Jack ignored his question and fired back more of his own. "Outside on the other side of the hotel there is a large overflow parking area. It has cameras installed on the four corners of the light poles around the perimeter. Each of them are facing inward toward the parking lot.

How long will it take you to pull up the footage of them for the last 90 minutes?"

"With the authorization of the hotel, minutes, but without it, I'm afraid I can't do anything."

He didn't have time for this and wasn't in the mood. "Who needs to authorize it?"

"Well Agent Chambers or Director Allen would have to sir. "

"Call Allen now. Tell him what I just told you and tell him that Jack Lawson said to do it. Where is the rest of your team?"

"Probably in their rooms or down getting breakfast."

"Get them together now. We don't have a lot of time. You calling Allen yet!?"

Jack paced the room and waited for the man to make the calls. He ran the last 4 days through his mind and everything they discussed. He could see the guy's hand shaking on the phone and hear the quiver in his voice as he spoke. It was a new era of the FBI he supposed. People had feelings now and everyone was treated equal. This poor guy probably never had anyone raise his voice to him since he was a kid and now he was ready to pee himself.

Jack looked out the window at the grey morning light. The sun was up now over the mountains burning the dew dropped from the evening before. Somewhere out there was Cathy and a mad man had her.

She knew the longer she could keep him talking the better chance she had of Jack finding her. At least that was what she was hoping. No doubt that by now he had realized she was gone and was looking for her. He would've figured out where she went to run. With any luck, some of her blood was left where she was tased and knocked out. That would kick Jack into high gear. What she was worried about was this guy and his methods. He didn't do anything without thinking it through and it's possible he already had her destiny mapped out. It was possible this guy was planning on all that and it didn't bother him because she wouldn't be alive when they got here anyway. He didn't make mistakes. Jack said that so many times. She prayed that this time he was wrong.

"Where are we?" She asked.

"We are in my storage unit, about 8 blocks from the harbor in Seattle." Vincent said to her.

"Why have you brought me here?" She asked trying to sound authoritative, but after hearing his answer she knew her fate was sealed. He didn't care what she knew.

"Well Agent Chambers, you have interrupted my work and caused me to regroup a little or possibly change things altogether. Because of your people sniffing around at the library, I needed to bring you here so we could discuss what the FBI knows about me. How much of my identity do you know and how close are you to finding out my location? If you answer my questions it will make things go a lot smoother for you and it will help me out a lot."

Cathy looked at him without breaking eye contact. "What are going to do with me if I tell you? I am assuming since I have seen your face and know your name that you have no intention of letting me live. What's the point in me helping you?"

"You are correct Cathy, you will not see tomorrow. That is an unfortunate guarantee for you, but how you leave this world rests solely in your hands and what you tell me. You see, I do not enjoy torture or needless killing for that matter. I know you don't believe me, but it's true. I do what I do because it is my job not because I get off on it like some freak. It's my purpose and calling to do the things I have done and I have a lot of work still to do and will not allow you or anyone to get in the way of that. Now, in saying this, please know that I have no problem with the latter part of my conversation and can make your last few hours on earth seem like an eternity if you don't share everything you know about your investigation with me. On the other hand I can also make it quick and painless. The choice is yours and to be honest it is something that very few people get to decide. So take pleasure in the fact that you are in control of your own destiny right now."

The man handed the phone back to Jack. "Sir, the Director would like to speak with you."

Jack snatched the phone from him. "Allen, listen to me. This guy has taken Cathy. I know don't have proof yet, but you gotta trust me on this. I need your team."

"Jack! Stop talking. I already briefed them to give you whatever support you need. Keep Cathy's phone with you. We will track where you are and send a team to your location. I will scramble them as soon as we get off the phone."

"What do you need sir?"

Apparently Allen was understanding enough with his request that he didn't argue when Jack requested the teams help. Maybe it was because it was Jack that did the asking or because Cathy was missing. It didn't matter. What did matter was time and every minute her chances of survival was fading. Allen obviously thought the same.

"Get the rest of your nerds in here. I need you to pull up the CCTVs of that parking lot and the other guys to start a search for this asshole. I am tired of chasing this guy. We are gonna find him today."

"Yes sir." The man said sitting at the desk, snatching up the phone and dialing. Within 10 minutes the rest of them were in the room and busy typing on laptops or using cell phones.

He was running his own little team and each man was searching something different. One was pulling up the cameras from the past 2 hours of the parking lot and streaming it in speed to see if an image of Cathy was recorded being put in a vehicle.

Jack had the other three searching while he spoke. "Ok, we are looking for a man between 30 and 50 years of age. He lives in the Puget Sound area and has for at least the last 10 years. He would have no children and never married. Anyone with relatives anywhere close by, scratch off the list. This guy is a loaner from birth. He wouldn't have a criminal record of any kind. Scratch any of those."

"That's still a pretty broad search sir." One of the men said while tapping on the computer.

"He wouldn't have a job. He either inherited the money or made smart investments a while back and is living off the dividends. Check for trust fund babies or large inheritance recipients. Come to think of it, this guy wouldn't have investments, forget that. Too easy to track. Go with the inheritance route and look for people that cashed it out. This guy stays off the grid because he doesn't use banks. Last word from Cathy was no connection between banks in the Seattle area being used to or from the locations of the murders in the other states. That means this guy uses cash. Most likely from a settlement or inheritance and he is budgeting himself to make it last."

"Sir, I have something!"

The man at the computer searching the camera footage was pointing at the screen like he had just found Waldo. Jack leaned in and saw Cathy. She was on her stomach being drug from the wood line like a hunter pulling a dead deer. A man with long hair and a hoodie was tying her feet to her wrists then lifting her into the back of a station wagon. The image was black and white, but the color of car was light not dark.

"Is she dead?" Asked the man at the desk.

"No." Jack said. If she was dead he wouldn't be tying her up. She is unconscious. Probably knocked out by a blow to the head. That would explain the blood I found on the trail. Watch the car and get a plate number and the direction it went."

He walked back to the three sitting around the room. "Search for owners of station wagons. It looks like a Ford Taurus, maybe mid-90s. Look for a light color, grey, silver, or beige. The registration would be clean and up to date with no tickets. Cross check that with the other parameters we have."

"I got a partial plate sir!" He shouted from the desk.

"Good" Jack said. "You, nerd 2, run with the partial number on the plate. Cross check it with whatever these guys find. Can you follow the car using the cameras at intersections to track where it's going from the parking lot?"

"Yes, I can, and my name is Karl."

"That's great Karl, if you stop doing what I tell you again to inform me of anything other than what I ask, you won't be able to say your name."

He turned back and kept typing not saying a word. The others continued their search without looking up. The room was filled with the sound of keys being hit and Jack waited.

CHAPTER 36

"So, Special Agent Chambers, have we decided what we're going to do today? I have a lot of work to tend to still and would like to get on with it if you wouldn't mind." Vincent said, looking at her tied to the chair.

There were no sounds coming from outside. No sirens or men shouting and beating at the door. She was alone. Even if Jack had discovered she was taken off the running trail, how long after she was gone did he realize it? How would he even know where to start looking? Hell, she had no idea where she was! She didn't want to give Vincent anything, but it seemed like the only way to prolong her life was to delay telling him everything she knew but it would come with a price. If he was going to kill her, she didn't see how he could do it here. The man was very careful not to leave trace behind at any of the scenes and this would be a scene hard to cover up. He must have a plan to take her somewhere else and do it, so the longer she remained here in the storage unit the longer she could stay alive and the better chance of Jack finding her would be. If that was even an option for her now.

"I will tell you whatever I know Vincent." She said.

"Oh, that is great." He said stepping away from the car and moving back to the work bench. He picked up the pliers and socket wrench and started again assembling the strange looking metal cage. "You go ahead and start from the beginning, I am listening. Don't leave anything out ok?"

"What are you building?" She asked trying to prolong the time she had.

"Cathy please. What did I tell you? I need to know what you and the FBI know. Not waste time discussing my own projects and try stalling for more time. What I do is inevitable and out of your control. Let's get that clear. What I am doing here may involve you in a way, but ultimately has nothing to do with what you tell me, so let's get back on track shall we and stop wasting my time."

She knew that he was aware of her trying to stall, but there wasn't much of a choice. The truth was they had virtually nothing on him to make an arrest. All they knew was the accounts started in Seattle at the Library. They assumed he lived in the area, but nothing was confirmed. They had no prints, pictures, DNA trace or witnesses. If she told him that now, he would be done with her and her end would be sealed. She had to prolong it even if it meant the worst.

"What do you mean it may involve me, what is it?" She asked again ignoring his last statement to cease the procrastination she was giving him about his requested information. "Don't you think I have the right to know what that thing is if it involves me?"

He set the socket wrench down sighing heavily while doing it. He walked over and stood in front of her again. This time directly in front positioning himself between her legs only a foot separated them.

"What did I tell you Cathy? I don't have time for this." Vincent said.

She looked up at him ready to respond and he grinned down at her. With his left hand he jerked her head back as far as it would go by her pony tail. It was straining the vertebrae in her neck to the point of snapping. The extreme angle forced her mouth open and she couldn't close it. He was pulling so hard on the hair that her Jaw was being hyperextend. She could feel the snapping point of her neck was being tested. He straddled her on the chair putting all his weight on top holding her down. With the pliers in his right hand he reached in and grabbed ahold of one of her top front teeth.

Cathy screamed as much as she could with a gaping mouth and thrashed against the chair, but it was of no use. The bonds were tight and the chair wasn't coming apart or moving with his body suffocating her movements. Vincent gripped the tooth so hard she could hear it crack under the pressure he was applying with the tool. He began twisting it left and right like pulling a cork. The pain shot through her head like a freight train. He continued to twist and pull. Blood filled her mouth from the roots tearing loose of the tooth deep within the gum line. She coughed and bucked backwards again trying to get him out of her mouth and off of her but it didn't work. The more she fought, the harder her squeezed and twisted.

She could feel her upper gums giving out under the pressure and angle he was pulling the tooth. With a final twist it came free and he let her go. The chair rocked back to the floor into a sitting position and she leaned forward vomiting from the pain. Blood and empty stomach bile landed between her feet. Vincent leaned back on the car hood and watched her recover and take in air. He looked at the jagged, broken tooth for a while between the jaws of the tool then placed it in his pocket.

"Ok, Cathy." Vincent said leaning against the car where he stood before. "Let's start again shall we. What do you and the FBI know about me?"

"I have a list for you sir." Said one of the IT guys from the couch. He was busy running the partial plate and came up with 127 options of plates in the Seattle area that had the same 3 digits at the beginning of the license. Jack leaned over his shoulder and scanned the list.

"Are any of these cars station wagons?" He asked

Karl minimized the screen and pulled up another. Inputting the data fast and hitting enter. A fresh list came up with 54 cars on it.

"Cut all colors except brown, silver, grey and white." He barked.

Fingers flew across the keyboard as Jack talked. He looked over at the other two on the couch that were busy typing. Nobody looked up from the screens. They just punched keys in a flurry like kids afraid to look at the teacher.

"Here it is." He said spinning the laptop so Jack could see. The list was still too long to pick from. 14 of the cars were the right make, color and style with the same starting digits, but nothing else to single them out.

"You" Jack said, pointing to one of the men on the couch. "Crosscheck the names on these 14 vehicles with the parameters I gave to search for our guy. See if any of them are close to a match."

This time nobody spoke up about his choice in naming them and he didn't think they would. Time was wasting right now and Jack knew it. If he was going to find Cathy alive it needed to happen soon or it never would.

If this guy was onto them and was watching what they did there was only one reason he would have to take her. He wanted to know what they knew. He needed to know if he should run or if he could stop this investigation now by eliminating the problem and continue on by simply changing his technique. The information wouldn't be easy to get out of Cathy, but he knew this guy would do it. He would get it any way he could and once he had it, she would be of no more use.

"I got a hit!" The nerdiest looking one of the group said sitting alone on the smaller of the two couches. He was raising his hand like he was in school waiting to be called on. Jack was beside him instantly looking over his shoulder.

"Right here sir." He said, pointing at the screen. "His name is Vincent Holbrook. It says he owns a beige Ford Taurus station wagon. Lives at D-33 Puget Sound Marina. Hang on one second, I am pulling up his financials."

Jack waited but didn't move from the spot. He pointed to the man next to him. "Get me directions to that place. Now!"

"Here you go sir. According to this, the man has no bank account, credit cards or anything current. He actually has no credit history to speak of within the last 15 years. The last transaction I have on him was in 2003 when he drained all his accounts into cash out of a bank in Illinois. Since then nothing. "

"How much are we talking about?" Jack asked.

"14 Million And change sir."

"That's him!" Jack shouted out loud. "Get everything you can on this guy now. Get ahold of Allen and let him know where the house is. You got that map for me yet? Tell him to send a team there ASAP!"

"It's printing now." Nerd #3 chirped.

Jack snatched it off the printer and looked at it. "It's a boat!"

"This guy is off the grid in one of the largest cities on the west coast in a boat. He could be mobile right now with Cathy and we would have no idea where."

"Sir, I have more information. Just got it. According to the city database he has a boat moored in the harbor and a storage unit about a mile away. Both lease agreements have been payed years in advance."

"Get me a location for the unit." Jack barked.

Just at that time, Karl, spoke up from the desk. "I have a video of the car sir, it left out of the west entrance of the parking lot. I lost it for two blocks but picked it up on a street cam heading onto the freeway."

"Does that road lead to the sound?" Jack asked.

"No sir, it's heading south."

The printer began to purr. Jack pulled the paper up and looked at it. He held one page with the location to the marina in his left hand and the storage unit where he obviously was keeping his car in the other. The two locations were about a mile apart from each other and in Seattle traffic the difference could mean life or death for Cathy.

Getting a team geared up and ready to assault the two locations would take hours, maybe more. There was no time to waste. He looked at the 4 men in the room.

"You guys have your side arms?" He asked.

The four of them looked at each other then back at Jack. "Yes sir." Said the one responsible for making the connection between Vincent and the car.

"Good, your gonna need them. Will this computer shit work in the van or does it need to be plugged in?" Jack said pointing to the computers strewn about the room.

"Yes sir, we can operate it all from our Mobile CP outside. It is equipped with the latest…"

"Great let's go!" Jack said cutting him off in mid-sentence before he wasted any more time throwing out multi syllable words that he wouldn't understand.

Jack was at the door barking orders at the men behind him while holding it open. "Let's go! I will take the storage unit with you. "He said pointing toward Karl. "The rest of you head to the Marina. Do not approach the boat unless you see Agent Chambers. Keep your distance and call Allen on the way. Send him everything you have on this guy and get him up to speed with what we are doing. Understand?"

They all nodded at him then back to each other. He saw they were scared. The last time they removed their weapon from the holster was probably when they qualified last year. Right now he didn't care about that. He couldn't be in two places at once and these guys were all he had to work with. He knew Allen would get a team together but knowing how this guy worked, it would be too late for Cathy.

They all crossed the parking lot together then peeled left and right. Jack and Karl went to his rental car and the others to the van. The day was clearing slightly with the sun burning the remaining morning away. He looked at his watch and saw it was already 0830. Cathy had been gone now for over 3 hours. His hopes had gone up slightly in the room when they found the guy and his location, but they dropped now with the hour. They had broken the case and found the guy but catching him no longer mattered to Jack. All he could think about was Cathy and if she was alright.

He started the car and pulled out of his spot skirting the edge of the parking area heading for the exit. He looked over at the three men climbing in the van heading for the marina as he passed by. Each of them had a phone to his ear talking when the Van exploded in a ball of fire.

CHAPTER 37

The tooth coming out was excruciatingly painful but the numbness after it was gone now filled her gum line. Maybe it was shock or her body's own way of protecting itself. She didn't know which but was happy it was happening regardless as the pain drifted away. She spat out another large saliva and blood mixture to the floor while probing the hole where the tooth was with her tongue. It was obvious that her pain meant nothing to him and her chance of making out of this unit alive was getting slimmer by the minute if not altogether gone.

Vincent was back at the table now working again on the metal cage like thing. He was paying zero attention to her and her suffering, but she knew he was watching her every move. The man was crazy, she thought, but not stupid. He had eluded her and the FBI for who knows how long and now that they were close he had snatched her up, making it seem effortless. Once she gave him what he wanted she was finished, but she didn't see how he could kill her here. This was a public storage unit and anything left of her here could lead to him. Not to mention, moving a body around without being seen was no simple task even for him. No, if he was going to kill her, it wasn't going to be here.

He saw she was looking at him again and spoke. "Well Cathy. What do you think? You want to tell me what you and the FBI know or should I practice my new found ability at dentistry again?"

"Please don't. " She heard the words come out of her mouth without knowing she spoke them. She sounded sad and pathetic. Like a woman beaten. That wasn't her. She was strong and capable of more than most. Her life was one she had earned through hard work and dedication. She wouldn't let this fucking psycho beat her, but she needed to play it smart and drag out as much time as she could. Whether or not Jack was looking for her, or the IT team back at the hotel, it didn't matter. What did matter to her was stretching out as much time as she could. Every minute she was here, breathing, tied to the chair, was better than the outcome he had planned even if it meant a lot of pain to pay for it.

"I'm sorry Vincent. I am just scared. You understand that don't you?" She half begged.

He looked at her but didn't stop the assembly at the table.
"No Cathy I don't. Not in any way do I understand that. You see that's the difference between you and me. I am in control of my life and all around me. Nothing scares me or controls me. It's actually quite the opposite. My entire life I have been the hunter, not the prey. I have devoted everything I am to weeding out the weak and unworthy of this world. Why should I share any of it with someone or anyone who is undeserving of it? From the air you breathe to the ground you walk on, you take it all for granted. Like it something you have rights to. You don't, none of you do unless you earn it."

He was crazy. She could hear it in his voice and by the tone he spoke. This guy wasn't mad or angry when he answered her. He was calm and well thought. It sounded like a professor in college giving a lecture he had done before a hundred times. He wasn't listening to voices in his head and following their instructions. He truly believed that what he was doing was right and just. She couldn't think of anything to reach him without sounding like a victim so she went back to her stall.

"Would you please tell me what it is you're building? It's all I can think about Vincent. I will tell you what we know about you and our investigation but, please, I've got to know what you're doing first."

He dropped the socket and pliers both this time. Instead of running over to her and inflicting more pain, which she was mentally preparing herself for, he turned to the table behind him and shuffled through some papers. With one selected, he approached her and laid it on her lap.

"Here you go." He said. "Now, let's continue please. What does the FBI know about me?"

Cathy looked down at the page resting on her legs. The top was titled Pacific Crab Pots, followed by a description of the materials used and a picture of the end result.

She looked up at him and he smiled down at her.

The explosion rocked his car to the right shattering the driver's side window from the blast and causing him to swerve into a parked minivan. He wasn't going fast enough when impact was made to deploy the airbags but it was enough for him to kiss the windshield. He was hoping the car was still operable. Karl was riding shotgun and was now holding his ears and screaming to himself. Jack didn't see any blood on him but he was definitely outside of his comfort zone and falling into his most primal of instincts. Obviously this guy wasn't on the fight end of the "Fight or Flight" spectrum.

Jack slammed the car into park and told him to get out. The man was so busy screaming and rocking back and forth in the seat he didn't hear him say it. Jack reached across the seat and jabbed him once in the jaw with his fist. Not hard enough to knock him out but enough to jolt him out of the state he was in and possibly loosen a couple fillings.

His head bounced off the passenger window glass from the strike. Maybe it wasn't the medical way to snap a person out of temporary hysteria, but the rap on the chin worked and shook him out of the screaming fit. Wide eyed, he looked at Jack, like a kid wanting an explanation to the appearance of the boogyman standing at the foot of his bed.

He was in shock. It was obvious. If it were any other circumstances Jack would've pulled him out of the car, laid him down, elevated his feet and called for an ambulance. He would even try fighting the blaze that was engulfing what was left of the three FBI agents with whatever means he could find. But things were different now. He didn't have time to coddle this guy or fight the blaze just to pull out 3 dead bodies. The situation around had already happened. Whatever he did now wouldn't change this, but he still had a chance to change Cathy's.

The bomb on the van meant this guy was more than just a serial killer whacking people in their homes by using FaceBook or abducting FBI agents at his leisure. It meant he was smart. Knowledgeable enough with explosives to set and wire a bomb to a vehicle without being seen in a very public place. Capable enough to do it all overnight with very little planning time and dedicated enough to execute it without thought. Finding Cathy alive was beginning to seem like a wish more than chance and the more time he wasted here with this sniffling Nerd the worse his chances were getting.

"Call this in and see if there is anything you can do for them!" Jack shouted at Karl standing outside the car pointing at the inferno that was just a moment ago a van with his friends inside. The man was in a dizzy state, floating between consciousness and passing out. He looked lost. He knew the guy didn't understand anything and was on the verge of tears, but he didn't have time to hold his hand. Jack had a slim 50/50 shot at where he would find Cathy and less of a chance that she would be alive when he got there and time was wasting.

"Call 911!" He shouted out the broken window at Karl.

Slamming the car back into gear and pulling around the minivan out of the parking lot. The wheel vibrated only slightly in his hands. The small collision probably bent the fender inward and took out a headlight. Engine sounded fine and the car responded to him without hesitation. He looked at the two maps lying on the seat next to him. One went to the marina and the other to the storage unit owned by the crazy bastard that had Cathy. Both were the same distance from where he was, give or take a couple blocks. But, if he made the wrong choice, it would take twice the time to get back to the other and he knew she didn't have time for him to be wrong. He prayed to himself swerving through traffic getting onto the highway that he wasn't late and she would be alive when he got there.

"Why are you building a crab pot?" She asked him already dreading the answer she was sure she already knew. Or worse, dreading his reply with more pain because she was still stalling and it was pretty obvious by now.

Vincent ignored the question and kept working. The Crab pot appeared to be nearly finished. At least from her angle it looked like the photo on her lap. It was large. Big enough for her to fit in and she was certain that was his plan. Why else would he be doing it? It's not like he stopped his killing spree and kidnapping to take up crabbing in the NorthWest.

The clicking sound of the ratchet echoed in the unit as he worked. Piece by piece he assembled the thing. He seemed totally focused on his project and didn't utter a sound while he worked. Only once did she see him look at his watch then back to the project at hand.

Behind him a tiny bell went off. It sounded like a timer on an oven indicating the food was ready. A simple 3 tone alarm that would seem normal anywhere but here. Vincent set the tools down and looked at his watch again smiling.

"Well, Special Agent Chambers, looks like we have run out of time. I was really hoping to find out more from you but it seems you just do not want to participate. Which is fine with me really. I don't mind. I was ready for you not to say anything and quite honestly, you have impressed me slightly. You are a strong person. I give you credit for that. But, unfortunately that bell means we must be leaving now regardless of the information you have."

"Where? Why did you build a crab pot? What was the bell for?" She was scared. His methods and attitude were so cold and calculated it was terrifying. She doubted he even saw her as a person. Just a means to get something done, a piece in a sick puzzle. Killing her would mean no more to Vincent than stepping on a bug. He was on a mission and she was simply a little cog in the machine required to accomplish it.

Vincent ignored her questions completely this time and walked past her, leaving the crab pot finished on the table where he was working. Pushing the button for the door to open he got behind the wheel of the car, started it and backed out of the unit. She sat silent watching him pull out. A tiny spark of hope filled her thinking maybe, just maybe he was done with her and going to just leave her here tied up to be found later. Maybe he had a change of heart and was going on the run. Maybe he would just disappear into the folds of criminal history and she would live. Then he stopped the car. Executed a three point turn and backed up until the rear hatchback was resting just inside the entrance.

He opened the rear of the vehicle and began moving things around to allow room for his newly built project. Within 5 minutes he was done and it fit perfectly in the rear of the station wagon. He must have known this upon purchasing it. The pot filled the space up to the bottom of the windows and did not stick up above. Driving down the road you would have no idea it was in the car. Cathy's heart sank at the site of it in the car. She knew she was going to be put inside and once there, she could only think of one place it was going.

He went to work cleaning up the remnants of his work. He never spoke a word while doing it. Maybe he was done with her. Maybe he really didn't need to know anything and his reason for keeping her here was different than what he said. Maybe he was going to load up the vehicle and leave. She lied to herself as she watched him.

After the car was loaded and the clean-up was done Vincent removed the top to a five gallon can of gas that was sitting on the shelves near the rear of the unit and began pouring it across everything inside. He doused the shelves, workbench, tool box and rows of items stack along them. He wasn't splashing it about in a hurry like a man being rushed by time, but simply pouring it everywhere to ensure all was sufficiently covered. After the can was empty he opened another and repeated the exercise.

Cathy began to shake in the chair.

CHAPTER 38

He took the next exit for the Marina off the interstate and floored the accelerator. Everything back in the Hotel room pointed toward the storage unit. That's where he kept his car so that would be where Cathy was for certain. He didn't have any place else to store a body or a car out of sight. But after the Van went up it changed things for Jack. This guy wasn't just covering his tracks and putting the screw to the FBI. He was planning on getting away. He may have taken her initially to find out what the FBI knew about him but she could also be used as a small bit of insurance to give him time to disappear if things went south. He could've taken her just out of pure revenge for getting too close and causing him to stop. If that was the case, the boat was the only possible place they could be and if she was still alive when he pulled out of the harbor for the Pacific Jack knew she wouldn't see land again.

Cathy's phone rang on the seat next to him. He saw the name Allen on the screen and picked it up. A green circle with the picture of a phone was flashing in sequence with the ringing on the front. Jack touched it once, hoping it would answer and not pull up some other worthless application installed on the thing.

"Hello?" Came from the speaker into his ear.

Jack let out a sigh of relief that he didn't screw up answering the thing and started talking. "Allen, its Jack, listen up. This guy has taken Cathy, his name is Vincent Holbrook. He has a boat in the marina down at the harbor in Seattle. I think that's where he's going. I'm on the way there now. You have 3 men down back at the hotel. Send Emergency Services as soon as you can."

"What happened?" Allen asked.

"The guy put a VBIED on their van and it went off when they started it. Not sure if he command detonated or if it was wired to the ignition system. Doesn't matter. I think he is making a run for it. Find out everything you can on this guy and get the Harbor Patrol and Coast Guard on the line to stop the boat from leaving. I should be there in the next 20 min but if I don't make it, this guy can't be allowed to get away."

"I will make the call and get EMS to the Hotel. I have a team heading to the storage units' location you sent me earlier. The Marina team is on the way as well, but you will beat them if you're already on the road. I will contact the harbor patrol as well, but it is a weekend and it's still early."

He knew Allen was worried about Cathy not to mention he was plagued with the unfortunate situation of being in charge and completely helpless. At least Jack was here and moving to do something. Allen was stuck on the East Coast hearing all this second hand and waiting for it to play out.

The fuel was covering the floor and pooling around her feet. It didn't bother Vincent that it was on his shoes or creeping toward the entrance of the unit and the rear tires of the car. He continued until he emptied 3 cans in the small space. The fumes inside were getting too much for her and she began to cough. Even with the large door open, the mixture of exhaust from the idling car just outside the door and the amount of gas was causing her breathing problems.

After emptying the last can Vincent removed a small square device from his pocket. It looked like a garage door opener. A simple thing no larger than a beeper. He pushed a button and it illuminated green on one side with a single audible beep. That's when he stepped in front of her and spoke for the first time in almost since he began his cleanup process.

"Cathy. In the back of my car is my newly built Crab Pot. As I am sure you have guessed, I made it for you. However, with my timeline being sped up slightly due to your friends back at the hotel, I need to change my plans slightly. Not a big deal and nothing I have not anticipated. The end results will be the same, but because I do have a small amount of respect for you I will give you an option. Mind you, this is a one-time offer and not open for discussion. A simple yes or no is all I want to hear from you. Do you understand?"

She was terrified beyond the ability to form any other response than the one syllable he was requesting. "Yes." She said nodding and blinking from the fumes.

"Good." He said, smiling at her. "That little beep you heard earlier was a notification that the explosive device I had wired to your FBI van back at the hotel had gone off. It is telling me that your men discovered you were gone and were leaving to come find you. I can only assume that through the cameras displayed around the parking area they discovered my car, saw me taking you, my plates and have found out my name. Therefore, we need to get moving. Do you understand?"

"Yes." She answered.

"That's good Cathy. Very good. I was planning on a little more time with you, but your peoples have appeared to be more capable than I gave them credit for. Surprising really. The men I saw at the library did not look like experienced agents. They all had the look of younger, less field worthy FBI. But, none of that really matters now."

Cathy listened to him. If what he was saying was true, the IT team was gone. He must've been watching them at the Library and Hotel. Most likely sitting in plain site because he knew they didn't have a description yet. He was right about the van and her IT team but he didn't mention Jack. Maybe he wasn't aware he was part of the search for him. If he planted something on the Van and nothing else, it means he thought they were it. Maybe Jack was on his way now? If he got a video of Vincent's car, he definitely would've been able to track him down using her team. Jack wouldn't have them leave if they didn't have a lead on her location. There was still a chance. She needed time. She needed to stall.

"So, here is my offer to you Cathy. It's very simple and please do not waste too much time deciding or I will decide for you." Vincent said.

The gasoline had covered the floor now and was running out the open door under the car, pooling in the low spot of the road between units. None of this seemed to bother him or concern him in any way. If this was a public storage unit, it was only a matter of time before someone came by and noticed the scene, but obviously that was of no concern to Vincent. He didn't do anything without planning it so this was just another step he was taking on his route. The man was crazy. Cathy was sure he was going to burn her where she sat along with the entire structure then drive away like nothing had happened.

"If you would like to climb into the crab pot in my vehicle I will cut your bonds and allow you to do so. I am sure you are aware of the fate that awaits you with that decision. Or, you can stay here in this chair and this timer will to go off igniting the gasoline and burning you alive. It is very simple Ms. Chambers. Do you want to burn or drown? Please understand that this is the day you are going to die, nothing will change that. But I will let you decide how out of respect."

The decision for her was simple. Have him cut her loose and she will fight her way out or die trying. If today was gonna be her last day and this guy was to be her end, she would make him earn every bit of it.

"I don't want to burn." She said, looking up at him. She was doing her best to sound beaten and spent. She was reserving all her strength for the moment he cut her loose.

"That works for me Agent." He said while setting the timer and placing it on the back shelf of the unit.

He walked back to the rear of the car, leaned in and propped the top of the crab cage up. She was almost certain it wasn't designed to do that and he had made modifications for the sole purpose of accommodating her to fit inside. With it open and waiting for her like a cartoon trap set for the road runner, he returned to the work bench and picked up a red cleaning rag and a roll of duct tape. He balled the rag up to the size of a baseball and stood beside her.

She knew he intended to gag her with it and there was nothing she could do to prevent it. They must be someplace where a scream would be heard and attract unwanted attention. Maybe she would risk a shout.

Before she could contest to the gag and get the scream out, he yanked her ponytail back again like before and forced the wadded up rag in her mouth. She fought with her tongue to keep it from going further down her throat and choking her. He was fast and efficient with the tape. Her head was wrapped so tightly the pressure was causing her vacant tooth cavity and head to throb in pain.

He was in a hurry. She could tell. After she was muzzled he stood between her legs again and removed a knife from his pocket.

"Let's make this quick, shall we Special Agent. I do not have all day and I am only doing this because I believe you have earned the right to choose you're fate. But make no mistake, if you fight me or delay me any longer than necessary, I will open you like a fish right here and burn what is left. Do you understand?" Vincent asked her in that cold and deliberate tone he used.

She nodded to him and blinked back tears. He was smart and was taking every precaution but it wasn't enough. The moment her bonds were cut she would show him how just how much of a predator she was! She readied herself to jump the second she was free. If he cut her loose from the front her plan was to slam her head into his nose, hopefully breaking it on the initial impact. She would follow it immediately by a shoulder under his chin forcing him up off his feet while she stood up and putting all her weight behind her smashing him to the ground. With any luck his larynx would be crushed between her and the gas soaked floor killing him or at the very least giving her a chance to get away.

If he cut her loose from behind, she would do the opposite but use the chair to pin him against the wall while cracking him as hard as possible with a backward head butt using the wall behind him to increase the damage. Then, instead of trying to subdue him, she would gain distance and take the idling car only 15 feet away. In either scenario, the chances of him lashing out with the blade and causing multiple injuries was going to happen but it was better than the other two options she had of burning or drowning. She tensed up slightly and waited for him to choose how to cut her loose.

Vincent smiled at Cathy with the same grin he did last time and sank the full 6 inches of the blade into her right thigh then the left.

CHAPTER 39

Jack found himself in the morning rush of Seattle traffic. He laid on the horn and flashed his lights but it did no good. It wasn't grid lock but moving slow and every person he saw was fumbling with a phone, a cup of coffee and a steering wheel. This along with the adrenalin he had pumping through his veins it seemed like he was standing still and the world was against him. Changing lanes and tying side streets to get ahead only resulted in the same slow drudge of morning commuters and gained him nothing.

According to the map he was only 3 miles from the Marina. He was hoping to be there in less than 10 minutes, but it wasn't looking promising. The thought of getting to Cathy in time started to weigh on him. The reality was he had no idea where she was or if she was even alive. He was trusting his gut now and running on instinct. The phone rang on the seat next to him. Scooping it up, hitting the green button again he answered.

"This is Jack." He said taking an open spot in the left lane that just appeared when a city bus turned off. He cut off another car and moved ahead 50 feet.

"Jack, its Allen. I have the Seattle Police heading to the storage unit and the Marina right now. They should be there in 15 minutes. A BOLO has been sent out on the car so if he tries to run he will get picked up. We are locking the Seattle area down. Where are you now?"

"Stuck in traffic, maybe 10 out from the Marina. If this clears up less. This guy is sharp Allen, make sure the PD knows to keep their eyes open. He already torched one vehicle. Wouldn't surprise me if he has something else waiting especially since he knows we are onto him."

"Understood. I received some background on the guy that one of our people pulled up. Turns out he has been bad since he was a child."

Jack swerved right to miss a parked car unloading a bunch of kids. He bounced the front fender off an SUV forcing it into another car in the next lane over. Horns and shouting erupted behind him, but it opened up a lane in front and he shot down it.

"What was that?" Allen asked through the earpiece.

"Nothing, don't worry about it. You were saying this guy was bad since when?" Jack asked piloting the car like he was in a demolition derby.

"I was saying his parents were murdered in their sleep almost 25 years ago on Halloween night. He was only 12 at the time and found sleeping in his room safe and sound the next morning. He was completely safe and untouched. A local contractor and landscape worker was convicted and got life without parole."

"You think this guy killed his parents when he was 12?" Jack asked, dodging a pickup truck with a canoe sticking out the back.

"Well, if this is the guy and it sounds like it is, his parents were loaded. Stupid rich. Makes no sense for some random landscape worker to kill them and take nothing.

Vincent took over the family business after graduating from college then sold it all. Even sold the house he grew up in. Then disappeared. Gone, off the grid until today."

"This guy has been off the grid all this time for one reason Allen. He has been killing anyone he wants for whatever reason he can think of that's why you have never connected him. He is straight batshit crazy and to make it worse, he is rich and smart!"

"Listen Jack, I know you want to find Cathy and you feel somewhat responsible for her but you are a civilian in this. I am supporting you because of your past and your help with the case, probably more because we have nobody else there right now, but as soon as the Police or FBI show up, you need to stand down and let them take over. Understand?"

Jack hung up the phone without answering and threw it back onto the passenger seat. He never really liked Allen anyway and if he thought he was going to stand down before he knew she was safe, he obviously forgot who he was talking to. He would worry about what laws he was breaking after he knew Cathy was safe. He braked hard then swerved to the left onto the sidewalk, blowing the horn.

People were jumping back into coffee shops and out into the street to avoid him barreling down the sidewalk. He was hoping not to hit anyone full on but if he did, he wasn't going fast enough to kill em so it didn't matter. A broken leg or two, maybe some emotional scaring would be worth getting Cathy back safe. They could all get together later and sue him with an army of lawyers. If he failed to get to Cathy in time, nothing else mattered.

A small sign ahead with an arrow on it pointing toward a dock and a boat on a trailer sat on the right side of the road across two lanes of traffic. Jack spun the wheel off the sidewalk hitting the front of a car sending it sideways into the next lane and shot down the street. He could see the water for the first time since he left the hotel. The tops of sailboat masts littered the horizon.

He was close.

Cathy screamed behind her gag when Vincent stabbed her and withdrew the blade. She bucked backwards, slamming the chair against the wall and tumbling over onto the side crushing her left hand between the floor and chair. She heard the bone snap in her finger on impact. The blood pumping from her legs soaked her legs turning them red and pooled around her on the floor. She choked back the rag in her throat while she inhaled from the pain and screaming. The fumes made her eyes water to the point of blindness being this close and she could feel the wetness of the gasoline on her cheek.

"Ok, Cathy, are you ready to get into my cage or do you want to stay here?" Vincent said, looking down from above.

She tried to nod her head yes that she wanted to get into the cage and no she didn't want to stay here at the same time. She was incapable of doing anything now except uncontrolled whimpers and twitches. Her legs would be worthless in a fight and even if she did, somehow get free, how far would she get?

Vincent knelt down and cut the rope connecting her hands to her feet. Then he separated the bonds holding her to the chair. She tried to stand, but wasn't capable and fell back to the blood and gas soaked concert floor. He had punctured the muscles in both thighs causing spasmodic reactions in her legs making her incapable of controlling them. They were limp noodles under her. Limp, bleeding appendages that would be the death of her if not treated soon.

Grabbing her like a rag doll and giving no care for her pain or injuries, Vincent left her hands tied behind her back and using them as a lifting point, he heaved her off the ground and tossed her up into the back of the car. Only the top half of her body made it over the side of the cage on the first attempt. Her legs crashed into the rear of the vehicle right where he stabbed her, shooting a new wave of pain through her.

The pain was so bad she had to swallow back vomit because she would surely drown being unable to get it out beyond the gag. The top of the cage came down from where he had it propped up by the impact and smashed her head down sending stars into her vision. Vincent folded her the rest of the way inside and shut the cage.

Her world went Dark.

The phone continued to ring on the seat next to him. He had no intention of answering it. The news on the other end could only be bad or worse and he could do nothing with either. He wasn't in the mood for anything but finding Cathy. If the Seattle PD found the storage unit and Cathy was dead, he didn't want to know. If it was Allen to tell him what to do, or what not to do, he wasn't listening. The only other option would be they did find her alive and that would mean Vincent was getting away. His boat was the only way he could do that and Jack wasn't going to let that happen.

Pulling into the marina parking lot, Jack was stunned at the amount of boats floating in front of him. Hundreds of them. As far as he could see were sitting neatly spaced and rocking in unison to the waves. He didn't have time to look for D-22. He didn't even know where to start. It could take hours to find the right dock and time was something Cathy didn't have right now.

At the end of the parking lot was a trailer with the word "Office" stenciled on the side. Jack locked up the brakes directly in front of the small building and slammed the shifter into park before the car was fully stopped. He snatched the phone off the seat and took off at a dead run, leaving his door open. The woman inside must have seen him coming because she was wide eyed and silent when he burst through the door.

"D-22, where is it?" Jack demanded in the calmest voice he could manage, but was sure that it came out as an order more than a request.

The woman was older but not in grandmother status yet. She was weathered like the building but had a tint of authority left in her.

"Excuse me sir, but may I ask, is there a problem?"

Jack pulled out Cathy's FBI again and flashed it to her while covering up the picture. "It's a Federal matter ma'am and I need the location of slip D-22 right now!"

Without giving the ID a second look or question him, she pulled a map from underneath the counter. It was littered with hundreds of identical, evenly spaced dash marks all divided by long arms. It looked like a giant comb with hairs growing out of the teeth. She circled one of them down near the end of a section consisting of six rows. "Right here." She said with attitude in her voice.

"What's the fastest way to it?" Jack demanded.

She rolled her eyes and sighed heavily then went back to the map. "You are right here! In my office!" She snapped. "You need to go around the front of the office, down to the wharf using this road and park in the owners parking area at the shoreline. From there you take the second dock on the right and it's the second to last slip on the left. D-22"

Jack grabbed the map and headed for the door.

"Of course you will need the key card to open the gate and only owners of moorages get those." She said as he was stepping out.

CHAPTER 40

Cathy woke to the sound of birds and scratching sounds. Her eyes adjusted to the light and the smell hit her. Saltwater, the ocean. She was outside. A seagull sat on the top of the cage only inches from her face. The tiny webbed feet sporadically dancing across the top then it was gone. The squelch and squawk of more birds filled her ears. She tried to raise her head to look but it was impossible. The cage was barely large enough for her to fit in. Stuck in a fetal position on her side with her hands behind her back, the only thing she could see was a portion of the ocean and what looked like the side of a wooden boat. Moving was impossible not to mention unbearably painful.

Waves of pain covered her like a blanket. The fresh wounds in her thighs pulsed in rhythm to her heart in beats of fire. Her head was swimming with blurs and random dots of light at the corners of her vision. She tried to focus on anything to get her bearings but in no time it would drift into another fuzzy image making her head hurt worse. She didn't remember being pulled from the car or getting on the boat. Only the storage unit and torture she just endured filled the grey space of her memory. The ride here was nonexistent and now seeing the water so close, she was sure Vincent was going to keep his promise to her.

"You have had a very eventful day Special Agent." Vincent said looking down into the cage at her. "You started with the closest you have ever gotten to me and meeting in person. Now you will end it by being the first person to have ever been on my boat since I have lived here."

From her perspective he looked like a huge black monster of a man. The sun was behind him blocking out his features and shadowing his form. The gag in her mouth was soaked with blood and saliva preventing any sounds from exiting. The mixture was flowing down her throat causing the gag reflex when she looked up at him from her soon to be watery coffin. Only turning her head down and allowing what fluids could drain, pour from her nose and around the soaked cloth would allow her to breath. Every time she sniffed in more of the liquid would shoot down the windpipe and cause a coughing fit that would get snuffed by the red rag and more gagging would ensue. She doubted she would last long even if she didn't go in the water.

If her breathing held and she could control it enough to survive she was certain bleeding out would occur within an hour. The wounds on her legs still pumped blood. She could feel the weakness in her from losing so much of the precious fluid already. Cathy had no thoughts of survival. No instincts she could go on or possible outcomes that in any way would render her living through this. The man was smart, and in total control of her now. He had won and there was nothing she could do but wait for it to come and Vincent to decide how.

"If you don't mind too terribly Cathy, I must make ready so we can push off. I don't want to send you to the bottom of the Puget Sound here. This area is littered with power cables, pipelines, and old wreckage of all kinds. If you can believe it, some people actually dump their waste right here in the harbor. I don't feel it fitting for you here. Instead, I will be dropping you out farther. Much farther. Someplace deep in the Pacific was my plan. Maybe between here and Hawaii. That part of the ocean is beautiful and full of the most amazing creatures I have heard."

She heard him walk away and begin to move things around on the boat. They were still moored somewhere, that was good, but she had no idea where and neither did anyone else.

She closed her eyes and prayed.

Jack flew around the corner of the office in the car, screeching to a stop inches from the gate. He got out and swiped the key card he secured from the less than helpful woman at the main office. The thing beeped once and started to lift. Getting back in, he was certain a call was being made right now to the Seattle PD about a man that threatened her at gun point and posing as an FBI agent had stolen her keys and was busy committing unknown atrocities in the Marina.

If he was wrong and Cathy wasn't here, he would gladly turn over the gun and himself to the authorities. It would mean she was gone, he had failed and it wouldn't matter anyway. His feelings for her that were driving his actions were surprising him. He must have more than professional care and loyalty pushing to get her back safely.

With the gate bar lifting up on a poorly oiled hinge, making it take twice as long as needed, Jack got back behind the wheel and shot under it before it was fully raised. The bottom of the drop arm gate scraped hard on the roof then crashed back down after he had passed under it. Great, he thought to himself. He is gonna have to buy them a new gate when this is over. Just tack that onto the long list of reimbursements he will be stuck with.

Down a steep hill to almost the water line was a parking lot large enough for small cars only. Nothing with a trailer was parked anywhere to be seen. This had to be the place owners of the boats moored here would park and leave their vehicles. Nearest the ramp, backed directly up to a dock was a beige Ford Taurus Station wagon. Jacks heart pumped harder in his chest than it had before. He was here. Which meant Cathy was here. He prayed he wasn't late.

A loud screeching sound bounced off the water and reached her ears. It was louder than a bird and lasted longer than it should. It sounded like metal being drug against metal and was out of place with the sounds around her.

Instantly, the pounding steps of Vincent on the deck of the boat approached and his shadowy figure appeared above her again. He stood motionless looking over her cage toward something beyond her vision. It seemed to be the direction of the sound she just heard. Vincent didn't move. He stood and watched.

Cathy tried to adjust her head in the cage to see out but it was impossible. The most she was able to accomplish was increasing the pain in her legs and wrists by doing it. The cage bumped hard and jarred her head against the side. The pain came back in a wave.

She looked at the deck of the boat under the bottom of the cage and saw it was moving. She turned her head back toward Vincent. He was pulling her. He was moving her to the edge to throw her in! This was it. He lied and wasn't taking her out to the middle of the Pacific he was going to drown her right now!

Cathy didn't know what it would do but she squirmed like a worm on a hook from inside the cage. She howled as loud as she could through the gag and moved whatever part of her body she could regardless of the pain in response to him dragging her closer to the edge. She couldn't die like this. Maybe he would slip and fall trying to pull her over. Maybe the cage would break and she could go in the water out of site. She was hoping and praying for anything when she saw the water below her and the cage stopped moving.

Cathy stopped squirming when it stopped and an eerie silence filled her head. The black water below her was so close now. Only a few feet away. Dark, deep and cold. It was lifeless and void of emotion. Just waiting for her to come in.

"Cathy. Cathy, can you hear me?"

Vincent was talking to her. She could hear him but it sounded so far away and almost fictional. Like a mediator in a children's book talking from the clouds.

She turned back to look the best she could and saw that he was kneeling beside her on the deck of the boat. He was so close to her now she could smell him. Bleach and oil gathered in her nostrils with bile, blood and salty sea air. He leaned in close to the cage like he was trying to whisper a secret that nobody would ever know because he would throw her over the moment it was spoken.

"Cathy, I am sorry for not taking you out to the ocean like I promised. I am normally a man of my word. However it seems my schedule must be pushed even farther ahead. I do hope you understand."

She tried to plead with her eyes but there were no more tears in her. She was broken and empty.

Vincent looked at her long and hard, then back up in the direction of the sound. He rose to his feet and walked away, all the while talking. This time loud enough for her to hear him without issue and possibly anyone within earshot.

"So, special agent Chambers I am gathering that you have not been working alone on this case. I suspect that you have had some help! Possibly from a man. A man from your past? A man that is not in the FBI!"

His words were bouncing around in her head like a spilled box of scrabble tiles. She was trying to put them together and understand it when the rumble from the motors of the boat began to vibrate underneath her. He had started the engines and was leaving. She would be dead any minute.

Vincent returned to the cage and reached for it. She squirmed away as far as she could but gained only inches. His hands only came through the webbing of the cage with fingertips while threading a rope in and out.

"I truly can't believe I am doing this Cathy. I really can't. But, as I said before, I do have a tiny amount of respect for you." Vincent said, finishing his knot and vanishing from her site again.

Jack slammed the car in park and bolted out the door with the pistol up and ready in his hands. He ran to the Taurus and found it empty. The doors were unlocked and the back hatch was still open. Inside he could smell gasoline and saw large smears of blood on the rear carpet like someone was dragged out. The site of the blood, knowing it belonged to Cathy turned his stomach.

Spinning to the docks and the direction the lady had indicated on the map by circling one of the slips, he saw movement and it caught his eye. At the far left end of the second dock, he saw a man standing up staring at him from the back of a large wooden boat. The man didn't move just stared at him, like he knew him. Jack watched him long enough to count the slips between him and read the dock sign to realize he was looking at D-22 and Vincent Holbrook.

Without a second thought, Jack took off in a dead run down the loading ramp onto the dock. He was 50 yards away and gaining, but with all the boats and pilings moored to them he could never risk a shot. 35 yards now, he passed a vacant slip and caught a glimpse of the boat again. It was moving, he was pulling out! Jack ran harder.

25 yards and the sound of the engine could be heard. It wasn't roaring or opened up like he was trying for a speedy getaway. It was deep and thumping at an idle out of the Marina. 15 yards and only 2 boats in between him and a clean shot at the man. Jack rounded the last boat and the entire boat came into clear view. Vincent was standing on the back deck of his boat only 15 feet away from the dock. He was smiling at him and waving his left hand.

Jack raised the pistol and lined up the sites in the center of the man's chest. He started to squeeze, but before he could fire Vincent kicked a large black cage off the side of the boat that he had been resting his foot on. The movement of the cage pulled his attention from the sites for a split second and Jack recognized Cathy's blue eyes staring at him from inside the cage then it disappeared under the watery blackness.

Time has the ability to make an event faster than you can see or stand still and seem like an eternity. Jack was caught in the slow speed of time while he watched it unfold in half speed only 15 feet away.

The image of Cathy crammed inside the cage, bloody and bruised with duct tape wrapped around her would be something he never forgot. Her crystal blue eyes filled with redness and tears were staring directly at him, helplessly before they vanished under the water. The man waving at him on the boat didn't speak a word, just pointed to Jacks feet then turned back to the front of the boat and walked away.

Either by the direction Vincent indicated or the movement at his feet that caught his attention, Jack looked down and saw the rope whipping into the water from the coil laying on the dock.

He dropped the gun and grabbed the last foot of the rope before it vanished under the waves. It jerked him forward with so much force that if the piling had not been there, stopping him, he would've been yanked off the dock with it. Jack pulled on the rope and began to haul it up. It was heavy and strained every muscle he had doing it. Hand over hand Jack heaved the heavy cage with Cathy inside closer to the surface. He prayed out loud for her to be alive and to have the strength to get her up in time.

With every pull on the wet rope he pictured her beaten and alone. The image of her took him back to the floor of that nightmare basement so many years ago. He saw her helpless again. He saw the crazy murdering bastard above her with the weapon. Jack could smell the smoke and blood in the air. He was sure the men on the stairs were dead. They had taken the full assault of death played out by the man waiting below in the dark.

Jack knew he was hit and could feel the warmth under his vest seeping down into his pants. He didn't know how bad it was but he could still function. He knew Cathy was helpless on the floor at his feet. Her weapon was out of reach and the fall had to of broken at least her arm if not more. She wheezed out a syllable but he couldn't understand it. All he knew was the man had reloaded and was now turning his attention toward her.

Jack raised his pistol and fired as he ran. The sound of his weapon drew the man's attention from her on the floor as well as the rounds impacting him. Being hit didn't stop the maniac and he raised the weapon in his direction. Jack felt the rounds hitting him but didn't stop his own firing. All he could think of was Cathy and stopping this man from hurting her.

Jack was oblivious to the sound of the engines roaring to life from Vincent's boat. He didn't care that he was heading out to the Pacific at full speed and would soon be gone. He didn't care what direction he was going or even to look up after him. The sirens from the Police cruisers arriving at the parking lot sounded distant and unreal to him as he pulled. Everything that mattered to him was at the end of this rope and he gave everything he had to get to it.

Like shouting in a tunnel, he heard voices barking orders at him from a distance. He didn't stop.

He wondered how long she could hold her breath. How long would she survive? She had to live. She was a fighter. She was strong he told himself. She lived through so much, she had to live. He yanked on the wet rope.

The voices grew louder the closer they got. Jack began to recognize what they were saying but he didn't care. They told him to stop, drop what he was doing and put his hands in the air. He didn't listen. Hand over hand he strained to get her up to the air again. The pounding of boots on the dock sounded like thunder to him and only made him pull faster.

Just when the men were only feet away, the edge of the cage broke the surface. Instantly the weight of the thing increased as the buoyancy provided by the water vanished and gravity took control of it.

Jack let go of the rope, dropped to his belly to grab ahold of the cage with both hands. It was large and bulky but he was gaining. He wouldn't let her slip out now.

The shouting in his ear was deafening as the first cop barked orders from directly behind him. Only seconds later did the man see what Jack had ahold of and helped him get the cage and Cathy onto the dock.

"Call an ambulance!" Jack barked at the two men.

The hum of the engines became more and more distant until they faded completely away into silence. Jack looked out to ocean and the direction Vincent went, but he was gone. Not even the trail from his wake was left.

CHAPTER 41

"Request accepted." He said to himself closing out of one screen and opening another. The search bar appeared and he began typing. All the while he smiled to himself and the thought of the hunt he was about to partake. Within an hour he was done and closed the laptop.

Leaving the café and walking the streets back to the marina, Vincent thought about the woman that just accepted him. He wondered who would be at the home when he got there and what method he would be given to end them when he arrived. Maybe it would be violent and bloody. Possibly using a machete. He had never used one before. The thought did appeal to him. Or maybe it would be quiet and subtle. Possibly strangle her and that would be it. She might try to fight back or just cry like most of them did.

The last few months of his life had been a great joy to him. As he continued on his path while honing his skills and abilities even sharper than before. Like the caterpillar evolves into something bigger and better, so was he. He thanked Agent Chambers for all her help she gave him in accomplishing this as well as the man Jack that had rescued her. He apparently was very paramount in locating Vincent. Without them he would have never learned the errors he had made. They helped him more than they realized. Now, with this new found power and knowledge he would travel the world doing his work and not be stagnant in one place like he was for so long before.

Life gives you opportunities, he thought to himself and he took full advantage of them. Perhaps it was a rebirth for him. Perhaps deleting all he had worked for so many years back in Seattle was a necessary cleansing for him and he came out anew. Emerging reborn from the crumble of his former self into a life better, stronger and more capable. Only in losing something does one truly appreciate what they have. Vincent was better and stronger now because of it.

The walk down to the harbor was short and easy. He didn't need to go far anymore to get a signal and find a worthy hunt. The world supplied him with WiFi anywhere he went now. The need for constant camera avoidance and disguises was a concern he didn't have. This area was ripe for his harvest and he was eager to spread his work wherever it was needed.

During spring break the area was full of the world's people. All different cultures merged here making his work international without having to travel. So many were here and oblivious to anything around them. He could be invisible standing directly in front of a person.

Privacy and seclusion were easily purchased in Mexico. Along with his ability to go completely unnoticed. Taking the water taxi out to his boat anchored off the Baja peninsula, Vincent wondered if this driver's wife was the one that had just accepted him. Would he be visiting her soon? Maybe he would see the man and his family in the next day or two. Would the man recognize him before Vincent ended him? Would he kill him before the woman or let him watch? The thought filled him with energy and anxiety. He loved the idea.

Tipping the man a moderate amount, not too much to raise suspicion and invite unwelcome attention but enough to keep his services when needed, Vincent climbed off the water taxi and aboard his boat then waved him off.

His new vessel wasn't as old as his last, but it was larger by another 15 feet and by all standards of society much nicer, as well as more modernized. He personally felt it was plain and without any character but, it blended perfectly with the others anchored around him so he made it home.

He purchased the vessel a couple months ago from a recluse millionaire he had befriended off the coast of California. The man was much like Vincent in many ways and longed for his privacy. Purchasing it with cash was easy for him and disappearing on the vessel was effortless.

The 70 ft. boat was at perfect harmony with the sea. It glided over the water without issue. The boat was capable of being manned by only one person thanks to all the automatic features and upgraded electronic modifications it had. The world would be at his disposal with the boat. Free to hunt wherever he felt the need.

After a day of wandering the street and finding his next hunt he was always famished. A good meal and maybe relaxing with a new book would be the best way to end his day before planning his hunt.

The evening sun was beginning to set and soon the Pacific coast line would be a marvel of color as the sun gave up its rights to the sky but before the moon took control. He would watch it after dinner from his viewing deck then go to bed.

In the Galley that was large enough for a full kitchen staff, he prepared a salad with grilled chicken and only a splash of oil and vinegar for flavor. It was accompanied with a fresh pineapple cut up and mixed with grapes and strawberries. Normally he wouldn't splurge like this, but he was having a marvelous day and a little extra fruit wouldn't hurt. Besides, he had no doubt the empty calories would be used up shortly.

After his meal was done and he had cleaned up, Vincent went up to the deck to take in the setting sun. Immediately he saw he had moved. His boat had slipped from its mooring line and drifted out of the bay deeper into the openness of the sea. With the rocking of the boat a norm and no windows in the galley below decks he didn't realize it had happened. From the looks of how far he was, he had been floating away for at least an hour now. It was a marvel he had floated past the other yachts without making contact.

Frustrated with the strength in the ropes he had purchased and sure that was the reason for the drift and not his ability to tie a functioning knot he went up to the main cabin to start the engines and bring the vessel back to the mooring buoy.

Vincent opened the door to the bridge and standing in the opening next to his captain's chair was Cathy Chambers, alive, well and aiming the Taser directly at him. She pulled the trigger and both prongs shot out imbedding themselves into his chest. Vincent fell backwards to the floor of the cabin in a spastic convulse of muscle and grunting sounds.

When the jolting current stopped and he was able to regain his senses Vincent attempted to get up. Raising his head first and getting to a half sitting position was all he could do when he heard a man's voice behind him that he didn't recognize. His world went black.

"How do you like Mexico, Vincent?"

He could hear two voices but only recognized one of them. He saw Agent Chambers on the bridge, but it wasn't possible. How could it be? How could she possibly know where he was?

Opening his eyes Vincent found himself on the rear deck of his boat. His hands were bound behind him and his feet were secured to his wrists. The sun had set and the moon was high in the sky. Vincent rolled his head around looking at the horizon but saw nothing. No lights, no land, nothing.

"Vincent, how are you liking Mexico?" Jack asked him again.

He loathed the man for speaking to him. He hated him and wanted him dead for stepping foot into his home. He would kill him and the woman. This he promised. They could not do this to him! This time he would cut her to pieces and make him watch.

"Why are you here? You have no jurisdiction here. You're not even in the FBI! A worn out FBI agent with a crush on a whore. That's all you are. Now get the fuck off my boat!" Vincent yelled.

"Don't waste all your oxygen Vince. Nobody out here but us. Won't do you any good." Jack said looking down at him while he cracked open a beer and took a long swig.

Vincent pulled at his hands but they were tight. Very tight. His feet wouldn't budge either. He was tied to something on the deck of the boat. It was like he was bolted down. The most he could do was lift his head because his entire body was tied up.

"Where are the lights and sirens Jack?" Vincent asked.

"Oh you probably won't be seeing any bright lights. I would imagine there will be sirens of a sort where you're going though. Don't worry about that." Jack said looking down at him again.

"Where is that whore I should've killed that shot me with the Taser?" Vincent spat out.

"That is a good question Vince, let's see. Hey babe? Where you at?" Jack called out.

"Coming" came a voice from below and out of site. It sounded like it came from his room. "I found it Jack. We're good to go!"

"Good deal. Hey, I'm gonna get on with this, you wanna watch or what?" Jack yelled back to her.

"Yeah, yeah, wait for me. Wait, wait, wait." Cathy yelled as she appeared from below the deck. "I don't want to miss it."

She was alive and much better than when Vincent last saw her. She looked like she belonged in tropical world they were in. Her blonde hair was long and wild surrounding her head. She had on a yellow bikini top under a white see through shirt. The scars on her thighs where he sank the knife were healed over and tan like the rest of her body. She wore a short pair of jean shorts with a pair of sandals on her feet. Her grin was complete. She must have had her tooth replaced with a fake. She looked healthy and happy. It infuriated him!

"What are you doing on my boat?" Vincent asked again. "And what did you find?"

Cathy bent over and lifted a large black duffle bag. "This, we found. It's more than I thought you have left,

Vincent. You must be doing more than murder down here."

He stared at them both full of hatred.

Jack stood up and stretched his arms out wide, like he was hugging the horizon.

"Bottom line here Vince is this. You're a ghost. You have worked your whole life at not being seen and blending in to the woodwork so that nobody would remember you. That's what going to make getting rid of you so easy."

"Let's get this going babe, it's getting late." Jack said to Cathy.

She smiled and gave him a wink as she walked to the side of the boat and dropped the bag over out of sight.

Vincent watched as it disappeared over the side and spat out a mouthful of curses aimed at them both!

Jack emptied his beer then tossed it over the side following the duffle. Picking up a flare gun from the seat beside him, he fired it down below into the bowls of the yacht.

"Bummer Vince, was a nice boat."

Vincent screamed at him and began to howl as loud as possible at the man and woman. His disgust and loathing for them was unmatched. He would watch them both suffer the worst death they could think of and they would die knowing they had failed and he was the one who killed them.

Cathy stepped over the top of him and smiled down. His curses and spitting didn't bother her in the slightest. She appeared happy and without a care as she kicked something with her foot and he heard the chain start moving. The sound grew louder and louder. Just when he recognized what it was, the anchor chain snapped tight and jerked his legs. The pull was so fast and hard it yanked his hip out of socket before his entire body slid off the deck and over the side.

Cathy smiled at him all the way out of site. The last thing Vincent saw before the inky wetness enveloped him was a large dog standing on his bag of money that she threw over the side. It was in a small boat tied up to next his. The dog watched him as he went under the surface and was pulled to the crushing dark depths below.

She woke to Max nuzzling her face and neck. He sniffed and pushed at her until she gave up the fight for sleep and got out of bed. Opening the bedroom door allowed all the smells of the crisp ocean air mixed with breakfast in and she was instantly hungry.

Entering the kitchen she saw him at the stove. He was cooking her eggs just how she liked them. He turned and gave her a wink. She smiled back at him with that southern grin he loved so much.

The End